Run For The Hills

JODI BURNETT

DEDICATION

I dedicate this book to all Military Service Members to whom we Americans owe a mammoth debt of gratitude. Thank you for putting your lives on the line and fighting for our freedom and way of life. You sacrifice so much and often come home broken. Your country owes you more than it can ever repay. Thank you.

I would also like to dedicate this book to the horses (the true equine-therapists) who steadfastly and patiently help people with all types of mental, emotional, and physical challenges to find peace and learn to trust again. We are blessed to have such gentle giants in our world.

ACKNOWLEDGMENTS

First, I thank God for blessing me with work I love, and for the inspiration with which to do it.

The idea for this story came from years of working as a horse-trainer partner to some truly wonderful and dedicated social workers at Adams County Social Services. Together we witnessed the incredible power of utilizing horses in therapy with at-risk teens.

I am enormously proud of my husband who is a retired US Marine. Some of the bravest and most skilled men and women I know, serve or have served in our armed forces. I'm honored to call them friends. Thank you all, and your families, for your sacrificial service.

Books often have one name on the cover, but they are written by many hands. I must thank, with deepest love and gratitude, all the writers in my critique group. You have taught me so much about writing, dedication, and perseverance. I'm grateful for your wisdom, support, and friendship. Another big thanks to my editor, Cate Byer, for her expertise and guidance. Cate, you found all the things, and I'm so glad I found you.

The support of my family has been priceless. Your encouragement keeps me afloat. Most of all, I want thank Chris, my husband and greatest cheerleader. On days when my self-doubt threatens to suffocate me and I want to give up, you never let me. You're always there with a hug and a kick in the pants to get me going again. Thank you for believing in me and being my partner in all things. I love you more than I can say.

CHAPTER 1

Onyx and Fargo indicated his presence before she saw him. Four velvet ears pointed in his direction and long nostrils flared. Joscelyn Turner's horses raised their heads, sniffing at his intrusion. Jitters niggled at the back of Joscelyn's neck as she held up a hand to shade her hazel eyes and squinted toward the object of their vigilance. His slouch, and the rickety manner in which he dangled a cigarette from his fingertips betrayed his identity. A mere silhouette in the Colorado sunshine, he perched atop his tuna-boat—a rusted out, '70s model Pontiac Bonneville. She recognized him and shivered, though he sat parked on the road, fifty feet away. Onyx rumbled an anxious guttural sound and stomped his hoof in the sand.

"Easy, Nyx." Joscelyn stroked his long black neck. Ignoring the young man, she turned her attention back to the equine-assisted-therapy session she was facilitating in her arena. Joscelyn loved this work because it was effective, especially with people resistant to traditional talk therapy. "All right, ladies," she addressed the two seventeen-year-old girls standing next to her horses. "We've been working on team building the last couple of weeks. How are things going in your foster home? Are you getting along any better?"

"Bonnie never does crap," said Teresa, a petite, dark-skinned girl. "She's so lazy, I always end up having to do her share of the work while she sits around staring into space."

Bonnie bunched her fists, leaned her six-foot frame down to glare into Teresa's face. "At least I don't steal your stuff."

"Shut up, you Amazon bit—," Fargo interrupted Teresa by tossing his head and Onyx pranced sideways.

"No name-calling, Teresa," Joscelyn admonished. She shoved her long, thick, wheat-colored braid behind her shoulder and reached to pat Onyx on his neck. "As you girls can see, the horses are reacting to your tension. Let's try to discuss your issues and keep them calm at the same time." Joscelyn ran a hand down the length of Fargo's tan nose. "It sounds to me like you don't trust each other much." The girls exchanged glares and Bonnie crossed her arms over her chest. "So, today, let's work on trust. Trust is something that must be earned. We do that by being consistent and by keeping our word. We're going to do some ground exercises with Nyx and Fargo and work on earning their trust by using clear and consistent communication." Joscelyn handed each girl a lead rope.

"I don't know why we have to get along. Why can't I just move out on my own already?" Bonnie snatched the rope from Joscelyn's hand. The tail end swung around and snapped Onyx on his chest. He threw his head up, and with wide eyes, backed up several steps. Bonnie flinched and threw her arms up to protect herself. Her dramatic movement caused Onyx to turn and trot away. "Even Onyx hates me."

"Bonnie, Onyx doesn't hate you. He simply doesn't know what to expect from you. He doesn't trust you yet, but you can change that by being calm and communicating clearly. Onyx will learn that you don't want to hurt him."

"That's right," a masculine voice interjected. A sharp jolt shot up Joscelyn's spine and her stomach clenched tight. "But when someone you trust behaves in an unexpected way, it breaks trust. Doesn't it, Joscelyn?" The young man's oily voice smoothed over his words. She hadn't noticed him approach the arena rail and her skin prickled.

Joscelyn drew in a deep breath, she swallowed and turned to face him. "Lenny, I'm in the middle of a session right now. It is not appropriate for you to be here."

He stared at her with his pale, watery-blue eyes. "You were in the middle of sessions with me too, but you quit. Talk about trust—what a joke."

"I didn't quit, Lenny. For now, I need you to leave. You can call me at my office tomorrow and we can discuss this further." Joscelyn realized she was in a difficult situation and wished for the hundredth time that she had an assistant. She needed to protect the girls' privacy, as well as Lenny's, but for safety's sake she couldn't leave her clients alone with the horses.

"No. You tried to pass me off to some psychiatrist, but I don't want to see Dr. Strauss. I want *you* to help me. I want you to do what you promised. You said I could *trust* you." He glanced at the girls and then smirked at Joscelyn. "Don't you practice what you preach?"

She clenched her jaw and followed his gaze to the shocked faces of her clients. They seemed uncertain and a bit frightened. Teresa hid behind her horse. Joscelyn took a step toward Lenny, inserting herself between him and the girls, and forced bravado into her voice. "Now's not the time, Lenny. Call me at my office, tomorrow." She *had* recommended that he see a doctor. It broke her heart she couldn't help him herself but now that he was over 18, a doctor could diagnose him more accurately. Joscelyn was sure he was sociopathic and may have other related mental illness that could be assisted by medications she didn't have the license to prescribe.

Teddy, Joscelyn's Bernese Mountain Dog, snarled and barked from his kennel next to the barn. Normally calm and friendly, his black fur stood up on his shoulders. Lenny lifted his chin toward the dog and snorted. "Some watch dog— what's he gonna do from behind that fence?"

"Lenny, you need to leave. I will talk to you tomorrow."

"I'm going, I'm going." He cocked his head and his eyes softened. His long straight hair, which he dyed a flat black, hung across one eye. "It's just that I miss you, Josce. I thought I meant something to you. I thought you cared." He was probably a good-looking kid once upon a time, and he could be convincing, but Joscelyn knew better. Leonard Perkins was manipulative and dangerous. "I even sent you flowers."

She remembered the cloying, saccharine-sweet, scent of the lilies and shuddered. "Yes, and I've explained that sending me gifts is inappropriate, but I *do* care. We'll set up a treatment plan tomorrow."

Lenny smiled, but his eyes grew cold and hard. "Whatever." He pushed himself away from the rail. "You disappoint me Joscelyn, but I'll be seeing you around. *Trust me.*" He turned and walked away in his loose-jointed manner and slithered into his huge car.

An icy wave of apprehension flooded through Joscelyn's system as she and her clients watched him speed away. When she was certain he was gone, Joscelyn relaxed her tense muscles and turned back to the young women. "I'm sorry for that interruption. You girls did a great job keeping the horses still and calm. You're already building trust by being good leaders for them to follow." Her voice sounded calm, but she thought, *there's no way I can recover the session now.*

"Let's put the horses up and move to the picnic table by the barn to talk. Remember to brush them out and then, if you want, you can give them a horse treat in their feed bin." She followed the girls into the barn and watched as they put the horses in their stalls.

Bonnie finished first and left the barn. Joscelyn waited for Teresa and when they went outside, they found Bonnie sitting in the dirt, punching the ground with her fist.

"Teresa, would you mind waiting for us at the picnic table?" She tilted her head toward the seating area but her eyes never left Bonnie. Joscelyn's heart squeezed tight as she watched the girl's inner pain play out.

Joscelyn sat down next to the large girl whose knuckles were bleeding. "What's going on?"

Bonnie shrugged and slammed her fist once again into the gravel.

"Please stop hitting the ground and tell me what you're feeling." Joscelyn's chest ached for the young woman who tried to appear so tough.

Bonnie wiped her skinned knuckles on her jeans and peered at Joscelyn with tear-filled eyes. "I don't want to go back to that foster home. No one likes me there. Teresa hates me."

"I know it's hard." Joscelyn rested a hand on Bonnie's shoulder.

"I wanna run away," Bonnie's voice broke.

Joscelyn bent her head so she could look Bonnie in the eye. "You can't always run away when things get difficult. Try to think of what good things could happen if you stayed. What if you tried to build a friendship with Teresa?"

Bonnie shrugged and covered her face with her hands. "I just want to find my dad. I wanna go live with him."

Joscelyn hesitated. "Your dad left when you were three. No one knows where he is." Joscelyn resisted the urge to put her arms around Bonnie.

Instead, she lifted the girl's injured hand and poured water from her water-bottle over the scrapes. Bonnie's mother was a meth addict and Bonnie had been in foster care since she was four. Joscelyn blotted her hand with a bandana.

Bonnie pulled away. "I know and I hate him for that—but I love him too." She took a wobbly breath. "Does that make me a freak?"

"No, not at all. Think of your love and memories as a gift, but don't let your loss keep you from loving others. You're scheduled to emancipate in two months. Let's see if we can make things work at your foster home for that long, okay?"

"I just want to disappear." Bonnie stood up and ran back into the barn.

Joscelyn rushed after her and drew in a sharp breath as Bonnie shoved Onyx's stall door open and flung her arms around his strong neck. A rebuke died on Joscelyn's lips and her mouth fell open as she watched her horse, normally high spirited and aloof, stand rock solid and allow the broken girl to cry into his mane. He stood firm until she finished and when she lifted her head and stroked his cheek, he nickered at her.

Bonnie smiled and turned back to Joscelyn. "Nyx understands." She kissed his nose and came out of his stall closing the door behind her. "I'm ready."

Joscelyn smiled and walked Bonnie outside. At the end of their session time they waited together for the girls' ride. Amy Gardner, a co-worker of Joscelyn's from Douglas County Social Services, arrived to pick the girls up and drive them back to their foster home.

As the girls drove away, Joscelyn shook her head. No matter how good a therapist she was, she would never be as intuitive and sensitive as her horses. Somehow, they just knew.

~*~

A ringing, at first distant and then blaring, crashed into her dream world. Joscelyn pulled herself out of the vivid imagery and fumbled with random items on her nightstand, searching for her phone. It slipped through her fingers and landed on the floor. The bright screen hurt her eyes in the dark. She stretched down to retrieve it.

"Hello?" Her voice cracked with sleep.

Silence.

Joscelyn rubbed her eyes and cleared her throat. "Hello?"

Silence.

She peered at her phone. The call was still connected to an unknown caller. "Hello? Is anyone there?"

Click.

Joscelyn groaned and flopped back onto her pillow. She set the phone back on the table and pulled up the covers. *What was I dreaming about?* It seemed like a good dream. She threw an arm over Teddy, who took up more than half of her bed, and pushed her fingers into his silky coat. Her eyes closed and her breath evened out. Her head had begun to float when the ringing startled her again.

"Who is this? You have the wrong number," she said.

Silence.

"Hello? This isn't funny."

Silence.

Joscelyn disconnected the call and turned her phone off so the prankster couldn't call again. She curled up with her back against Teddy. Isolation ran its cold, bony fingers across her body. *I hate being alone.*

Tired and groggy from broken sleep, Joscelyn stumbled out the door of her tiny, clapboard, ranch-style farmhouse on her way to the barn, for morning chores. Even though it was spring, a crisp chill in the air forced her to pull on her faded Carhartt jacket. Joscelyn smiled as she heard the first meadowlark's song of the season. Her dad used to say the song sounded like the bird sang "Do you want licorice?" Lost in her memory, Joscelyn almost stepped on a dead magpie laying on the front door mat. *The barn-cat must have thought I needed a present.* She nudged the bird off the porch with the toe of her boot and headed toward the barn. Onyx and Fargo whinnied when she opened the door, demanding their breakfast hay. The scent of dried grass and manure filled the air.

"Good morning," she sang. Passing by the tack area, her eyes caught sight of a gash across the seat of her saddle. Joscelyn scrunched her brows together and ran her fingers across the damaged tack. *How the hell did that happen?* She let out a hot sigh and looked around, trying to figure out what might have caused it. The cut seemed too clean to have come from a rodent or an owl. *Did something fall on it?* She looked at the floor around the saddle rack. Her chest constricted, sick at the thought of the repair cost.

Angry about her saddle, she tossed hay to her horses, pausing only to run her hand along their shoulders. She threw feed out to the chickens and filled the cat's bowl. Not wanting to be late for work, she rushed to the driveway. At first, she didn't see the blood smeared on the door of her red truck. When she touched it, a dawning reality jarred her tired brain. Her eyes dropped from the sticky blood on her fingers to the ground beneath the door. The victim, a rabbit with its throat slit, lay with its eyes wide open, staring at nothing.

Panic surged into Joscelyn's throat, stealing her breath. She spun around to make certain no one was there. Every incident crashed into her consciousness at once: Lenny showing up, the middle of the night phone calls, the bird, the saddle, the bunny. Her heart galloped as she rifled through her purse for her phone to call the sheriff.

CHAPTER 2

Joscelyn spoke with a woman in the regional dispatch office. She explained what happened during the night and the weary voice on the other end of the line assured her that a deputy would call within the hour. Joscelyn went back inside. Her hands shook as she poured herself a cup of coffee and sat down at the small kitchen table to wait.

The phone rang just as Joscelyn took a fortifying sip. She swallowed too fast and the bitter, hot liquid burned her throat causing her to cough as she answered the call.

"This is Deputy Cook, ma'am. I'm calling to take a report of the vandalism and the dead rabbit you found this morning."

"You're going to take the report over the phone?" Joscelyn wanted him to come out to the ranch, hoping his presence would help her feel safe and less isolated. Not to mention the appearance of a cop car could be a deterrent.

"Yes, ma'am. It's a mighty big county, a phone report is much more efficient. Why don't you tell me everything that happened, starting with the middle-of-the-night phone calls?"

Joscelyn recounted the details as she experienced them. When she finished, she waited for the deputy to complete his note taking.

"All right, Ms. Turner, do you have any idea who might have done these things? Anyone in particular who's mad at you or who'd want to scare you? Say an ex-boyfriend?"

"I think it might be an ex-client of mine."

"Ex-client?"

"I'm a therapist with Douglas County Social Services." Joscelyn answered. "This particular ex-client is angry because I ended our regular sessions and referred him instead to a psychiatrist."

Deputy Cook pressed on. "Alrighty, then. Can you give me his name and a brief description?"

Joscelyn shoved her chair back, strode to the kitchen counter, and leaned against it. "I can't do that. His privacy is protected under the HIPAA laws."

"Alrighty then. Who else lives with you at your place? Husband? Children?"

Joscelyn sighed and squeezed her temples between her thumb and middle-finger. "No one. It's just me." She heard the deputy tapping on a keyboard.

"All right, here's the thing. With no real proof or specific evidence, you're gonna have to give us this guy's name so we can go talk to him. Otherwise, an investigation simply can't take place." He cleared his throat and continued, "You might like to get some exterior lighting, if you don't already have it. If you do, make sure it's turned on at night. The only other thing I would suggest is to set up a camera. They make motion-sensing cameras for hunting. You could get one at Cabela's or maybe even find a cheap one at Walmart."

Joscelyn closed her eyes and sighed. "Is that all you can do?"

"Well, I've got everything you've told me written down. I'll add an increased patrol request to this report and we'll have deputies drive by your place every couple of hours. At this point that's all we *can* do unless you tell me a name."

She rubbed her arms against a sudden shiver. "Thanks anyway, Deputy."

"You're welcome. Call me if anything else happens." He gave her his work cellphone number.

Joscelyn swallowed her frustration. Maybe she couldn't *prove* it was Lenny, but deep in her core she knew it was him.

By late afternoon, Lenny still hadn't called her office, so Joscelyn contacted Dr. Strauss to ask if a client of hers had perhaps called him directly to make an appointment.

"I don't believe anyone has called, Ms. Turner. Is this concerning a referral?" Dr. Strauss asked.

"Yes, I have a client whose issues are more involved than I am equipped to help with," Joscelyn answered. She skimmed Leonard Perkin's file, noting his tendencies toward anger and control—the incidences of manipulation and hostility. Amy, Joscelyn's co-worker, stopped at the door of her office. Joscelyn held up her index finger and continued with her call. "I've asked him to contact you, but he is resistant to seeing a new therapist." She considered his narcissism and extreme desire for admiration. Joscelyn knew Lenny could be charming and engaging, but those traits were superficial, even deceitful. Amy leaned in and mouthed the word "coffee?" Joscelyn nodded, closed her eyes, and smiled.

"Let me put you on hold for a moment and I'll double check with my receptionist," said Dr. Strauss.

"Thanks." While she waited, Joscelyn flipped through the pages of the file and read her notes from their last session. *When Lenny doesn't get what he wants, he displays destructive, argumentative, and at times, even cruel behavior.* She tapped her pen on the file. *Lenny displays an inability to acknowledge responsibility, and shows a complete lack of empathy and remorse. He also presents addictive behaviors. Lenny feels helpless, hopeless, and angry. He believes that professionals—me in this case—minimize his problems.* Joscelyn pinched the bridge of her nose. She hoped she could convince Lenny to get the help he needed.

Dr. Strauss came back on the line. "No, there haven't been referral calls. Are there specific symptoms causing you concern?"

"My client is displaying symptomatic behaviors of narcissism and anti-social personality disorder." *In other words, he is potentially dangerous.* Joscelyn kept the last thought to herself.

Amy returned with two cups of coffee and handed one to Joscelyn who mouthed, "Thank you." She blew on the surface and continued, "It's why I thought it would be beneficial for him to receive psychiatric care. He may also need medications I'm unable to prescribe."

"I see, but as you know, it's hard to convince a narcissist to agree that they need help. All we can do is hope your client reaches out. I will keep you informed on that front."

"Thank you, Doctor. Have a nice afternoon."

Joscelyn took a big sip of the hot drink. It seared her mouth and throat where she burned it earlier that morning. In her hurry to set the cup down she spilled coffee on the file. *Damn it!* It had been a long day and Joscelyn rubbed her temples. She blotted the spill and put Leonard's file back in the cabinet. She read through several other case files before the clock announced it was time to go home.

Joscelyn waved at the security guard in the lobby as she left and went out through the double glass doors to the parking lot. When she opened the door of her truck, hot air poured out. The cab was as scorching as a kiln after basking in the Colorado sun all afternoon. She climbed in, closed the door, and baked in the heat for a few minutes before cracking her window to cool things down.

Joscelyn shook her mind free from thoughts of work. It was an hour drive from the Douglas County Social Services building in Castle Rock to the ten-acre ranch she rented in Kiowa. Eager to get home, she wanted to check on her animals, and enjoy a cold beer. The deputy hadn't called, so she assumed that all was well. She pulled out onto I-25, cranked up the country music station, and gunned the engine of her aging F-250. Once she left the traffic of the city behind, her tension eased.

Joscelyn enjoyed her commute through the countryside. She loved the fact that her way home was a beautiful drive through rolling, wooded hills.

Joscelyn glanced in her side-mirror and spotted a wide, beige car behind her—two cars back. She braked reflexively and peered into the rearview. The beige car slowed down and fell further back, causing an SUV behind it to pass. An icy-cold wave flushed through her, raising bumps on her skin. *Is that Lenny's car?* Joscelyn turned left into a neighborhood of five-acre properties. She drove through the winding roads, wondering if the large car would turn in and follow her. After five minutes of twists and turns, she didn't see any other cars on the road. Joscelyn laughed aloud. *Now, I'm being paranoid.*

She relaxed, found her way back out to Highway 86, and turned east. Tim McGraw strummed his guitar through her speakers and she sang along. As she drove by the post office, she saw him. Their eyes clashed across the distance and her stomach clenched like she'd been punched. Sharp jabs spiked through her scalp but a surge of heat behind her eyes shoved her fear aside. Lenny had the audacity to grin at her when she saw his face. Without thinking it through, Joscelyn pulled over on the shoulder of the road, ready to confront him. She threw open her door and jumped down just in time to get hit with a spray of sharp gravel as Lenny peeled out from the lot and raced away.

Joscelyn climbed back into her truck and stared straight ahead, gripping the steering wheel until her breath slowed and her blood cooled. Once her heart settled, she pulled her phone out of her purse and checked to see if she had coverage. Her hand trembled as she dialed Deputy Cook.

He listened as she described the incident. "When did you first notice he was following you?"

"Not until I was just this side of Castle Rock. I don't know when he started following me though. It could have been at my office."

"And you're sure it was your ex-client?" he asked. "Sure it wasn't a simple coincidence?"

"Look Deputy, I know I sound paranoid, but I'm a therapist. This man was a client of mine. He has a lot of issues and I believe he is dangerous. He's angry with me for referring him to a psychiatrist. It's very likely he's the one who killed those animals at my ranch."

"I know you're scared, Ms. Turner, but you don't have any proof that this was the guy out at your place last night and he didn't break any laws when you saw him today. He might have simply been mailing something at the post office. He could have had any number of reasons for being in the area. If you would tell me his name, I could interview him and find out what he was up to. Where did you say he lives?"

Joscelyn gritted her teeth. "I didn't. I don't know where he lives and I couldn't tell you if I did."

"Alrighty ma'am, if you won't give me his name or address there isn't much I can do other than increase the extra patrol request. I'll add today's incident to your report. Try not to worry, all right?"

Joscelyn leaned her head back against the seat rest. "Easy for you to say."

His voice softened. "Call if anything unusual happens. We'll come right out."

"Sure." Joscelyn ended the call and shook her head. It was always the same. Her dad used to say, "You can't rely on others to take care of you." Obviously, she would have to protect herself.

~*~

Her phone didn't ring that night, but even so, Joscelyn didn't sleep well. She lay awake, listening for any unusual bumps in the night. Teddy stood on the bed and barked a couple of times, but when Joscelyn got up to look out the window, she didn't see anything out of the ordinary.

Strong, black coffee bolstered her as she gulped it down on her way to the barn the next day. Teddy trotted at her heels. The morning was chilly, but promised to be another beautiful, spring day. She passed the chicken pen and turned toward the barn door.

It was open.

Joscelyn never left the barn door open. The hair on the back of her neck bristled and her senses flared to full alert. She set her coffee cup on the picnic table. When she got to the door, she stopped outside and listened. The horses were munching on hay. Hay she had not yet fed them. Concern propelled her through the door. It took a minute for her eyes to adjust to the dim light of the barn and she walked into something dark hanging from the rafter above. Her arm flew up to deflect the object. Soft, sticky fur brushed her hand and her

18

body jerked back before her mind registered what the object was.

A shriek tore from her throat. "Oh, no! Felix!"

Joscelyn's eyes focused in the darkness and she took in the gruesome sight. Her little barn kitty was hanging by the neck and was sliced from his throat all the way down his belly. Blood dripped from his exposed intestines into a dark pool at her feet. Joscelyn's heart constricted and her eyes burned. A sour, slightly metallic odor caused a wave of nausea to rise up her throat and she ran outside to be sick. Joscelyn spit out the bitter bile and wiped her mouth on the sleeve of her jacket. She pressed her fists to the sides of her head. Swallowing hard, she brushed tears out of her eyes and ran back into the barn to check on her horses.

Onyx and Fargo were out of their stalls, in the main passageway of the barn, eating hay from the stacked bales. The lid was off the grain bin and Joscelyn raced over to cover it. She noted a large amount had already been eaten, and she worried her horses would colic. Her office would have to do without her today. She took a halter and lead rope and slipped it over Fargo's head. He followed her back into his stall. Next, she went to catch Onyx.

"Hey, Nyx. Good boy." Joscelyn reached up to stroke his dark neck and the whites of his eyes flashed. Onyx threw his head up and wheeled away from her.

"Whoa, Nyx. Easy boy." Joscelyn waited for him to calm down before she approached him again. She cooed at him as she reached for his neck. It was damp. She pulled her hand back and her fingers were slick with blood. Adrenaline slammed into her brain once again. She slipped the halter on his head and led him out to the light. Onyx had three shallow cuts sliced into his neck. Blood seeped from the wounds.

"Nyx, what happened, boy?" Joscelyn swallowed against a hard gnarl of pain, fury, and guilt trying to lodge in her throat and turned on the hose to rinse off his cuts. Her eyes blurred and Joscelyn wiped them with the back of her hand. Her chest ached when Onyx flinched as she dowsed the cuts with Betadine. "I'm sorry, buddy." She patted them dry with gauze from the first-aid kit. The slashes were superficial and wouldn't need stitches, but that didn't alleviate Joscelyn's horror. When the blood stopped oozing, she closed Onyx in his stall and pulled her phone out of her pocket. Unable to control the tremor in her clammy hands, she punched the numbers and called both Deputy Cook and the equine vet. Once help was on the way, she reached for her utility knife to cut the baling twine that held the cat suspended, but changed her mind and left him for evidence.

When the deputy arrived, Joscelyn was walking her horses in her round pen, keeping them on their feet trying to prevent grain-colic. "This is really scaring me, Deputy." Joscelyn's voice cracked. She gestured toward the dead cat. Fresh tears warmed her eyes, and she blinked them back.

"Try to calm down and tell me what happened." He took out his notebook and pen, ready to take another report.

After she finished her story, Joscelyn approached the deputy and gripped his sleeve. "I want to file a restraining order."

"You can go to the court and get a protection order if you want, but it won't do you much good."

"Why not?"

His jaw bulged and he ran his hand down over his face. "They'll need his name and want a photo. If you won't go against HIPAA and provide those things, then you're at a standstill."

"There has to be some other way to stop this." Joscelyn's squeezed the words through her thickened throat.

Deputy Cook's face flushed with frustration. "When you finally decide his actions are enough to be considered an imminent threat and you tell us who he is, we can do something." He looked away and took a deep breath. "Look, I know what happened here last night is upsetting. I'll take pictures of the cat and your horse's injuries. Afterward, I'll get the vet's input and I'll put everything in your report file. But, so far we don't have any actual proof that your ex-client did this."

Joscelyn stepped forward to interrupt, but the deputy held up his hand and continued, "I know you feel certain he did, and I believe you. But still, we need actual proof."

"Well, what the hell am I supposed to do, then?"

"As I told you, a motion-sensing camera would catch the culprit in the act and would provide visual proof. Maybe an alarm system would help too." Joscelyn nodded at his ideas and waved to the vet as he pulled into the property.

Deputy Cook took pictures of the cat, the barn, and Onyx's neck. He spoke with the vet and gave him his business card. He watched Joscelyn walk her horses for a few minutes before he said, "Ms. Turner, call me when you're ready to give this guy up." He tipped his hat at the vet and climbed into his Bronco.

Joscelyn led the vet to Onyx. He gave the horse a thorough check-up and examined the lacerations. He assured Joscelyn that Onyx would be fine, and that she did a good job cleaning his cuts. After he left, Joscelyn grabbed a shovel and went out behind the barn to dig a small grave for Felix.

That night, Joscelyn closed and bolted the stall-run doors, locking her horses inside. Peering up, she checked the newly installed motion-sensing camera. She anchored and locked the sliding barn doors and threw the deadbolt on the entrance door. Next, she turned on all the outdoor lights on the property and at the house. Inside, she checked the locks on all the windows and doors.

Joscelyn turned the tumblers of the combination lock on her gun safe and pulled out her guns. She cleaned and oiled both her 12-gauge shotgun and her 9mm, semi-automatic Ruger. With an angry calm, she loaded her weapons. She propped the shotgun inside her bedroom door and set her pistol on the nightstand. She didn't dress for bed. Instead, she wolfed down a quick ham and Swiss with a glass of milk, and lay down on top of the quilt in her jeans with her boots on. She knew she wouldn't sleep.

After midnight, her phone rang. "Who is this?"

Heavy breathing answered her, and she hung up. Several minutes later, it rang again.

"Lenny, I know it's you. Why are you doing this?" she yelled.

Laughter rang out over the line before it went dead. Joscelyn's heart pounded. She jumped off the bed and looked out the window toward the barn. Everything was quiet, so she sat back down. By 2:00am her eyelids grew heavy. Her head bobbed up and down several times before sleep won the battle. Joscelyn didn't know how long she'd been dozing when she woke to the sound of tires crunching gravel on her drive. Teddy snarled and barked, running back and forth from the front door to her room. Joscelyn's blood raged through her veins. She could hear the pulse in her head as she tucked her pistol in the back waistband of her jeans and lifted the shotgun. She wiped her damp palm on her thigh before she gripped the stock.

Joscelyn took a deep breath and forced her legs to walk toward the front door. She unlatched the chain and turned the lock. Flinging open the door, she marched out onto the porch

CHAPTER 3

"Get off my property, Leonard!" Joscelyn screamed into the night.

Maniacal laughter sawed through her nerves. Lenny's huge car floated toward her. She saw his face glowing green in the dashboard lights, and like an evil goblin, he kept laughing. Joscelyn stepped forward and cocked the shotgun, the 'crack-pop' of the round ramming into the chamber, a telltale threat. Lenny stopped the car. For one long moment, they stared at each other. Then Lenny floored the Bonneville. It lurched toward Joscelyn. She aimed low, at the grille of the car and fired. The kickback nearly knocked her off her feet. Her ears rang from the report and the spent gunpowder stung her nose.

Lenny slammed on the brakes. The shot left a smattering of dark, dented spots in the paint and chrome, and shattered his left headlight. Pure grit took over and left Joscelyn's fear on the sidelines.

She cocked the gun once again, and this time aimed it directly at Lenny's windshield. He threw the car into reverse and squealed backwards down the drive. The tires swung around and Lenny sped out the gate and onto the road. He honked and hooted as he drove away, leaving Joscelyn to collapse on the steps, trembling. Teddy licked streaming tears from her cheeks. She threw her arms around his furry body and held tight. Finally, she went back inside, found her phone, and dialed 911.

Steam from their coffee cups swirled up into the pre-dawn darkness. Joscelyn spoke and again, the deputy on duty wrote the details of her most recent fright.

"The detective will be here soon and we'll get a crew out here to hunt for paint chips and any other evidence. Can you positively identify the man in the car as your ex-client?"

"Yes."

"Do you want to press charges for trespassing and attempted vehicular assault?"

"Yes, I do." Joscelyn closed her eyes, sorry it had come to this. The man who tried to run me down last night is Leonard Perkins.

When the detective pulled in, the deputy met him at the door to fill him in on the situation. He wrote a few notes on a pad, then took off his cowboy hat as he entered the house. He sat down with Joscelyn to rehash the events. "What do you suppose Perkins wants from you?"

"All I know is that he's angry that I won't see him in therapy anymore. I referred him to a psychiatrist who has more experience to help him than I do. Now he feels betrayed."

"Do you think he has feelings for you?"

"It's more like he thinks *I* should have feelings for *him* and is angry that I don't." Joscelyn clamped her teeth together and pressed her temples with her fingers. She was still under the obligation to protect Lenny's private information. She began again. "He's trying to manipulate me with violence and fear." Joscelyn took a sip from her mug. "I'm afraid the violence will escalate along with his frustration at not getting what he wants."

"Do you think he wants to kill you?"

"I think he just wants to scare me."

The detective said, "We'll go to his residence and put out an APB with a description of his car. In the meantime, is there any place you can stay for a while? I'll make sure the deputies continue to check on your property regularly."

Joscelyn closed her eyes and thought of her lack of family and close friends. The emptiness was like a deep bruise that never healed.

"I'll figure something out. You have my phone number in case anything else happens out here?" The detective held up his pad and nodded.

"I guess I'd better call my landlord too." She jammed her fingers into her hair and gripped tight, exhaustion and anxiety taking their toll.

The detective stood to go and Joscelyn walked him to the door. "Keep your doors locked and your dog inside with you. Let me know where you end up. I'd prefer you were gone by this afternoon." He put his cowboy hat back on his head. "Oh, one more thing. Can I ask why you aimed so low with your shotgun?"

Joscelyn shrugged. "I didn't want to kill him."

He smiled. "Yeah, but the car wasn't the threat—the maniac driving it was." He gave Joscelyn a reassuring pat on her shoulder, nodded, and left.

Joscelyn locked the door behind him. She stroked Teddy's head and sat on the sofa. The sky brightened though the sun wasn't up yet. It would be several hours before she could start making calls to find a place to board her horses and take the chickens. She figured her co-worker, Amy, might let her sleep on her couch, but she wasn't sure if Teddy would be welcome.

~*~

Joscelyn found a barn in Castle Rock that agreed to board her horses in their pasture but she had to pay by the month, in advance. She moved her chickens to her nearest neighbor's coop, and Joscelyn and Teddy went to stay with Amy. They'd been there almost a week the morning Joscelyn went out to the parking lot and found all four of her truck tires sliced.

A wave of red heat swept across her eyes and down through her body. Joscelyn placed a call to her roadside service agency. She paced and pressed her palm against her forehead as she spoke. They assured her someone would be there within the hour to haul her truck in for new tires. Joscelyn let down the tailgate for a place to sit while she waited. The sight that assailed her caused her body to recoil. She clamped a hand over her mouth. Smeared all over the bed of the truck were the blood and feathers of three headless chickens whose bodies were piled in the corner.

He found me.

Joscelyn whipped her head around in all directions, looking to see if anyone watched her. She shivered. Not wasting any time, she ran back to Amy's apartment and locked herself in. She pulled her handgun locker off the shelf in the guest room closet and opened it. Joscelyn had a concealed carry license, but she rarely took her gun around with her. That policy had changed.

When she called the detective, he told her to call the local police. Since Castle Rock was out of his jurisdiction, they would have to cooperate on the case. The CRPD sent a crime scene investigator who dusted the truck for prints. He took several photos before helping Joscelyn dispose of the chicken carcasses. The tow truck arrived as they finished bagging up the mess and loaded Joscelyn's truck. She filed a new vandalism report with the police officer and gave him the case history.

As soon as the official business was complete, Joscelyn went back inside, packed her things, and left a note for Amy. She and Teddy took a cab to the tire shop to pick up her truck. They drove it through the nearest car wash—

twice. Joscelyn rushed out to her ranch to pack more clothes and a few necessities.

When she called her landlord to explain she would be gone for several weeks, he groused, "You better be on time with your rent or I'll evict you and rent to someone else. I have plenty of offers."

"Thanks for understanding." Joscelyn rolled her eyes. She was paid up through the end of the month so she had at least that long to get things settled. Joscelyn's next stop was the barn where she boarded her horses. She hooked up her trailer, loaded Onyx and Fargo, and headed for the highway. She turned north on I-25. Her only plan was to get far away. She couldn't put the people or animals she cared about in danger any longer.

Once she was on the north side of Denver, Joscelyn's tension eased enough for her to call her boss. "I need to take an emergency leave of absence. I'm not sure when I'll return, but I'll keep you posted."

"Are you all right, Josce? What's happened?" her boss asked. "Come into the office so we can talk about this."

Joscelyn scanned the traffic in her rear-view mirror. "I can't come to the office. I'm fine, but I'm being threatened. The police haven't been able to help me, so I need to get out of town for a while." She sighed, "I have an active case with two teens preparing for emancipation. Would you please turn the case over to Amy and tell her I'll be in touch?" The director said she would, and Joscelyn ended the call before her boss could question her further. Joscelyn couldn't tell anyone where she was going, chiefly because she didn't know herself.

She pulled her truck and trailer into a McDonald's in Cheyenne at dinner time. Joscelyn hopped out of the cab and stretched. Teddy followed suit, then sniffed the small grassy lot, marking it as he saw fit. After her dog ran a full inspection of the area, Joscelyn succumbed to her gnawing stomach begging to be fed. When she opened the passenger door and asked Teddy to load-up, a large tan car sailed into the parking lot and pulled in behind her trailer.

Her breath caught and sharp pinpricks skittered across her scalp. She grasped the latch on the glove box, but it was locked. Joscelyn always kept it locked when her gun was in there. She scrambled for the key, jammed it in the entry and jerked open the compartment. The cool metal bolstered her nerves as her fingers closed around the pistol grip. She pulled out the gun and turned just in time to see a young family emerge from the sedan.

"I want a Happy Meal," shouted a little girl, pulling on her daddy's hand.

He laughed and swung his daughter up to his shoulders. "That's the plan, sweetheart."

Joscelyn's whole body went limp and cold. Her heart skipped and stuttered. *What is the matter with me?* She threw the gun back into the glove box like a hot rock and locked it up again, then she held her face in her hands until she could catch her breath.

A soft breeze soothed the warm evening as Joscelyn ate her fast food at a lone table outside. She googled local hotels with horse facilities and found one in Laramie, so after checking on the horses and tossing a ball for Teddy a couple of times, they packed up and headed west.

The ranch hotel was outside the city and only one other horse owner was staying there. The manager helped Joscelyn unload her horses and settle them in their stalls for the night. Then, she and Teddy were shown to their room. Constant vigilance and tension knotted Joscelyn's sore muscles, so she tried to relax now that they were safe, far away from Denver. Certain that she had escaped unnoticed, Joscelyn slept soundly in the quiet Wyoming countryside.

She was in no hurry to get back on the road in the morning since she still didn't know where she was going. The hotel served a big ranch-style breakfast of eggs fried in salty bacon grease, hash-browns, and stout coffee in the main house. She enjoyed the meal before taking a long, hot shower. Joscelyn jerked her jeans and top on over still-damp skin, gathered her hair into a messy bun, and pulled on her cowboy boots.

She threw a ball for Teddy in the bright morning sun. His tail swept back and forth when he ran. Once he tired, Joscelyn loaded her animals up and pointed her truck in a general westerly direction. They stopped to buy some dog food and a few groceries before driving to Rock Springs for lunch. From there, Joscelyn turned north and meandered along the country roads.

With a constant eye on the rear-view mirror, it irritated Joscelyn that she couldn't relax and enjoy the beautiful drive. Every car that slightly resembled Lenny's, caused her heart rate to surge. Thoughts of the work she was missing and the fact that a violent ex-client forced her out of her daily life kept the muscles in her back and neck bunched up. Her head throbbed.

The steering wheel gave a sudden jerk and Joscelyn reflexively gripped it tight, steadying the truck. She felt a heavy drag on the engine which surged against the resistance. Down shifting with one hand, while fighting to keep in her lane, Joscelyn slowed down and pulled to the shoulder of the highway.

"Damn it!" Joscelyn peered in her side mirrors, checking her tires. The left trailer tire was shredded. Black rubber ribbons scattered the road behind them. She let loose a frustrated sigh, told Teddy to stay in the truck, and stomped to the trailer's tack room to get the tools she would need to replace the tire.

Joscelyn pumped the jack and released the pressure off the good tire of the pair as a car pulled over and parked in front of her truck. A thin, gangly man got out and came toward her. The evening sun, bright behind him, kept her from seeing anything but his dark form. He tossed his long bangs out of his eyes with a flick of his head and Joscelyn's blood went cold. She recognized that gesture. Her fingers closed around the lug wrench, preparing to defend herself.

"Got a flat, huh?" The masculine voice said with a chuckle.

Joscelyn squinted her eyes at the shadowed shape and she took two steps back, gripping her weapon now with both hands.

"Looks like you've got a good start. Want some help?" White teeth flashed when the man smiled at her, and instantly she realized he was a stranger. Probably a friendly stranger, but she would have to let go of her lug wrench to allow him to help her.

"I think I've got it. Thanks, though."

"It's no problem to lend you a hand. Hold on, let me grab my gloves and tell the family I'll be just a few minutes." He turned back to his car.

Joscelyn leaned her back against the side of the trailer and drew a long breath. She felt a tremor in her hands and she eased her grip. She narrowed her eyes and bit down hard as heat flashed through her head. *I've got to stop suspecting everyone of being Lenny. He's terrorizing me without even having to try. Stop acting like a victim!*

With the help of the good Samaritan, Joscelyn and her animals were back on the road in a half hour. They stopped in Jackson, Wyoming for the night and the next morning, she drove through Yellowstone, marveling at the grandeur of the Tetons and the wilderness. Teddy barked at the bison grazing alongside the road.

"That's a fight you wouldn't win, buddy." Joscelyn roughed up the fur on his head.

She found a horse camp in the park and let her animals take a break from standing in the trailer. Pretzels and a beer made up her dinner while she watched the sun set—a mulberry, tangerine, and refined-gold masterpiece painted over the mountains. That night she and Teddy slept in the gooseneck part of the horse trailer.

The following morning her muscles were even tighter and her neck pinched where she'd slept on it wrong. She hadn't prepared for camping before she left home, and the floor of the gooseneck loft was scratchy, hard, and unforgiving. Her stiff neck screamed when Joscelyn pulled a bale of hay down from the rack on top of the trailer.

Back on the road, continuing north, Joscelyn's strain and stiffness eased. She hadn't seen anyone following her in the past three days. The mountains towered around her as she drove across the border into Montana. She stopped for a late lunch in Butte and consulted the map on her phone. Somewhere along the drive, Joscelyn started thinking less about running away, and more about where she might end up. She knew she couldn't drive forever.

The road eventually led upward and soon Joscelyn found herself in another mountainous forest. She rounded a bend and came upon a beautiful, smooth, and peaceful lake. A large, scenic overlook made the perfect place to pull over. It offered plenty of room to get her horses out and walk them. After stretching their legs and tying them to the side of the trailer with hay-bags and water, Joscelyn grabbed a beer from her cooler and sat on a huge log to watch a group of bald eagles swooping and diving into the glistening lake. The majestic birds mesmerized Joscelyn. Unimpressed with majesty, Teddy chased squirrels and rabbits into the brush.

The peacefulness of the water reminded her of when, as a girl, her dad took her fishing. Smiling, she thought of him helping her tie a hook onto a line on a stick. "This is the way Huck Finn did his fishing," he said as he showed her how to slide the hook through a worm. "No fancy rod and reels back then." Joscelyn could almost hear the sound of his voice. Her heart still ached for his presence. It had been almost fifteen years since he was killed in Iraq but she still missed him. Then only five years later her mom had succumbed to breast cancer. Time softened the sharp edges of her grief, but a dull, purple pain still bloomed heavily in her chest whenever she thought of them. Loneliness overwhelmed her.

Joscelyn's phone rang, and she pulled it out of the back pocket of her jean-skirt to check the screen. She didn't recognize the number and without thinking, Joscelyn answered the call.

"Hello, this is Joscelyn Turner."

"Montana, huh? Do you seriously think you can hide from me?" The greasy voice slapped her hard, back into reality.

CHAPTER 4

"Lenny?" Joscelyn's heart vaulted into her throat so fast she choked. "Why are you doing this? Leave me alone!"

A wicked laugh answered her. "You'll never get away from me, Joscelyn."

As though bitten by a snake, Joscelyn threw her phone down. She figured he must be tracking her through the device somehow. His laughter echoed from the dirt and she crushed the terrifying sound with the heel of her boot. She stomped once more and swiveled her heel for good measure before picking up the mangled phone and throwing it into the lake, the thought that she no longer had Google Maps occurring to her only as the water splashed and the lake swallowed the mini-computer.

"Damn it!" she yelled. Trembling, she loaded her horses as quickly as possible, startling at every car that drove by. She pulled back onto the road, wanting to get away from this place—the place where Lenny located her. Joscelyn prayed he couldn't track her now she no longer had a GPS. Her truck wasn't new enough to have a navigation system, so she needed to drive to the next town to buy a road atlas.

Joscelyn surged past the gold-streaked lake that reflected the late afternoon sun, before the road descended into a steep, winding, mountain pass. It was difficult to maneuver with the trailer and she took it slow so the horses wouldn't lose their footing. Joscelyn wished she hadn't drunk that beer as she gripped the steering wheel. She traveled almost two hours of white-knuckled driving, feeling the weight and tug of the horse trailer behind her before the road leveled out. The sky was hinting at dusk when up ahead she saw a lone ranch with a few lights on.

Joscelyn slowed to a stop before turning left through the gate. A wrought iron sign that read, "Stone Ranch" hung over the drive. She watched the sides of the trailer as she eased through the gate, careful not to scrape the posts. Then she continued up the drive toward a worn, white, two-story farmhouse to ask for directions to the nearest town. On the right side of the gravel road stood a large red barn with stalls, runs, and a corral. An arena extended off the far side of the barn. Joscelyn pulled to a stop along the fence and killed the engine. Leaving Teddy in the cab, she hopped out, straightened her denim skirt, and headed toward the house.

About twenty feet from the porch, Joscelyn hesitated. The front screen-door flew open so hard it hit the house and bounced back into the cowboy who had shoved it. The man's sky-blue eyes flashed with anger as he strode across the porch and down the steps. Right behind him, a small blonde woman wearing high-waisted shorts and a blouse tied at her midriff ran out, slamming the door in the same manner. With her hair rolled up in a 1940s style, she looked like a pin-up girl.

"Don't you walk away from me, Trent Stone," she yelled. "You know it's true. You're such a jerk. You'll kiss anything wearing a skirt!"

"Yeah?" The man turned back toward the woman and as he did, he spotted Joscelyn. His eyebrows lifted in momentary surprise before his gaze traveled from her face, over her cotton blouse, her short denim skirt, and on down to her boots. He took his time ogling her before his eyes rose back to hers. A grin lit his handsome face, and he hollered to the screaming woman, "I suppose you're right."

The man strode up to Joscelyn and without warning he pushed his cowboy hat back, took her face in his large hands, and kissed her. It wasn't merely a peck either. He kissed her good. Stunned into paralysis, Joscelyn gaped at the stranger.

The woman following him shrieked in anger. When he released Joscelyn's face, a clenched jaw replaced his previous mirth. He looked at her then, deep into her eyes for a second or two, before he turned and stalked off. Joscelyn stood frozen in shock. Her eyes moved from the man's retreating figure to the woman who marched up to Joscelyn and slapped her hard across the face before running after the man. Joscelyn lifted her hand to her stinging cheek and watched the man leap into a huge, dark green Ram 3500 dually. He gunned the engine and roared away. The woman jumped into an old, yellow, Volkswagen Thing and peeled out after him.

Joscelyn's mind fumbled to make sense out of what had just happened. Before she could pull her thoughts together enough to react, the screen door opened once again. This time the hinges squeaked but the door was not flung.

"Oh, my goodness. You poor thing." A woman with white hair stuffed into a banana clip at the back of her head, came down the front steps. The rounded figure seemed comfortable in her jeans and blue-plaid flannel shirt. She reached her arms out to Joscelyn as she moved toward her. "Are you all right?"

"I…" Joscelyn couldn't find any words and she lowered her hand from her face. "Yes, I…"

"Are you a friend of Trent's?" The older woman patted Joscelyn's arm with a strong and calloused hand.

"No. I'm not from around here. I just pulled in to ask for directions to the nearest town. I lost my phone, so I don't have a map."

"Oh." The woman's brows scrunched together. "Well—don't pay those two any attention at all. They're like wet cats in a barrel, fightin' all the time."

Joscelyn gave her head a slight shake and said, "It's fine, really. They just surprised me, that's all." Forcing strength back into her voice she held out her hand and continued, "My name's Joscelyn Turner."

The woman thrust out her hand and gripped Joscelyn's. "I'm Mary Stone. The fool in the cowboy hat was my grandson, Trent. The banshee with the pink streak in her hair chasing him is his girlfriend, Tonya. Or, I suppose she's his ex-girlfriend now." Mary chuckled and then sobered, her gaze moved beyond Joscelyn and took in the truck and trailer. One of the horses stomped with impatience and she smiled. "How many horses you haulin'?"

"Two, and they've about had it for the day." Joscelyn smiled.

Squinting her eyes, Mary asked, "What're you doing out in the middle of nowhere at this time in the evening with a loaded trailer and no place to stay?"

Joscelyn's cheeks flared with heat and she was glad for the darkening sky. It *was* foolish to haul horses around without a plan. She opened her mouth to answer, but no words came.

Shaking her head, Mary said, "The next town is quite a-ways away, and it's too late to be hauling a trailer full of exhausted horses anyhow. Why don't you allow me to make up for my grandson's awful behavior by letting you turn your horses out in our corral for the night? You and your dog can sleep in my spare room."

"I couldn't do that. You don't even know me." Joscelyn understood country hospitality, but this was over the top. "I'm sure when your grandson returns, he wouldn't be happy to have a stranger staying in his house." She was still shaken by Lenny's call and her strange welcome at this ranch, but Joscelyn found Mary's company comforting and wished she could stay.

Mary's laugh was low and soothing. "First of all, it's *my* house, and Trent won't be home tonight. They have plenty more fighting to do before they figure things out. If you aren't comfortable staying in the house, you can camp out here in your trailer, but I don't recommend you drive into town. There isn't any place to turn your horses out there."

Joscelyn was exhausted from travel and the tricky drive down the canyon. "If you really don't mind, I will take you up on your offer to camp here." She rolled her achy shoulders. "You are so kind, thank you. We won't be any trouble and we'll be on our way first thing in the morning."

"Good. I'm glad you see reason." Mary opened the gate of the corral. "As soon as you get them unloaded, come on up to the house. Dinner's about ready and I planned enough for three." She waved her hand toward the gate. "Since those two left, I have plenty."

Joscelyn's belly rumbled in response and Mary smiled at her. "I guess I can't try to tell you I'm not hungry."

"Nope." She grinned. "Come on up. We're havin' roast and mashed potatoes." Mary turned, went back up the steps and into the farm house.

The soft yellow walls inside the house gave the home a cozy feel. More than with decoration, Mary filled the rooms with a sense of being lived in. It was a home. A fresh spear of loss punctured Joscelyn's heart. It had been a long time since she'd been anywhere that felt like home. Joscelyn perused Mary's bookshelves while she waited in the front room to be called for supper. Sprinkled among the books were framed snapshots of three boys at various ages. She recognized the man who kissed her. He had been a cute teenager, the only fair-haired boy between two darkly handsome brothers. Joscelyn ran her fingers over books on cooking and gardening mixed in with books on bovine and equine home-veterinary care. Several shelves held novels, from classics to bodice-ripping romances. *You can tell a lot about a person by the books they keep on their shelves.* Joscelyn smiled to herself.

"You like books?" Mary entered the room.

Joscelyn nodded. "You have some of my favorite classics. I read *Jane Eyre* at least once a year and *Little Women* every Christmas. My folks gave me a collection of classic books when I turned thirteen." She thought of the box packed in the backseat of her truck. Her forced displacement rankling her once again, she turned away from the bookshelves.

"I can always tell a kindred spirit." Mary wiped her hands on a towel. "Come on in for dinner. You can pick out a book to read later."

Joscelyn sat down at the kitchen farm table to a plate filled with delicious, savory-smelling food. A rich, brown gravy covered the meal, and swirled together with a pool of melted butter on top of the potatoes. Mary bowed her head and said grace.

"Amen," Joscelyn responded. "Thank you so much for this wonderful meal." Her fork was already filled with meat on its way to her mouth.

"Where you headed?" Mary asked.

Joscelyn took her time chewing before answering, thinking about how much she should say. "I'm not exactly sure. I'm looking for a job and an inexpensive place to live, so I guess I'm headed to wherever I can find that."

"Where you from?"

"Colorado." Joscelyn took a large bite of potatoes so she wouldn't have to say more.

"You got family there?"

Joscelyn shook her head and scooped another quick bite into her mouth.

Mary considered her for a long moment and then nodded. "Running from somethin'?"

Joscelyn swallowed her bite before it was well chewed and coughed. "I just need some time away. I'll be going back in a few months."

"Well, don't you worry, in spite of being greeted with a kiss and a slap, you're safe here. In fact, I wish you would let me convince you to stay inside tonight. It's supposed to be a cold one. It's no problem at all. In fact, I'd be grateful for the company."

Joscelyn looked over at Teddy curled up and snoring in front of the fire. "That *would* be nice, Mary. If you really don't mind, I will. Thanks."

Joscelyn slept soundly on the soft bed under the down comforter and a handmade quilt. She woke with the sun and the cock-a-doodle-doo of a rooster in the yard. Rolling out of bed, Joscelyn grabbed her cosmetics bag and headed toward the bathroom. A nice hot shower would be just the thing before hitting the road.

She leaned back in the stream of water to rinse her hair when she heard the bathroom door open.

"Hello?" she called out.

"What the hell?" A man's low voice rumbled.

A cold wave of fear doused Joscelyn under the hot spray. She grabbed the edge of the shower curtain and held it across her chest as she peeked out to confront the intruder.

"Well, good mornin'." The man from last night smirked under elevated brows. His handsome dark-blond looks only improved by the rough morning stubble on his cheeks. "Fancy meeting you here... in my shower."

"Would you mind giving me some privacy? I'll be out of your way in a minute."

He grinned a charming, lopsided grin and his eyes sparkled. "You're not in *my* way. I'll just brush my teeth and wait till you're done."

Joscelyn gave him an icy glare. "Do you mind waiting in the hall?"

Trent chuckled and cocked his head. "I suppose I could do that." He glanced at the toiletries she left on the counter and picked up a jar of face cream, pretending to read the label. "Women sure are mysterious creatures."

Joscelyn let out a frustrated groan, reached out enough to snatch the jar out of his hand and whipped the curtain closed. Trent laughed again and left the room. She finished her shower as fast as she could and wrapped a towel around her hair and another larger towel around her body. She would finish getting dressed in her room—with the door locked. Joscelyn stepped into the hall and found Trent leaning against the wall, waiting.

"Finished?" He pushed himself up. "Did you leave me any hot water?"

Joscelyn lifted her chin and strode by him as if he wasn't getting under her skin.

Once dressed, Joscelyn went down to the kitchen and joined Mary who greeted her with a mug of strong, hot coffee. The scent of bacon filled the house and Joscelyn's mouth watered at the sight of a stack of pancakes at the center of the table.

"Smells delicious." She breathed in and she sat down.

Trent rounded the corner, tucking the last of his shirt into his jeans. He buckled his belt and winked at Joscelyn. He sidled up behind his grandmother who flipped pancakes on the stove, put his arms around her, and kissed her cheek.

"You make the best pancakes in the world, Gran."

Mary pretended to bat at him with the spatula. "Stop your nonsense. You'll get fed without it, you know." She grinned, obviously pleased at his attention even as she chased him off. Their familial affection washed over Joscelyn in a melancholy wave that accentuated her loneliness.

Trent poured himself a cup of coffee and took his place at the table. "So, here's the mysterious woman with the bag of potions." His smile dripped charm. "I suppose since we've kissed and I've seen you with no clothes on, we should introduce ourselves." His teasing smile broadened, and he held out his hand. "I'm Trent."

Joscelyn's face heated as she glanced at Mary. "I had a towel on." She glared at Trent.

"Don't pay him any mind," Mary called over her shoulder. "Trent, behave yourself. This is my friend, Joscelyn—a guest in this house, I might add." She gave Trent a meaningful look. "Joscelyn, this is my ornery, good-for-nothin' grandson, Trent." She stacked more pancakes on the plate and put a hand on Trent's shoulder. "He's all charm, but no harm." She laughed at her own joke. "You know, Trent, you need to settle down and stop chasing women. You're always looking for the next best thing to come along when you already have what you're looking for right in front of you."

Trent looked offended. "Don't you believe her for a minute. I'm full of harm." He winked, and though Joscelyn was sure he knew Mary meant Tonya, he gave her a lascivious grin. "But I couldn't agree with you more about wanting what's right in front of me, Gran."

"Get on with you, Trenton. I mean it." Mary smacked the back of his head with the spatula and he rubbed the spot, chuckling. She flipped two more cakes and said, "Trent, will you please let Joscelyn follow you into town today? I want you to show her around a bit. She's looking for a place to land and I think Bob is still looking for help in the library."

Trent raised his eyebrows at Joscelyn. "You planning on moving here?"

Joscelyn had the uneasy feeling she was losing control of her situation. "No, I *hadn't* planned on it."

"Don't make any decisions till you see Flint River. It's a nice little town and didn't you say you love books?" Mary turned a pointed glance toward Joscelyn.

"I do, but…"

"Perfect. You love books, we need a librarian and bookshop clerk."

"I'm not a librarian, though. You have to go to school for that," Joscelyn argued.

Mary scoffed, "That may be true in Denver, but this is Flint River. We make our own rules."

Trent smiled, "I'll be happy to show you around. Don't bother trying to argue with Gran though. It hasn't worked for me or my brothers our whole lives."

"What about Teddy and my horses?"

Mary turned toward the table. "Leave them here for the time being." She waved her spatula around like the wand of a country fairy-godmother. "Trent, you run Joscelyn into town in your truck. After you give her the tour and talk to Bob, you can bring her back out here. That's better than making the horses stand in a hot trailer all morning, don't you think?"

Trent shrugged, "Sure thing. I have to run into the feed store, anyway." After he polished off a large stack of cakes, he wiped his mouth and pushed his chair back. His appraisal meandered over her frame and his mouth curled into a crooked grin. "You ready?" His eyes sparkled with mischievous intention.

CHAPTER 5

Western Montana was beautiful country, and Joscelyn was glad she stayed at Stone Ranch and didn't miss the scenery by driving through it at night. Her gaze panned over valleys carpeted with rolling, brome-grass pastures dotted with Black Angus. The verdant fields led up to thick, darker green forests of pine that blanketed the foothills. Beyond them, the peaks of the Pintler Range stood sentinel. The vast views were unending.

"What kind of cattle do you raise?" Joscelyn asked.

Trent gestured to a large herd. "This is still our land, for another five miles. Those are my Black Angus there."

"Wow. This sure is gorgeous land up here."

"Yes ma'am. It's a good place to be from. I couldn't live anywhere else." His gaze caressed the pastures. "We're about fifteen miles from Flint River. Gran told me not to pester you with questions, but can I at least know where you're from? Your truck has Colorado plates."

Joscelyn's nerves snapped to alert, and she studied Trent. She had no reason not to trust him, but she'd rather not trust anyone right now. Any little piece of information could be something that gave her away. Her dad always used to say, 'Loose lips sink ships'. "I come from a little town southeast of Denver."

"Good thing you're used to small. Flint River only has a population of about 900."

"That's about the same as my hometown." She spotted the quaint little village coming up on the right. "What a cool place. It looks like we're driving into another era—back into the days of cowboys and Indians."

All the storefronts were painted fresh and gave the impression of an old mining town. Only the cars parked out front gave the year away. Trent drove down Main Street and pointed out the diner, the grocery market, a drugstore with an old-fashioned soda fountain, and the library. He avoided mentioning the beauty salon and Joscelyn realized why when she caught a glimpse of Tonya glaring at them from inside the front window as they drove by.

"Isn't that your girlfriend?" Joscelyn leaned forward to get a better view.

Trent shrugged. "Not anymore." He moved on past the bank, coffee shop, and the Sheriff's Office, stopping in front of the town square at the end of the road. The courthouse perched on a slight hill overlooking the town. Gardens flanked the building, filled with flowers preparing to bloom.

"That's the grand tour. Doesn't take too long." Trent winked.

Joscelyn took in the granite courthouse and then turned to look out the back window at the town. "It's charming."

"Let's go find Bob Tillman. He owns the hardware store and is president of the town council." Trent drove around the courthouse loop. "He's the one to ask about the library/bookshop job."

"I'm not ready to look for a job, Trent. I haven't even decided if I want to stay."

"Can't hurt to check out your options."

Exasperated but also curious, Joscelyn decided to go along for the ride. The wave of Stone determination had bowled her over.

Bob Tillman left his shop without locking the door to show Joscelyn the library. He hurried his large, overall-covered frame up the street. The seams of his camouflage hunting shirt strained with each swing of his arms. Joscelyn and Trent had to step-it-out to keep up with him.

"So, *you're* the mystery woman Trent's been seeing on the side, huh?" Bob puffed over his shoulder.

The air rushed out of Joscelyn's lungs and her cheeks burned. Small town gossip traveled like the Pony Express. She turned wide eyes to Trent who smiled and shrugged. He wasn't any help. "No, actually I'm *not*. I only met Trent this morning."

Bob stopped in front of the storefront library and assessing Joscelyn, he cocked his head to the side. "That's not the way *I* heard it."

Great, I haven't even been here for 24 hours and I'm already the town floozie. Joscelyn glared at Trent, silently urging him to defend the truth. His eyes sparked with mischief and he said nothing.

"I don't know what you heard, Mr. Tillman, but I have only known Trent Stone for a few hours."

"Don't get fussed now. It's good to meet you either way, Miss Joscelyn. Always nice to know a fellow bibliophile, no matter the circumstances."

Joscelyn resisted the urge to stamp her foot and insist on her innocence. Instead, she went with the new subject. "I do love books, Mr. Tillman, but you should know, I don't have any library training." Ribs of panic rolled up her throat and she swallowed to push them back down. Everyone she met seemed certain of her future here in Flint River, a town she planned on driving through, stopping only for gas. "I worked in a bookstore once, in college, but that's all."

Bob unlocked the front door to the library. "Perfect. That's more than Erma, our previous librarian had when she started. You'll already know how to run the bookshop side of things. The library part will grow on you. How hard can it be to write down the books people check out?"

Joscelyn shook her head and raised her eyebrows in question at Trent. He smiled and shrugged, holding the door open for her to follow Bob inside. The musty library/bookshop hadn't been dusted in a long time, but the alluring scent of books drew her further in. It was a small space, laughable even, for a library. The library half of the space was to the right of the entryway. There were only three rows of bookshelves including one along the wall. A curved counter stood at the back and looked ready for a librarian to take up position behind it. The original woodwork emanated a warm, antique, honeyed glow.

Joscelyn asked, "What happened to Erma? Why did she leave?"

Bob faced her and held his beefy hands together as if in prayer. "Well, she died three months ago and the library's been closed ever since. Erma was 88 years young, bless her heart."

Trent feigned solemnity. "Yeah, bless her heart." He shook his head and put a hand over the left side of his chest. He chased his false grief away with a wink and a smirk at Joscelyn.

She gave him a sidelong glare with a raised brow and followed Bob back through the entranceway to the left side of the space. "The bookshop is on this side. There are both new and used books here." He gestured at a couple of shelves and a large reading table.

There were even fewer books in the shop section, but it was a welcoming space with a small cozy sofa flanked by two overstuffed chairs and a low coffee table. The comfortable looking furniture faced a small, wood-burning fireplace. Something in Joscelyn's heart relaxed. She could picture herself reading, snuggled up by the fire in that room.

"There's a small kitchen area in the back and a counter for coffee if folks want." Bob smoothed his hand over the counter and wiped the dust on his pant leg.

"Mr. Tillman, the truth is, I wasn't planning on staying here in Flint River so I'm not really looking for a job." Joscelyn said the words but her hands itched to glide along the covers of all the books.

Bob harrumphed. "Don't you like Flint River? You won't find a better place to settle down."

"No. I mean… yes. I love your town. It's just that…"

Trent nudged her arm. "You don't have any other plans, you told me so yourself. This morning, you told me you weren't sure *where* you were headed. Why not give this a try? If it doesn't work, no harm done."

"What about my horses? My dog?" Joscelyn couldn't resist re-shelving a book that had fallen to the floor. "I'm actually a social worker. A therapist—not a librarian." Her hand flew up to her mouth as if to shove her personal details back inside. Trent's brows slid together and he cocked his head. She blinked her eyes at the men in consternation.

Heedless of Joscelyn's anxiety, Bob said, "That fits right in. People always want to find someone willing to listen to their problems. What better place than the library?" Bob held out his hands, palms up and shrugged.

Joscelyn had to laugh at that reasoning, even as she worried Lenny might track her more easily if she gave away too much information.

"You can board your horses at my place," Trent chimed in. "In fact, I'll trade you, board in exchange for you doing the nighttime feeding. It won't cost you a dime."

Joscelyn spread her hands on her hips. "What about the cost of hay?"

Trent's mouth tilted up on one side. "I grow my own, and I always have more than I need. Of course, if you want to give them grain, that's on you. Same with farrier and vet care."

She was losing the battle but wasn't too upset about it. It might be fun to lie low and play librarian until the police caught up with Lenny. She tried one last argument. "I don't have anywhere to live."

"Plumb didn't think of that," Bob said.

"What's the pay for being a librarian, Bob?" Trent asked. "Alice might rent that apartment over her garage."

"I honestly don't think the small wages the town can offer would cover rent with enough left for groceries and gas." Bob pulled a handkerchief out of his pocket and wiped his fleshy face. He paused as his fresh-mopped eyes settled on a closed door across from the front entrance. He stared at the door and a slow smile plumped up his cheeks. "I have an idea. I'm not sure it'll work but hear me out." Bob pointed to the narrow door. "That door leads to the attic stairs. We've used that space for storage for so long, I have no idea what's up there. Maybe we could clean it out and make it livable?"

Without waiting for an answer, he hurried over and threw open the door. Dust filled the air, dancing in the sunlight.

"Wait. I can't live in an attic. What would I use for a kitchen or shower? This is all happening too fast." Joscelyn decided to stop the steamroller. "It seems like we're pushing beyond common sense to make this happen."

"Let's see what we find." Bob pulled a string attached to a bare bulb and disappeared up the stairs. Joscelyn and Trent followed.

It was determined, primarily by Bob and agreed upon by Trent, that the tiny attic space would make a perfectly adequate 'loft' apartment. Someone had lived in the space before, though that was likely fifty years ago or more.

"It just needs a little sprucing up. I own the hardware store, for crying out loud. How hard can it be?" Bob assured Joscelyn they could finish the work in a day or two, provided she would go through the storage boxes and organize what should be kept and what could be given or thrown away.

"I don't know," Joscelyn hemmed. "I don't have any furniture."

Bob clapped dust from his hands. "How much furniture does one girl need?"

"Well," the word came out on a rush of breath. "At least a bed and a place to sit." Joscelyn narrowed her eyes and shook her head.

"I think Gran has some old furniture in storage out at the ranch. You could borrow stuff until you get your own things. I think it'll work," Trent said as he looked around the attic. Sunlight spilled into the room through the wavy, antique, leaded-glass in the tall windows overlooking Main Street. The top of each window was accented with panes of stained glass that dripped colored pools of light onto the floor.

"We need to discuss rent and the pay for a librarian-slash-shopkeeper." Joscelyn wasn't completely against the crazy idea but she was low on cash and wouldn't get paid during her sudden leave of absence. It might be a good thing to land in Flint River for a while. She had to stop running at some point and this particular point came with a job and an apartment. *Okay, it would only be one room with a sink, a hotplate, and a microwave for a kitchen, with a closet bathroom. Worse, the apartment was across the street from Tonya's beauty parlor.* Indignation flared up, heating Joscelyn's ears. *I didn't do anything wrong— damned if I'll let Tonya's gossip chase me away.*

Bob interrupted her thoughts. "I'm sure we can come to an agreement about the rent. Maybe if we reduce your pay, you could live here rent-free, except for utilities." All his teeth showed as he smiled at this plan.

A smart grin spread across Trent's mouth. "You could always stay at my place, if this is too small and you want to be with your horses."

That sealed it. Joscelyn pursed her lips at Trent. "No, thank you." She addressed Bob. "What do you say if I try this for one month?" *I'm going to have to decide what to do about my place in Kiowa by then, anyway.*

"I think we can manage a trial period, Miss Joscelyn." Bob stuffed his hands between the bib of his overalls and his shirt.

"Who will show me what you want done and how to do it? How will I handle the money from the shop, for example?"

Bob rocked back and forth on his heels. "As far as job training, I'm sure you're better qualified to figure it out than anyone in town. You've worked in a bookstore before. I'm sure you'll do fine." He reached out with a big, beefy hand and patted Joscelyn's shoulder.

Her mouth fell open. She would be in over her head with this job and didn't seem to be able to convince Bob or Trent of this fact. She shook her head. "But—"

"I'll be back this afternoon with a few instructions, how does that sound?" Bob said, and on his way out the door he handed Joscelyn the keys.

As much as they coerced her into her new situation, a raw energy filled her body at the thought of trying something completely new and unexpected.

Back inside Trent's truck, Joscelyn pulled a notepad from her purse and began a list of items she would need. The first thing she wrote was "cleaning supplies".

"A therapist, huh? Why do I get the feeling you didn't want anyone to know that?" Trent turned the key.

"It's not that. Never mind. Anyway, it looks like I'm going to be a librarian now." Joscelyn kept her tone airy. Hoping to move the conversation away from her past.

"It's not like it's something to be ashamed of… is it?" Trent didn't take the hint. "Did you screw somebody up or something?"

Joscelyn's heart bumped and she swallowed. "No. I'm just taking a break."

"A break. Not a vacation? Why a break?"

Scrambling for an explanation that would stop the questions, Joscelyn answered, "A vacation is only two weeks, and you get paid. I'm taking the summer. That's why I brought my animals and I need a job and a place to stay."

Trent's eyes narrowed slightly. "So, you loaded up all your animals and took them with you on your *break* without any kind of plan?"

Joscelyn swallowed and nodded. Her eyes met his, and she sensed him waiting for her to be the first to look away.

When she didn't, Trent raised his brows and shifted his truck into reverse. "I'll see what furniture Gran has stored away at the ranch. Why don't I leave you at the market so you can get what you need? I've got to get to work. I'll feed and do barn chores tonight since you'll be getting settled. Then, later I'll take you to dinner." Trent said it all like it was a given. And in fact, it was the easiest thing in the world for Joscelyn to allow herself to be swept away by such a good-looking guy. *Way too easy.* "I'll have one of my hands bring your truck into town this afternoon."

Joscelyn straightened her spine. "Hold on. You're assuming I'll go out with you."

Trent blinked his eyes lazily and gave her a knowing grin. "You're assuming I'm asking you on a date." He lifted his hands in mock surrender. "I was just trying to be neighborly. You can do it all on your own if you'd rather."

Embarrassed, she rubbed her hands over her face. "I'm sorry Trent. You're being very kind. It's just this whole thing is a little crazy. You know that, right?" Joscelyn peered at him.

He shrugged. "You'd know. You're the therapist. But it seems to me like it's just good luck for everyone."

"Thanks, Trent—for everything." Joscelyn sat back against the seat. "People here are so willing to help me even though I'm a complete stranger. It's unbelievable."

"Small town livin', can't be beat." He chuckled. "Of course, Bob's getting plenty from you too. Don't be fooled." He dropped her off at the market, which was only one block away from the library. "See you tonight."

Armed with vinegar, rags, rubber gloves, and a broom, Joscelyn got to work. She went through the storage boxes first. They were mostly filled with papers and files. They might have some value to the town, so she stacked them by the stairs. Perhaps the museum had a historical society. Several of the boxes housed books. Joscelyn resisted delving into that treasure trove until she was being paid to add them either to the library shelves or the shop. She swept and dusted, saving the window washing till last. The evening light caused the wood floor to gleam and Joscelyn knew she would be very comfortable here as soon as there was somewhere to sit.

"Anybody home?" The bell on the front door tinkled and Trent's voice rang up the stairs.

Joscelyn jumped, her pulse sharp against her temples. *I've got to stop freaking out over sudden noises.* She glanced at her watch and was surprised to see that it was so late. She hollered, "I'm up here."

Trent took the stairs two at a time, carrying her bag in one hand and a lamp in the other. Teddy almost knocked him over as he squeezed past him to run to her.

"Hey, buddy!" Joscelyn patted his head and kissed his nose. His fluffy tail wagged. She looked up, "Thanks for bringing him."

"Sure. He's a good dog." Trent set the lamp on a box and wheeled her luggage to her. "I have a table, a stray chair, and a mattress with box springs for tonight. Gran sent sheets and towels, along with some food. She always sends food." He smiled when he spoke of his grandma. Joscelyn liked that about him. "My hand, Randy, drove your truck. It's parked out front. We'll bring the furniture up— then will you be ready to go?"

"Yeah, just let me change and freshen up a little." Joscelyn was glad to have her dog and truck back, not to mention relieved to reunite with her Ruger and shotgun. She would leave the 12-gauge locked underneath the back seat of her truck, but she wanted her 9mm inside with her, even though Flint River seemed safe and friendly.

Safe as long as Lenny doesn't find me.

CHAPTER 6

Trent opened the door for Joscelyn and followed her into the town's local brewery. Tall stainless-steel vats stood side by side across the brick wall in the back. The pub was more crowded than she expected, only two tables were still open. Conversation and laughter filled the warm taproom. Joscelyn made her way across the worn wooden floor, to a high-top table and sat, hanging her purse strap over the back of the tall chair.

Trent pulled out the chair next to hers and handed her the beer list. "Hope you like beer. I don't think they serve wine."

"I do. There are hundreds of craft breweries around Denver, so I'm a bit spoiled by good beer." She read through the list.

A woman approached their table and without taking her eyes from the menu, Joscelyn said, "I'd like to try the August Amber, please."

"You'd obviously like to try more than that," the woman snapped.

Joscelyn's brows shot up and she jerked her head around. When she realized the woman wasn't the waitress, her eyes narrowed at Tonya, the woman who had slapped her the night before. Tonya looked vulnerable in her pale green, 1930s-era drop-waist dress. The color in her cheeks matched the pink streak in her fair hair. Joscelyn opened her mouth, but before she could speak, Trent jumped in.

"Don't start in, Tonya. We're just having dinner." He signaled for the pub's waitress.

Tonya ignored Trent and addressed Joscelyn. "Who are you, anyhow? How do you two know each other?" She fisted her hands and set them on her hips. "I knew something was going on last night when you showed up at Trent's place." Her eyes bore into Joscelyn's.

"Listen—Tonya, is it?" Heat rushed to Joscelyn's head. "You've got it all wrong. I didn't know Trent before last night."

"Oh sure. You expect me to believe that? Why'd you kiss him then? Make it a habit of kissing strange men, do you?"

Rather than try to take their order, the waitress busied herself wiping an already clean table while canting an ear in their direction. Other customers turned and gawked at the escalating scene.

Trent spoke, his frustration hardening his tone. "For God's sake, Tonya, that whole thing happened because you were harping at me about being friendly to other women."

Tonya gaped. "*Friendly*? Is that what you call it?"

Trent stood and leaned down to speak into Tonya's ear. "This isn't the time or place to cause a scene. We're over. That's what you said you wanted, so if you'll excuse us…"

The color in Tonya's cheeks deepened and her eyes threatened a downpour. "Fine, Trenton Stone. This is it. It *really is* over this time." She spun around and rushed toward the door. In her hurry, she caught her hand in the long string of beads around her neck and rammed her hip into the corner of a table.

Joscelyn didn't know what to do or say. She felt bad for the woman but she wasn't the cause of their problems. Although, it obviously looked that way to everyone staring at them. *Not an ideal impression to make in a new town.*

Trent sat down. "Sorry about that. She loves to put on a show." He picked up a menu.

Joscelyn wished they could leave, but wasn't about to let Tonya's drama chase her off and make her look guilty.

~*~

The next morning, after a couple hours of organizing books and boxes, Joscelyn took a break to go to the hardware store to buy a mini-fridge. She also needed to order a new phone. Overwhelmed by the possibility that Lenny could track her down by her credit card, Joscelyn waited as long as she could, before making any purchases. Tired of being oppressed by such thoughts, she pulled the library door closed with enough force to rattle the ancient glass. A frenetic energy twisted its way up from her thighs, through her torso and wrenched her stomach before it rooted in knots at the base of her skull. She pressed her forehead against the cool window and waited for the sensation to recede. She took several deep breaths before stepping off the stoop toward her truck.

"Good morning, Miss Joscelyn," Bob greeted her. "How do you like your new place?"

"Fine, thanks, but I realized I need a fridge."

Bob rang up her purchase and helped load the box into the bed of her truck. "My sons should already be at your place, starting to fix her up. How's the library organization going?"

"I'm focusing on that today. Hey, Bob, would you mind if I borrowed your phone? I lost mine and haven't had a chance to get a new one yet."

"Well, of course, you can, young lady." He stretched the opening of his overall pocket with his hefty hand and pulled out his phone, handing it to Joscelyn.

"Thanks. I'll just be a minute." She gestured that she would make her call a few steps away. After searching for the number for the Castle Rock Police Department, she dialed and asked for the detective on her case. They bounced her around on hold a while before she finally spoke to him.

"I wondered if you've found Leonard Perkins yet?"

"No ma'am, not yet. We went to his apartment, but he hasn't been there in days. We're following up on a few other leads and I assure you we're doing everything we can. Until then, be sure to let us know if he tries to contact you in any way."

Joscelyn lowered her voice. "Lenny called my phone two days ago and said he knew I was in Montana. When he told me that, I panicked and threw my phone in a lake."

"How close is that lake to where you are now?"

"About a two-hour drive."

"So even if he was tracking your phone, he doesn't know where you are currently. We'll find him Ms. Turner, it's only a matter of time."

Joscelyn's sternum grew cold like a shaft of ice. "Will you please keep me informed? I left Denver to stay safe, but I can't be gone forever."

"Of course, ma'am, I'll let you know. Thanks for calling."

"Wait! You have no way to reach me without my phone. I'll call back as soon as I get a new one and give you the number."

"That'll be fine, Ms. Turner. Don't worry and have a nice day." The detective ended the call.

Joscelyn returned Bob's phone.

"Everything all right, Miss Joscelyn?" Bob pursed his fleshy lips.

She strained to act normal but Joscelyn felt like she was in a bubble under water. It had been a week and Lenny was still at large. *Where could he be? On his way to Montana?*

"I'm fine. Thanks for letting me use your phone." She turned, and in a daze, left the shop.

The grocery market was right across the street. Joscelyn waited for a Gator utility-vehicle to pass before she stepped off the curb. The driver was a thin man with dark, lank hair and Joscelyn drew a sharp breath. Cold pricks spread across her upper arms.

Once the sun hit his face, Joscelyn realized the man didn't resemble Lenny at all. She closed her eyes and released her pent-up breath. Rubbing her gooseflesh away, she crossed the street, noticing a good number of residents drove the smaller vehicles around town instead of using cars. If she was going to jump at every slight, dark-haired man she saw, she may as well have stayed in Denver.

Shopping for a few staple items, Joscelyn gathered milk, cereal, and sandwich fixings in her basket before perusing the produce aisle. Heading for the apple bin, she almost ran headlong into Tonya's grocery cart.

"Well, look who it is." Tonya sneered. "The other woman."

"Tonya." Joscelyn breathed in and swallowed her irritation. "Listen, if there's another woman, it isn't me." She offered her hand. "I'm Joscelyn Turner, by the way, and I'm going to be staying in Flint River for a month or so. While I'm here, I'll be working at the library."

"That's right across from my beauty shop."

"I wondered if that was your shop. That's great." Joscelyn said, hoping they could smooth things out and start again.

Tonya assessed Joscelyn's messy-bun hairdo, before she let her gaze flow down across her "Will Work for Hay" t-shirt and her dirty work jeans. In comparison to Tonya's vintage blouse and long lace skirt, the woman's perusal made Joscelyn feel grungy.

"You should stop in when you get a minute. I can try to help you with…" Tonya made a vague sweeping motion that might have included all of Joscelyn's appearance.

Sure, and I'd come out scalped. Regardless of how it was intended, Joscelyn decided to take the suggestion as a peace offering. "Thanks. I'll see you around."

Joscelyn spent the rest of the day in the library devising a system to check out books without the use of a computer. The old manila check-out cards came to mind, and she scribbled 'black ink pad and date stamp' on the running list of items she needed. The bell on the front-door chimed. A sweet buttery scent filled the room followed by a middle-aged woman carrying a plate of cookies.

"Hello?" the woman called out.

"Hi. Welcome." Joscelyn stood and went around the counter to greet her visitor. Teddy sprang to his feet and offered the newcomer his cold nose.

"I'm Sharon Cline." The woman flattened her lips and backed away from Joscelyn's dog. "I own the quilt store down the street." She lifted the goodies toward Joscelyn. "These are to welcome you to Flint River." Her eyes darted around the library before she let go of the plate.

Joscelyn accepted the cookies and set them on the counter. "How thoughtful, thank you," she said before introducing herself.

Sharon peered down the hall to the shop. "I'm glad to meet you and am so excited to have you opening the library. You're just in time." She slid her fingertips along a bookshelf and glanced to see if they came away dusty.

"In time for what?"

"The Annual County Quilt Contest. It's always held in May and the quilts are displayed in here." Sharon gestured at the walls of the library/bookshop.

"Oh?" Joscelyn bit her lower lip. "No one told me."

Sharon placed a hand on Joscelyn's forearm. "Yes, and I was hoping you would start up the community book club again too. Let's have a cup of coffee and I'll tell you all about it."

Joscelyn was glad she bought coffee that morning. "Let me make a pot."

"Two spoons of sugar, please."

"I'm sorry, but I don't have any sugar yet." Joscelyn wiped her hands on her thighs.

Sharon's eyebrows drew together and she shook her head. "Never mind then. Next time. You should be prepared, however, most of the other gals use a ton of creamer. The hazelnut kind."

"Good to know." Joscelyn noted the additions on her grocery list before she started a fresh pot.

Trent ambled through the door at 4:30 that afternoon and removed his straw cowboy hat. "How's the prettiest librarian in Montana?"

"You're a such a cornball." Joscelyn laughed at his smarmy line and lopsided grin. "I've made some progress on the lending system but there's a lot more to this job than I thought." She crossed her arms. "I've also met several new people today and I don't think I'm making a great first impression on the folks here."

"This job isn't anything you can't handle, and you shouldn't worry about what people think, anyway."

"I don't know about that, but as long as there's no annual chili cook-off taking place in the bookshop I can screw up, I think I can manage."

Trent licked his lips. "Mm, Chili—that sounds like a good idea. But don't worry, the cook-off happens in the park." Joscelyn rolled her eyes. "I stopped in to tell you, your buckskin is lame—left, hind."

Joscelyn set a stack of books on the counter. "Fargo? What happened, do you know?"

Trent shrugged. "There's no injury I can see and no heat. He probably strained something on the long trailer ride or by kicking something when you turned him out. I thought you might want to take a look."

"Yeah, let me lock up. I'm headed out there to feed anyway."

"I'll drive you. Then we can get a bite to eat after we check on him. Sound good?" Trent set his hat back on and tilted his head toward the door.

Joscelyn shook her head at his easy confidence. She thought of her empty refrigerator and the lone, cast-off plate in the cupboard. Grateful for the company, she agreed. "Okay, but tonight we go Dutch."

"Not on your life. Gran would have my hide if she found out I let a woman pay. It's not worth my skin. My treat, come on." He gave her another one of his trademark grins and she grabbed her purse.

"There's a barbeque place about thirty miles west of my ranch. We can head there after we take care of Fargo. How does that sound?" Trent held the door for her.

"Great. I love barbeque." Joscelyn double locked the door behind them when they left.

CHAPTER 7

On Tuesday, Joscelyn treated herself to breakfast at Alice's Diner, French toast smothered in butter and draped with thick maple syrup that tasted more like dessert than breakfast. Joscelyn savored a bite as Trent came through the door. Female voices from around the restaurant called out to him in greeting.

"Mornin', ladies." He doled out his charm, smiling, nodding, and even waving.

Oh, brother. Joscelyn rolled her eyes so hard her chin rolled with them.

Trent took the stool next to Joscelyn at the counter. "Coffee, please, Alice," he gave the older woman the same flirtatious grin he shared with the other women. "Extra sweet." He winked.

"You're really something, you know it?" Joscelyn arched an eyebrow at him.

He chuckled. "Well, thank you."

Again, she rolled her eyes with exaggeration. Alice brought Trent's coffee and topped off Joscelyn's.

She took a sip. "How's Fargo today?"

"Less sore. Your hosing down his leg the last couple of nights is helping. He just needs to rest. I have him confined in his stall."

"Thanks."

A woman in her mid-fifties, with bobbed, steel-gray hair worn in a uniform curl at her jawline, rose from a booth by the window. She straightened a dark business suit over her stout figure and approached them. "Good morning, Trent." She rested her hand on Trent's back. "Do you mind if I take a minute of your time?"

Trent turned his head. "Good morning, Mrs. Bell. How can I help you?" He moved to stand.

"Sit. I won't be long." Mrs. Bell patted his shoulder.

The woman smiled at Joscelyn. "Hello. I'm Margaret Bell, the school principal. Aren't you our new librarian?"

Joscelyn nodded and stretched out her hand in greeting. "Joscelyn Turner."

"I'm looking forward to the book-club starting up again. When is the next meeting?"

"I'm still getting organized, but I was thinking Thursday evening. I'll put out a flyer."

The woman nodded and turned back to Trent. "I'd like to speak with you about your niece."

"Is she okay?" Trent's expression gathered in concern and he swiveled his stool to face her. Mrs. Bell hesitated and glanced at Joscelyn. "It's all right, you can talk in front of her."

Mrs. Bell pursed her lips and leaned in. "Sadie has been acting out at school lately. I've tried to call her father, but he never answers the phone and he doesn't return my calls."

Trent's face turned grim. "What's she been doing?"

"For the past several months, she's been smarting off, not participating, and generally being a distraction to other students. Nothing too bad though until yesterday, I caught her with a group of other girls skipping class and..." Mrs. Bell peered around the diner and lowered her voice, "smoking marijuana."

"Sadie? None of that sounds like her."

"I'm afraid she and the other girls are making some bad choices."

Trent dragged a tan, worked-roughened hand over his mouth and chin. "Thanks for letting me know. I'll talk to her and I'll go see Cade."

Mrs. Bell gave Trent a grim smile and a nod. After she left, Joscelyn sipped her coffee in silence while Trent mulled over the situation with his niece.

Several minutes passed before Joscelyn cleared her throat and said, "Did I tell you I worked with at-risk teens in Colorado?" Trent considered her out of the corner of his eye and she continued. "A lot of times, I used horses in therapy with the kids. It's effective."

Trent's head snapped around. He raised his chin and narrowed his eyes. His voice took on a steel edge. "You think Sadie's at-risk and needs therapy?"

"I didn't say that, Trent. Take it easy. I don't know Sadie." Joscelyn's shoulders lifted in a slight shrug. "Some kids experiment with pot once or twice and that's it. They go back to being kids who try to stay out of trouble for the most part and try to succeed. 'At-risk' is a term that basically implies a kid is not likely to transition into adulthood successfully. They need extra help to navigate through their teen years."

Trent shook his head and sighed.

"What's Sadie's life like at home?"

He peered at her before turning to stare into his coffee cup. "It's not really any of your business."

"Okay." Joscelyn held up her hand. "I'm sorry. I was only trying to help." She reached for her purse to pay her bill.

Without looking up from his cup, Trent answered, his voice low. "It's a mess. Her dad—my brother—hasn't been the same since he came back from the war and her mom abandoned her while Cade was in Afghanistan. Gran took Sadie in until Cade came home."

"That's a lot for a young girl to handle." Joscelyn placed cash on the counter.

Trent's eyes flashed. "I suppose you think we're letting her down?"

"No." Joscelyn touched Trent's arm. "I don't know anything about your family's situation and I'm not making assumptions."

The muscles across Trent's back and shoulders were as tight as his jaw. For a second, she considered running her hand across his shoulders in comfort, but he returned his glare to his coffee, dismissing her.

She sighed. "You could try to talk to her. Ask her what's going on." Joscelyn folded her napkin and set it on top of her plate. "How's her relationship with her dad?"

He surprised her by answering. "It's been hard for Cade but it's not his fault, he just needs some time."

"So, not great?"

Trent pulled in the corner of his mouth and shook his head.

"I'm sorry, Trent. Let me know if there is anything I can do."

~*~

Book Club night arrived and Joscelyn turned on several lamps in the sitting area of the book shop. It was too warm for a fire, but Joscelyn thought the setting would certainly be cozy with one. She brought in a few extra chairs and made a circle. Seven women rsvp'd, but she made room for more, just in case. Joscelyn brewed a pot of coffee and had plenty of sugar and hazelnut creamer on hand. She looked forward to meeting some other women.

Margaret Bell arrived first. She bent down to accept Teddy's welcome with a scratch behind his ears. Joscelyn called her dog and let him out back to a fenced-in patio area. She poured Margaret a cup of coffee as three other women she hadn't met yet came through the door. By seven o'clock, nine women including Joscelyn, sat with their refreshments, ready to begin.

"I love what you've done with the shop. It's never looked so welcoming," said an elegant woman in her mid-thirties.

An older lady sitting next to her lifted her coffee mug toward Joscelyn. "Thanks for hosting book club. I like having it here in the midst of all these books."

"You're welcome. I'm glad you all could come. Are these all the members of the group?"

Margaret answered, "There are a few others that come and go, depending on what we're reading."

"What book are you discussing tonight?"

"It's called XO, by Jeffery Deaver." Alice held up her copy. "It's about a famous country singer and a psycho fan who stalks her."

A hard shudder ran the length of Joscelyn's entire body. It shook her so hard she wondered if anyone saw the ripple. "I haven't read that." She swallowed. "Do you normally read thrillers?

The elegant woman held up an old coffee can. "Not necessarily, we all put our suggestions in this can and we draw a title out each time to read for the next month."

"Oh, good." Joscelyn took her coffee behind the counter and snuck a shot of whisky into the brew while the ladies dove into their thoughts about their current read.

At the end of the meeting the women chatted as they gathered their things. Joscelyn joined in while she collected cups and napkins.

"What're you doing about Tracy's detention?" one mother asked another.

"We've grounded her. I can't believe they were smoking marijuana. Where do you suppose they got it?" Joscelyn's ears perked up, and she wondered if these were the girls who were with Trent's niece.

"We sat Dakota down and made her tell us. I hate to say it, but she told her dad and me that Tracy had it."

The first mother's face turned bright red. "What? That's a bald-faced lie. I can't believe Dakota's blaming Tracy as though *she* is Miss Innocent. Tracy told us it was Sadie's idea, and that didn't surprise me at all."

Margaret stepped in. "All the girls who were caught smoking are being equally punished. We need to help them *all* make better decisions."

"Some more than others, I think." Dakota's mother glared at Tracy's mom.

Margaret turned to Joscelyn, her eyes pleading. "Mary Stone told me you are a therapist and did work using horses with troubled teens in Colorado?"

Joscelyn nodded as she stuffed the paper cups in the trashcan. Trent must have told Mary about their conversation.

"I was wondering if you might come during detention one day this week and talk with these girls. They're good girls, they just did a stupid thing. I'm hoping we can get them back on the right track."

Joscelyn smiled at the women but was met with skeptical glares. "I'd be happy to do whatever I can—if everyone agrees. How many girls are involved?" Joscelyn missed working with kids.

"Four. Sadie, as you know, and their daughters," Margret gestured toward the two mothers, "Tracy and Dakota, and a fourth girl named Lisa. Detention is held in the school office from 3:00 to 4:30."

The moms both crossed their arms over their chests. Tracy's mother spoke to Margaret without taking her eyes off Joscelyn. "Joscelyn doesn't know our girls. She's really just a stranger. No offense, Joscelyn, but you don't even have kids of your own. I don't know why we would suddenly trust our children to your care." Heat radiated into Joscelyn's face and she clamped her teeth together to keep her mouth closed. She balled a paper napkin in her fist.

Dakota's mom moved her hands to her waist. "Are you afraid the truth will come out? That you'll find out your daughter is a drug pusher?"

"Ladies, please." Margaret held her hands together in front of her chest. "I'm sure everyone in this room wants what's best for all four girls. We're not trying to find blame. I thought it might be wise, since we have an expert available to us, to ask for Joscelyn's help."

The room grew silent while everyone waited for a decision. Finally, Tracy's mother acquiesced and shrugged one shoulder.

Joscelyn forced her ire back down her throat. "The library is closed on Sunday and Monday, I could come by on Monday afternoon." Joscelyn said. She turned to the mothers. "I know it's tempting to want to assign blame, but that only puts up walls and defenses instead of getting to the real problem. Let's try to work together to help these kids. Okay?"

CHAPTER 8

High schools nationwide all smelled the same—an odd mixture of canned green beans left from hot lunch, glue, paper, copy-machine toner, disinfectant, and adolescent sweat. Joscelyn slid into the comfortable scene like she would her slippers. She entered the office, and the secretary paged Mrs. Bell on the intercom.

"Thank you for coming." Margaret buttoned her gray blazer as she came out of her office. "The girls are in here." She led Joscelyn to a small conference room next door to the nurse's clinic.

Joscelyn assessed the teens when she entered the room. Four girls slouched back in their chairs as though they were bored out of existence. Three of them wore trendy clothes—leggings under tiny skirts or skin-tight jeans with layered shirts, high heels, and messy buns. The fourth girl wore baggy jeans with rips in the knees and thighs. Safety-pins haphazardly strained to hold some of the holes together. Her feet were encased in black, lace-up, paddock boots. Joscelyn assumed they were the girl's attempt at combat boots. An army-green, man-sized jacket completed her statement. Her rich, coffee-colored hair didn't look washed, and she rimmed her nut-brown eyes with half-a-pencil's-worth of kohl.

Nothing unusual here.

"Girls, this is Ms. Turner. She's a teen counselor visiting Flint River from Colorado. Your parents and I have asked her to come and talk with you today." Margaret glowered at the tallest blonde who rolled her eyes at the introduction and continued to tap on the screen of her phone with long, purple fingernails. "Tracy, rudeness will only increase your detention."

Uncertain eyes darted toward the rebellious girl who Joscelyn figured was the ringleader of their little circus. Tracy ignored the principal.

Margaret sighed and pulled down on the front of her suit coat. She introduced the girls, indicating each one as she said their name. Lisa, a petite pixie no one would guess was over the age of eleven, wore her black hair twisted up in two space-buns on either side of her head. Tracy looked like she would grow into a beauty one day, if she could lose the sneer cutting across her face. The country-looking girl with sand-colored hair was Dakota. She regarded Joscelyn with a direct blue-eyed gaze from an open face.

It surprised Joscelyn that the somber girl hiding behind the large coat was Trent's niece, Sadie. She didn't resemble Trent at all, with his blond good looks and easy smile. This girl seemed uncomfortable in her skin and her black-rimmed eyes stared resolutely at the table.

"It's nice to meet you girls," she said. "You can call me Joscelyn."

"Do you need anything?" Margaret clasped her hands in front of her stomach as she spoke.

"No, I think we've got it from here. Thank you, Mrs. Bell." Joscelyn pulled out a chair. Anticipation fed by the obvious challenge gave her a sense of fulfillment. This was the work of her heart. At the thought of her job, Joscelyn's chest tightened and her nostrils flared. Lenny had forced her away from the one and only thing in her life that gave her purpose. She shook her head and forced Leonard Perkins from her mind.

Margaret turned to go. "I'll leave you to it, then."

Joscelyn sat down and crossed her ankle over her knee. She looked at each of the girls before she spoke. "First things first. All cellphones face-down in the center of the table." Joscelyn pulled her own phone out of her back pocket and led by example. Lisa and Dakota followed suit. With their action Joscelyn identified the rule followers.

Joscelyn waited for the other two. "Sadie? Tracy?" Sadie reached in an oversized pocket and tossed her phone across the table. It slid into the other phones and came to a stop. Tracy tapped and swiped. "Tracy, this is detention, not social hour. Please put your phone on the table."

The eyes that met Joscelyn's were hostile as they narrowed to mascaraed slits. Joscelyn held her stare until with a sneer, Tracy tossed her phone on the table, face up.

"Turn your phone over, please."

"Gawd! What difference does it make?" Tracy said, but she flopped her phone over with a groan.

"Thank you." Joscelyn waited until she had all their eyes on her. "So, why are you ladies in detention?"

The girls exchanged glances, but no one answered. Joscelyn allowed the silence to expand. "Let's make a deal. What we talk about in here is private. I won't share it and I am asking each of you to agree not to share anything outside of this group either. This a safe place to be open and honest. Okay?"

Finally, Tracy looked at Joscelyn as though she was the dumbest person on earth and spoke up. "We got caught smoking weed—which you already know. Big deal."

"You don't think it's a big deal?" Joscelyn asked, careful to keep her tone level and without surprise or judgement.

"No." An ornery glint flickered in Tracy's eye. "You're from Colorado, aren't you? Weed's legal there." She smirked.

"Not for thirteen-year-olds." Joscelyn raised a brow and cocked her head. "Why do you suppose that is?"

Tracy rolled her eyes and jutted her chin. Ignoring the question, she said, "My mom warned me about you. Brand-new to town and think you can come here and fix everyone."

Joscelyn held Tracy's glare until the girl shook her head with what Joscelyn took as contempt. Tracy looked away. Lisa and Dakota stared at the table. Only Sadie met Joscelyn's eye.

"What do *you* think, Sadie?"

The girl shrugged with an air of defiance and held the stare.

"Well, I have to tell you, I honestly don't think having you girls sit in this room after school every day is doing much to help you think about the choice you made." Joscelyn paused. "You know, every choice we make has consequences. Some good, some bad, and some neutral." All four pairs of eyes gradually turned toward Joscelyn. "What were some of the results of your decision to try pot?"

Tracy sprang to answer, her smug sarcasm in place. "We got high—which was awesome. It's just something to do. School's boring." Her glare was an open challenge.

Joscelyn gave no outward reaction, knowing she had to be patient through the adolescent "tough-guy" act until she could build trust with them. That didn't lessen the sting from the girl's attitude though. She stood, picked up a dry-erase marker, and wrote the word "Consequences" across the top of the white board mounted on the wall.

"All right, so a couple of consequences of smoking pot are getting high, and it's something to do when you're bored." She wrote the responses under the heading. "What else?"

The girls peeked at each other out of the corners of their eyes. Lisa's arm rose as if on its own and Joscelyn smiled. "You don't have to raise your hand, Lisa. This is just a conversation. I want to help you look at why you made the choice you did and the effect it had. So, what do you think?"

Lisa's voice was soft. "Well, obviously… detention."

"Okay." Joscelyn wrote that down and turned to face the girls again.

Dakota cocked her head. "My parents were really pissed. I'm grounded for a month. I can't even go to 4-H." Joscelyn wrote "grounded" and then "missing out on fun activities".

"Yeah, but the ninth-grade boys think we're cool," Tracy argued. Without hesitating Joscelyn wrote, "Might be perceived as cool".

"Anything else?" Joscelyn asked. "What about you, Sadie? What consequences can you think of?"

Sadie stared at Joscelyn for a few seconds before her dark eyes grew shiny and she threw her gaze out the window. The muscles in her jaw tightened, and she closed her eyelids. When she opened them again, she continued to stare outside.

"Sadie?" Joscelyn prodded.

Sadie swung her head around to face Joscelyn and snapped, "I don't have any other consequences. My dad wasn't even mad that Mrs. Bell called."

Bingo, Joscelyn thought. She asked, "Did that surprise you?"

The silence reverberated. The glare pierced.

"He doesn't care what I do," Sadie's voice was so low it was barely audible. Her eyes flashed and she swallowed. Her face hardened. "It doesn't matter. Whatever—I did it because it was cool."

Joscelyn's heart hurt for Sadie as she turned to the board and wrote, "it's cool". She redirected to take the pressure off the girl for a minute. "What's cool about the act of smoking pot? Do you think it looks cool? Smells cool? What exactly?"

"It's what the popular kids do," Lisa offered.

Joscelyn wrote, "popular kids do it". "Do *all* the popular kids smoke pot?" No one answered. Joscelyn snapped the cap back on the pen. "Remember, what we talk about in here is private. This is a safe place."

After glancing at the other girls, Dakota answered, "Not all of them do, but when we didn't do it, some of the kids called us pussies."

Joscelyn nodded, wrote "peer pressure", and sat in her chair. "So, it sounds like there's a lot of concern about what other people think and about their reactions or," she glanced with compassion at Sadie, "their *lack* of a reaction. How much do you value their opinions? These are valid things you need to consider and while you're thinking about them, also consider whether the people you're concerned about want what's best for you—or not." She leaned forward, resting her forearms on the table. "I don't want you to give your answer to me, necessarily, but I do want you to think about this until we meet again."

Joscelyn stood and returned to the board. She erased what she wrote and while she rubbed she asked, "Do you girls like horses?"

"Yeah," Dakota answered immediately. Joscelyn smiled to herself before she turned and looked to the others for their answers.

Tracy nodded. "Dakota, Sadie, and I have horses. Lisa doesn't because she lives in town."

"But I like them." Lisa grinned.

"How about, next time we meet, we do it in an arena with my horses? It's way more fun to have these kinds of conversations outside while we're doing something interesting. I have some things I want to show you." The girls stared at her with wide eyes. Dakota's jaw dropped. Joscelyn imagined that this was not an expected consequence for them. "I'll have to get your parents' permission and they'll have to drive you, but If everyone agrees, we will meet again next Monday, after school. Spend some time thinking about what we talked about today." Dakota and Lisa were smiling when Joscelyn picked up her phone and slid it in her purse. "See you next week." Tracy shrugged in a posture of indifference and Sadie responded by pulling her hood over the side of her face.

The following Monday, Joscelyn leaned her forearms on the top-rail of Stone Ranch's arena and watched a white Suburban pull into the property. Dakota's mother drove the girls to the ranch for their session. Lisa hopped out of the car first. She didn't bother to disguise her excitement and waved when she saw Joscelyn. The other girls went for "too cool to care" and sauntered up to the fence.

"Hey, girls," Joscelyn greeted. "I'm glad you're here. We're going to start today by observing."

Tracy slid her mirrored aviator sunglasses from the top of her head down the bridge of her nose. She turned her back to the arena and leaned against the rail. Dakota sent nervous glances between her mother and the friend she wanted to impress. She finally settled on a hybrid of leaning forward but pasting a bored expression on her face.

Joscelyn waved at Dakota's mom. "Thanks for bringing them out. You can pick them up in two hours."

"I thought I'd stay and watch," the woman called out the window.

"I'd like to work with the girls without distraction, but there will be a show-and-tell, of sorts, with parent participation in four weeks." Joscelyn stood firm.

The woman drew in her chin and raised her eyebrows. "I'm not comfortable leaving Dakota and the girls out here with you alone and I want to see what you're doing. I'll stay in the car."

"I'm sorry, but we need you to leave. You and your husband agreed to that stipulation when you signed the permission slip. Don't worry. Mary Stone is home if we need any help and I have your phone number."

Dakota's mom glared at Joscelyn as she elevated the driver's side window half way up. "Fine. I'll be back in two hours." Her tires chewed gravel as she sped away.

Lisa stood on the bottom rung so she would be tall enough to lean on the top rail. Her curious study took in everything. Sadie's gaze was alert in her 'numb to life' affect, but she hung back, her hands stuffed in the pockets of her large coat.

Joscelyn's horses, along with two of Trent's, were turned out in the arena. "Sadie, please come up to the rail and join us. Tracy, turn around. I'd like to know what you see."

Tracy turned around with more drama and attitude than a film star in an old black-and-white silent movie.

"Tell me what you see," said Joscelyn.

Teenage incredulity flowed thick. The group waited for Tracy to answer. Eventually, with utter exasperation, she said, "Four horses—duh. How stupid do you think we are?"

"I don't think you're stupid at all. A bit lazy maybe, but not stupid." Joscelyn climbed over the rail and stood next to them on the outside. "What else do you see?"

After a long pause, Lisa ventured, "They don't seem to be paying attention to each other. Are they friends?"

"Good observation, and also a good question. What do you think?" Joscelyn asked. Lisa shrugged, and the girls watched for a few more minutes.

Sadie broke the silence. "My uncle Trent's horses and the buckskin are sniffing around for food but the black horse is watching us."

"That's interesting. Why do you think he's watching us?"

Tracy smirked. "He's probably asking the other horses dumb questions about what they observe." Her sarcasm didn't produce the laughter she went for, and she rested her chin on her hands on the rail.

Dakota, who had grown up around horses answered. "He's the protector of the herd. He's watching to make sure the others are safe."

"Good job, Dakota. I think you're right." Joscelyn pulled two leaves of hay out of a wheelbarrow. "Now watch." She tossed the hay out into the arena. All four horses trotted over to get a bite. There was some head tossing, and air-nipping. Equine ears flattened back. Fargo swung his hind quarters around and kicked toward Trent's two horses. Those two moved off without getting any hay. Onyx took his stand right in the middle of the hay pile and leisurely munched while Fargo snatched at bites near the edge.

"What a jerk." Lisa said. "The black horse is hogging all the hay."

Joscelyn smiled at her. "Keep watching and while you do, I want you to think about how this scenario is similar to what you see in the cafeteria at school."

All four girls leaned forward on the rail, studying.

"The black horse is the dominant horse in the herd," Dakota said.

Joscelyn nodded. "Then why is the buckskin the one chasing the others off?"

With a wry expression, Tracy lifted her sunglasses back to the top of her head. "Because the black one is on top. He's like the king. Someone else has to do the dirty work."

"Hm." Joscelyn turned back to watch. Before long, Onyx had his fill and he moved over to the water trough.

"Wow. As soon as the black horse left, the buckskin let the other two have some hay." Lisa was amazed.

Sadie spoke, "The leader of a herd eats first, then he'll stand guard again while the others eat."

"That's right, Sadie, but why is it the buckskin who is enforcing the pecking order?" No one answered, and they stood watching for several minutes. "How is this scene like the lunchroom?"

Dakota jumped in. "The popular kids sit wherever they want."

"Yeah, and their suck-up, wanna-be's push everybody else around. Sometimes, they even knock over the nerdy kid's trays," Lisa added.

Joscelyn cocked her head. "Why do they get away with that?"

Tracy pushed off the rail and stood tall. "Because they can."

"That's not a complete answer. Any other ideas?"

Sadie pulled the hood of her jacket over her head but answered, "Because we let them. Everyone's afraid to stand up to them 'cuz they don't want to be the next victim."

"So, they lead by intimidation?" Joscelyn asked. "They get away with it because, in a way, the rest of the kids chose them as leaders, out of fear."

All the girls, including Tracy, nodded.

"Is that the same or different from what happened in the arena?" Joscelyn leaned over and picked up a halter and lead-rope from a pile of tack on the ground.

"The other horses *weren't* afraid. They were being told to wait. The leader eats first so he can watch out for the rest of the herd," said Dakota.

Sadie's voice sounded muffled from inside her hood. "Yeah, with horses it's about respect. With the kids at school it's about being assholes."

CHAPTER 9

Joscelyn whistled and held up her hand. Her horses came to her and she put a halter over the big black face. "I'd like to introduce you to Onyx. I call him Nyx for short." She picked up another halter and slipped it on her buckskin. "This is Fargo. As Sadie said, the other two horses are Mr. Stone's. Horses are excellent at choosing reliable leaders. If they lived out in the wild, their existence would depend on it." Excited, Lisa reached forward to pet Fargo's nose but Tracy glared at her and let out a derisive puff of air. Lisa withdrew her hand and lowered her head. Tracy's defiant gaze challenged Joscelyn.

Joscelyn continued. "It's not a bad thing to be a follower, but it is crucial to carefully consider who you *choose* to follow and why. Are you following someone who bullies or intimidates? Or will you choose to follow someone who makes good decisions and has your back? Also, think about your own motivation. Are you wanting to have a real friend, or just impress someone and hope you fit in?"

Joscelyn let the questions sink in a minute before she asked Dakota and Sadie to catch the other horses. "Next, I want those of you who are already comfortable around horses to teach Lisa how to groom while keeping herself safe. There are grooming buckets by the hitching posts." She handed Fargo's lead-rope to Lisa and demonstrated how to hold it and lead a horse. "Sadie, will you show Lisa how to tie a quick-release knot?"

For the first time since Joscelyn met the girls, Tracy's confidence seemed to be faltering. "Tracy, would you like to work with Onyx?" Joscelyn figured Tracy would want the flashiest horse, but he was also the most intimidating. She knew it would benefit the process if she kept Tracy out of her comfort zone.

Tracy swallowed. "Can Dakota help me with him?"

Dakota's mouth opened and she stood taller, looking pleased to be needed. "Sure, I can do that."

Joscelyn watched as the four girls worked together, teaching and learning from one another. She smiled to herself. This was a good start. Next week they would face the real issues.

After the girls left, Mary came out to the barn. Joscelyn finished the evening feeding, and the women stood, listening to the relaxing sound of horses munching their hay.

"I love that sound. It's almost hypnotizing," said Mary. She reached down to scratch Teddy's head.

Joscelyn nodded and leaned against a stall door. "Sometimes, after a hard day at work, I sit in the barn with a cold beer and let that sound soothe my tension away."

"I came out to invite you to stay for dinner. I have more than enough and it *is* that time."

"Thanks, Mary." Joscelyn righted herself and brushed hay off her jeans. "That'd be great. I'm starving. What can I do to help?"

"You can set the table while I put the food out. Trent's running late, so we'll start without him."

Joscelyn set out plates and silverware while Mary pulled out a large chicken pot-pie with a flaky, golden crust. Joscelyn's mouth watered in anticipation. "It is a real pleasure to have a home-cooked meal and a friend to share it with. Thanks again for having me."

Trent arrived during dinner and Joscelyn felt her pulse stir as soon as she heard his truck outside. His smile lit the room when he saw Joscelyn at the table. He stopped to say hello to Teddy before he washed up and sat down for dinner.

"This is a mighty nice surprise, coming home to *two* beautiful women at the end of a long day." Trent wolfed down two helpings of pot-pie before the ladies finished their first.

"We were talking about Sadie," Mary told him while he ate.

He stopped in mid-chew, glanced at Joscelyn then faced his grandma. "Is she all right? How'd the meeting go today?"

"I'm worried about her, Trent." Mary placed a hand on his arm. "Have you talked with Cade lately?"

"I talked to him today, but not about Sadie. I offered to send his cattle with mine to the feedlot again this year. He's still not taking much of an interest in his herd."

Mary shook her head and looked at her plate. "I wish he'd show more of an interest in Sadie. She's hurting too. Do you think I should have her move back here?"

Joscelyn listened with interest. Trent finished his last bite and set his napkin on the table. His cheeks darkened and he set his jaw. "Cade just needs a little more time, Gran. He'll come around."

"I'm not so sure." Mary picked up her plate and stacked it on Trent's. She gave Joscelyn a weary smile. "Cade used to be so full of dreams and ambition before he went to Afghanistan." She carried the plates to the counter.

Joscelyn's chest tightened. Memories of her dad coming home from Iraq filled her with empathy for the Stone family. She stood and collected the glasses. "Let me do the dishes tonight, to thank you for such a nice meal."

"Trent will help you." Mary gave him a pointed look.

Joscelyn washed and Trent dried. They talked about the horses and the afternoon with the girls.

"Want to have a cup of coffee with me out on the back porch and watch the sun go down?" Trent's half smile enticed her.

"Sure, if you'll make mine herbal tea."

They sat on a glider and Trent rocked it as they sipped. Joscelyn asked, "Do you mind if I ask what's going on with Sadie at home?"

He hesitated, a muscle in his jaw twitched and he took time choosing his words. "It's been hard. Cade's a Marine." Trent paused for a swallow of coffee. "While he was in Afghanistan, his wife left them and Sadie had to live here until Cade came home. Now he's home, but he's having a hard time. I mean, anyone would. You know?" He set his mug on a side table. "He just needs some time to adjust."

Joscelyn listened and wondered about Sadie's dad. It seemed he had a lot to deal with and might need a little more than just time.

Trent rested his arm along the back of the glider and sat with his thoughts. The sun dropped low on the horizon, a clamshell-pink and tangerine-orange ball against the periwinkle twilight. He brought his hand up to Joscelyn's cheek, and he held her gaze for several seconds before he lowered his mouth to hers. Joscelyn's blood surged in her veins. It seemed as though every nerve ending in her body shot through her abdomen. She returned his kiss. It had been a long time since she'd kissed anyone and Trent made a welcome change. A nice, *great-looking* change.

Responding to her acceptance, Trent deepened the kiss. Without stopping, he took her tea cup out of her hands and set it on the window ledge behind her. He pulled her closer, his hands caressing. Trent slid his hand up her side and Joscelyn sat up, pulling back.

"Whoa. Let's slow down. Okay?" Her voice tripped on her breath.

Trent leaned his head to the side and grinned, his eyes sultry in the twilight. "We're just kissin'." He leaned toward her again.

Joscelyn put a hand on his chest and pushed. "No, I mean it, Trent. We hardly even know each other." Her physical desire for him wrestled with her desire for self-protection. She ached to be with someone, to no longer be alone, but the fear of getting hurt flashed warnings deep from within her soul. On one hand, Trent *was* gorgeous, and he helped her get a job, and a place to live. He housed her horses. He made her feel wanted. He'd been a good friend. She shook her head to stop that line of thinking because on the other hand, Trent was a player—she knew it and she needed to be careful.

"Let's take it slow. You just got out of a relationship."

He lifted her hand to his lips and kissed her knuckles. "All right. I promise to behave." The glint in his eyes promised her everything but.

~*~

The warm afternoon invited Joscelyn to prop open the library door and slide open a window in the back, in hope of a cross breeze as she worked out the bugs in her library lending system. Her apartment needed a lot more attention, but that would have to wait.

Sharon Cline stopped in. "Are you about ready for the annual quilt contest?"

"What exactly are you expecting from me?" asked Joscelyn as she set her pen down.

Sharon gave her an exasperated look. "We always display the quilts in the library. I don't have room in my shop for all the entries and it seems more impartial to display them here. You have all this great wall space." She gestured at the blank walls. "All *you* need to do is hang them."

Joscelyn glanced up. "I don't really have time to hang quilts all over the walls. Can't someone from the quilt committee do it?" The walls were tall and empty, except for a few posters that could easily be removed but she didn't want the responsibility.

Sharon pursed her lips. "The committee members are all women in their seventies. Do you really want them climbing ladders?"

The now familiar sense of small-town coercion rolled over Joscelyn and she clenched her teeth. "When is this contest?"

A self-satisfied grin hovered over Sharon's lips. "Quilters will start dropping off their entries any time. They need to be labeled with the name of the pattern on the front and the quilter's name on the back. The final judging will take place before Founder's Day, at the end of June, so the display will be up until then."

"Who judges them?" Joscelyn swallowed hard. "*I* don't know anything about quilts.".

"Obviously." Sharon laughed. "There's a group of experienced quilters from the committee who judge them. Then the prize is awarded at the Founder's Day Picnic."

"Okay." Joscelyn shrugged. "I guess I can hang them." Her eyes flew grudgingly to her long to-do list.

Sharon looked smug. "Thank you." She patted Joscelyn's hand and went on her way.

Quilts started arriving throughout the following week. Joscelyn needed to get something to hang them with from the hardware store. Until then, she stacked the entries on a chair by the front window.

Wednesday afternoon, Sharon slammed through the front door. "What are you doing?" she shouted.

Stunned, Joscelyn turned away from a patron. "What do you mean? What's wrong?"

Sharon raced to the window and snatched up the large pile of quilts and swung around.

"You absolutely *cannot* set these quilts in the sun. They will fade. What were you thinking?"

Joscelyn put a hand to her mouth. "I'm sorry, I didn't know."

"They must be hung. And not on walls with any direct sunlight." Sharon's eyes darted around the library searching for a safe place to set her load.

"I'm going to the hardware store today to get some nails."

"Nails?" Sharon's eyes popped.

Suddenly unsure, Joscelyn's voice wavered. "I didn't think tacks would be strong enough."

"You would ruin these quilts with nails." Sharon looked horrified. "There are quilt hangers in the shed out back. See if Bob will help you. He knows what to do."

Joscelyn felt heat expand in her cheeks. She didn't appreciate being chastised. She swallowed. "I'm sorry, Sharon. I didn't know."

Sharon gave Joscelyn an impatient groan. "Thank goodness no harm was done—yet. I'm glad I caught you before you hung them."

"Me too."

Joscelyn wrenched opened the shed door in search of the quilt hangers. *Is this what my life has become? Now I'm a quilt hanger? Damn Leonard Perkins.* The shed smelled like cigarette smoke. On the floor were several ground-out cigarette butts. Joscelyn waved her hand in front of her nose and shook her head at the stupidity of someone smoking in a wooden shed. She opened the door wide for fresh air. She found at least fifteen wooden quilt hangers. This was much more complicated than her original plan. Maybe she could borrow a ladder from Bob.

Trent stopped in right before closing time. "I just came from the hardware store where I overheard Ms. Cline telling Bob that you almost hung the contest quilts up by driving nails through them." He snickered.

"Oh, for crying out loud. How am I supposed to know how quilts are hung? She could have told me." Joscelyn said in a huff.

"Need some help?"

Relief flooded through her. "That'd be really great."

"Bob sent a ladder over for the effort. It's in my truck. Be right back."

Trent went to work hanging the quilt racks in place. At seven o'clock, Joscelyn turned the open sign to closed, but that didn't deter a group of women led by Sharon Cline. They marched in and began directing Trent's efforts. Joscelyn busied herself closing the bookshop's accounts for the day and tidying up the library. She watched the ladies flirt with Trent. He fielded their bold comments, eyelash fluttering, and giggles with ease. Obviously, Trent was used to the attention. Joscelyn, determined not to be irritated, decided to go upstairs and make a sandwich for supper.

The laughter died down about an hour later and she heard the ladies leaving. She went back downstairs to say goodbye, but the shop was empty. When Joscelyn went to lock the front door, she saw Trent talking to one of the women outside. The redhead stood next to her midnight blue SUV. They laughed at something together and then the woman, growing serious, stepped toward him. She placed a hand on Trent's chest and gazed up at him. Joscelyn drew in a sharp breath and retreated to the shadows of the library door inset. Trent and the redhead stood locked in a silent communication. He took her hand and held it on his chest a few seconds before he finally ducked his head and reached to open her car door. The woman placed a lingering kiss on his cheek.

Trent helped the woman into her car and shut the door. He gave the roof of the SUV a pat and waved as the woman zipped off. Whistling, he set off toward the brewery. Joscelyn noticed Tonya watching the scene from the beauty-shop window across the street. Their eyes met and held for a long moment before Tonya shook her head and left her window.

Joscelyn locked the door and turned out the lights. It disconcerted her to watch Trent with that woman in the street. Was something going on between them? Then she reminded herself that she and Trent didn't have any kind of understanding. But the resigned look on Tonya's face bore a solid warning.

Her phone rang. "Hello?"

"Hey," Trent's smooth voice caressed the line. "I'm over at the brewery. Want to join me for a beer?"

Heat pulsed in Joscelyn's temples. She couldn't believe his audacity. "No, thank you."

"Come on, sweetheart, I wanna see you."

Whatever! "Not tonight." Joscelyn poked the red button on the screen of her phone. Missing the satisfaction of slamming a phone into its cradle, she jabbed the faded red button three more times for good measure and threw her phone on the bed. Her irritation at Trent exacerbated her loneliness.

CHAPTER 10

Monday rolled around, as it always did, and it was time to meet with the four teens at Stone Ranch. They gathered in the arena where Joscelyn asked them to stand side-by-side in a straight line between two orange traffic cones. On the other side of the arena, opposite each other, stood two open-ended squares constructed with ground-poles, supported between the middle arena rail on one end and jump-standards on the other. Onyx and Fargo wandered loose, without halters, inside the arena.

"Hi, ladies. How was your week?" Joscelyn stood before the small group.

Dakota answered, "Same-ol', same-ol'." The others shrugged. Tracy pretended to be fascinated with imaginary dirt under her fingernails, and Sadie pulled on the strings of her hood, further hiding her face.

"Today, we're going to play a game. Who has ever played pool?" Joscelyn asked. The girls indicated with nods that they had. "Good. We're going to play pool with the horses. See the open squares on the other end of the arena? Those are the pockets. Your job is to get the horses into those pockets." Joscelyn paused to be sure she had the girl's attention. Tracy pretended not to listen, but Joscelyn knew she heard.

Joscelyn held up her hand with her fingers spread wide. "There are only five rules. One, you must stay in a line between these two cones unless it is your turn. Two, you will take turns and each of your turns will last thirty seconds. Three, you may only speak when it is your turn. Four, you may not touch the horses in any way, and five, if you break any of the rules, you will face a consequence."

The girls looked confused, so Joscelyn repeated the rules and added, "The good news is you get to come up with your own consequence. It has to be something that can happen immediately, right here in the arena."

The four girls huddled together. Dakota said, "In gym, if we do something wrong, we have to do laps."

Tracy shook her head, "I don't want to do laps. Let's make it easy, since we get to choose our own punishment."

Joscelyn leaned in, "It's not a punishment, it's a consequence."

The girls discussed ideas for a few more minutes. Tracy wanted the consequence to be getting a candy bar.

Sadie murmured, "It has to be something that can happen *here and now*."

Lisa narrowed her eyes in thought. "How about we have to count to twenty?" The girls bobbed their heads, looking smug, like they were getting away with something.

"Okay, does everyone agree? If so, get in line and I'll start the timer. Dakota, you get the first turn. Ready go!"

Dakota looked startled. Then she stood clapping her hands and shouting at Fargo. "Go on, Fargo. Get up." The horses flicked their ears, but Fargo was too far away and didn't move. Dakota tried this same tactic until the end of her turn.

"Time." Joscelyn clicked the timer. "Lisa, your turn. Go!"

"This is stupid." Tracy put her hands on her hips. "They're never going to go into the pockets."

"Stop." Joscelyn stepped in front of their line. "Everyone, freeze. Tracy, you must do your consequence for talking when it wasn't your turn."

She counted to twenty with abundant sass and sarcasm. By the time she finished, Lisa's time ran out.

"Sadie, your turn." Joscelyn hit the timer.
Sadie didn't move.

"Sadie?" Joscelyn's gut tightened, bracing for a refusal or a possible altercation. Seconds ticked by.

Finally, Sadie stepped forward and asked in a voice almost too low to hear, "Can we leave the line during our turn?"

"Yes, ma'am." Joscelyn grinned, glad that someone was listening and thinking. Sadie trudged in the direction of the horses, her hands jammed in the pockets of her large coat. Onyx stood closest to a pocket, and she picked him. His dark head lifted and he turned away, trotting to the far end, without going into a pocket.

"Time." Joscelyn shouted. "When I shout 'time', get back in line and the next person's turn starts immediately." Sadie plodded back to the line as Tracy stepped out.

She faced Joscelyn. "We're never going to do this if we have to stay all the way down here? *Obvi* you're just trying to make us look like dumb asses."

Joscelyn chose to ignore the slur. "*I* never said you had to stay all the way down here. There are only five rules." She held up five fingers and repeated them again. Joscelyn could see a light come on in Tracy's mind, but by the time the girl turned to talk to the others the buzzer went off. "Time!"

Tracy glared at Joscelyn who shrugged her shoulders. It was Dakota's turn again. She ran forward and tried to herd the horses into one of the squares. They moved off and stood by the side gate.

Joscelyn sensed their frustration building. "Time."

Dakota groaned and returned to the line. Lisa stepped forward and turned to face her friends. "I don't know how to move the horses, but when Joscelyn told us the rules again, I realized that she said we had to stay in a line between the cones, but," she looked at Joscelyn, "can we move the cones?"

Joscelyn's face opened in a wide smile. "There is no rule about the cones, other than you must stay in a line between them." She looked at the clock. "Time."

Lisa clapped her hands, her dark hair swinging as she skipped back into line.

Sadie bit her lip as she stepped forward. "Dakota and Tracy, you guys pick up the cones. Stay in a line but follow me." The group moved slowly toward the horses.

Joscelyn breathed in deep and released her breath with a pleasant sigh. She loved the moment in this exercise when kids realized there were fewer restrictions on them than they originally assumed. At times, the girls became frustrated and struggled. They often spoke out of turn and had to count to twenty, delaying the game. In the end, they managed to get Fargo into a pocket but Onyx eluded their efforts.

"All right girls. That's all the time we have with the horses today. Let's talk about your experience before you have to leave." Joscelyn had camp chairs set up in a circle in the shade of the barn. She passed out water bottles as they all sat down.

"Were you successful?" she asked.

"No," Dakota and Tracy said in unison. Sadie, unresponsive, stared at the bottle in her hands.

"We *did* get Fargo into a pocket," Lisa said. "I think that's successful. At least we're getting the hang of it. Next time, we'll do it for sure."

Tracy scoffed. "Lisa, you're such a nerd."

Lisa lifted wide, dark eyes to Joscelyn. Joscelyn tapped her water bottle against Lisa's in cheers. "I like your attitude. What happened once you girls realized you were limiting yourselves to staying in one place with your line when that wasn't actually a rule?"

"I felt stupid," Sadie answered.

Lisa sat on the edge of her chair. "Yeah, but then we got lots of ideas."

"You know," Joscelyn leaned forward, her forearms resting on her knees. "It's a common thing to assume we have limits where none actually exist. People do it all the time. The trick is to learn to recognize when that's the case. Instead of focusing on what we *can't* do, it helps to think of things we *can*."

Sadie pushed her hood back and appraised Joscelyn through her kohl-darkened eyes.

Finally engaging, Tracy said, "It was so frustrating when we had to stop to count. I mean, it wasn't hard, but it got in the way and wasted time." She took a swig of her water. "Once, we almost had Nyx in the pocket but we had to stop 'cuz I said something out of turn and when I was counting he ran off."

"So, your consequence got in the way of your success?" Joscelyn asked. She held her breath a moment while the girls reflected on her question. Tracy peered at Joscelyn and pursed her lips. "How could the things you've learned today apply to your lives?" She took a pull from her water bottle. "How about the smoking pot thing?"

The girls didn't answer though their faces gave away their understanding. Finally, Lisa spoke. "Our detention was a waste of time. Until we got to come out here, anyway. We could have been doing something fun."

Joscelyn enjoyed watching this small girl step into a leadership role within the group. She was bright and wasn't afraid to speak up. "What about the unspoken limits you originally put on yourselves? Can you think of a time you've done that before?" No one answered.

"Let me ask you a question. Why did you choose to skip class and smoke pot?" Joscelyn looked each girl in the eye. "When I first met you, you told me you thought it was cool—something to do when you're bored. The cool kids did it and if you didn't, they would think you are, uh... pussies, I think you said. Right?" The girls nodded. "And what were some of the consequences?"

"Detention and being grounded," said Dakota.

"Right. What about the consequences you hoped for? Do the cool kids think you're cool?" The girls squirmed and glanced at each other.

Sadie slumped farther down in her chair. "Is it the only option to keep you from being bored?"

"No," Lisa answered. "I guess we limited ourselves to what we thought would make us fit in."

"Okay." Joscelyn waited until all four girls looked at her. "You girls are smart. You learned to stretch beyond what you thought were limits and touch success. Seems like you feel good about what you accomplished and you had fun." She looked over her shoulders, one way and then the other. "I don't see any other kids around, cool or otherwise. Just you four amazing young women. You did great today and no one else's opinion can take that away from you. What you think about your own lives and the choices you make is what matters. Don't give yourselves false limitations." She stood as Lisa's dad pulled up in a minivan. "Great job today, ladies. I'll see you next week."

Lisa, Tracy, and Dakota chattered and laughed as they loaded into the van. Sadie followed and glanced back at Joscelyn, giving her a slight smile. Joscelyn's chest expanded with a pleasing warmth, gratified to see teens grasp large, positive concepts regarding their potential. She hummed to herself as she went into the barn to put away the equipment and feed the horses, hoping she was reaching Sadie.

"Having a good day?"

Joscelyn jumped and let loose a garbled shriek. Her nerves fired hot and sharp causing her to flinch. She peered into the darkness of the tack room, expecting to see Lenny lurking in the shadows.

"Hey… it's just me." Trent stepped out. "Why are you so jumpy?"

She laughed at her nerves, her heart thumping. "You startled me, that's all."

"Sorry. You were humming—did you have a good talk with the girls?"

Not wanting to say why she was jumpy, Joscelyn was glad for the change of subject and answered, "I think so. They're great kids."

Trent hung a bridle on its hook and stepped from the tack room into the barn's breezeway. "I wanted to apologize for the other night."

Joscelyn tossed hay into a stall then faced him. "Oh?"

"Yeah." He looked down as he scuffed the dirt floor with the heel of his boot. "It seemed like you were pissed at me when I called."

Joscelyn didn't answer.

"Maybe you saw me talking to Melinda?" Trent kept his head down but looked up at her from under his lashes. Joscelyn lifted her brows and cocked her head.

"Melinda and I've known each other forever. We dated for a while before she got married."

Joscelyn gave him a scowl. "She's married?"

Trent shoved his hands into his pockets and tilted his head up at her. The smile that crinkled his eyes was probably the same one he gave his mother as a little boy. The one that got him away with all sorts of trouble. He lifted his shoulders. "Yeah, she is. Sometimes we flirt a little, but we don't mean anything by it. It's not like we're having an affair or anything."

"But it's wrong, Trent. I feel awful for her husband." She threw two flakes into Fargo's stall and almost hit her horse in the face. He tossed his head and grumbled. Joscelyn said, "Sorry, boy."

"Dalton and I are friends. He knows Melinda and I flirt. He doesn't care."

"Sure. Did he tell you that?"

"No, but he never says anything. We've all been friends since we were kids. It's just the way we are together. But if it bothers you. I won't do it—ever again."

Joscelyn rolled her eyes. She didn't have the right to demand anything from him, but it did bother her. It was wrong.

Trent caught her arm and gently pulled her to face him. His eyes grew serious. "I really am sorry. I'd like to see you. You know—date. I promise I won't flirt with anybody but you." A mischievous glimmer shot through his eyes and he claimed a kiss before she could resist.

Man, but that boy could kiss. Joscelyn felt her indignation melt a tiny bit.

"So, will you let me take you to dinner tonight?" he whispered in her ear, sending shivers through her body.

She did need to eat, and another lonely frozen dinner was all that awaited her at home. Not to mention, Trent certainly made nice dining scenery. Joscelyn knew better, but it wasn't a hard sell to her conscience to allow him to buy her dinner. She didn't have to trust him to eat with him.

~*~

"What's good here?" Joscelyn asked while skimming the Silver Spur Chop House menu.

Trent's phone buzzed and he pulled it out of his back pocket to glance at the screen. The corner of his mouth flicked up for a beat. He turned the screen off and set the phone face up on the table next to his knife and spoon.

"Hm?" He looked up at her.

"I asked what's good to eat here?"

"Oh, sorry. It is a steak house so that's the obvious answer. I always order the T-Bone. What are you hungry for?"

"Have you ever had—"

Trent's phone buzzed again. His eyes flew to the screen for a few seconds before returning to her. He raised his brows. "Had what?"

Joscelyn finished her question through a tight jaw. "The Ahi?" She tapped her fingers on the table.

He laughed. "Nope. Isn't that a Hawaiian fish? I stick to beef. I am a cattle rancher, you know." He winked. "Order it. If you don't like it, you can always get something else."

Buzz, glance, smirk.

"Do you need to answer that?" Joscelyn inclined her head toward his phone and clenched her teeth.

Buzz, buzz, glance.

"No, I'm having dinner with *you*."

Joscelyn arched one brow. "Are you?" A low burn ignited behind her sternum.

Trent made an apologetic face. "Okay, hold on. Let me answer and then I'll put it away."

While he tapped the small screen with his large fingers, the waitress approached the table. Joscelyn ordered Pinot Blanc and the Ahi, then told the waitress Trent would have the T-Bone.

He glanced up to utter, "Medium rare with baked potato, all the fixin's. Oh, and a Lagunitas IPA." His thumbs kept typing.

Buzz, chuckle, type, buzz, buzz.

"Seriously? Who is that?" *He does that again and I'm outta here.*

"Nobody. Sorry." He grinned, pushed send and shoved the phone into his back pocket. "Now, it's just us." He snapped the cloth napkin before he spread it on his lap. "How did your session with the girls go this afternoon? You said 'good' but didn't give me any details."

Joscelyn stretched her neck to release the knots and smiled softly. "It *was* good. The idea is to set up a metaphor using the horses as a learning tool. Then I help my clients see how the lesson can relate to their actual lives. It's a powerful way to teach and it's effective in therapy." Their drinks arrived at the table and Joscelyn set her napkin on her lap. "Today, we learned about communication and to recognize when we put artificial limits on ourselves. The girls also discovered a little bit about leadership and choosing worthy leaders if they happen to be more of a follower."

"Seems like a lot to take in. How'd they do?"

"Great. They're participating without too much teen drama." Joscelyn winked. "I think they're having fun. Hopefully it will be more helpful than sitting them in a room doing nothing for hours on end."

Trent took a swig of his beer and pierced her with his bright blue eyes. "How's Sadie doing?"

"She's obviously struggling with a lot more than experimenting with pot in order to fit in, but she's coming around." Joscelyn sipped her chilled wine. "You said her mom abandoned her?"

Trent nodded, took a drink, and leaned back in the booth, draping his arm across the back. "Yeah. I still can't believe she did that. How can a mother just leave her kid?"

Joscelyn rolled her lips in between her teeth and nodded. "And her dad? He's a Marine, just back from Afghanistan, right? How long has he been back?"

"Almost two years, now."

Joscelyn disappeared inside her head for a minute, remembering her own life as the daughter of a Marine. She took another sip of wine. "Do you see him much? I don't think I've ever seen him in town."

"He mostly stays out at his ranch. He comes into town, now and again. He doesn't come to my place because he and Gran get into arguments about how he's raising Sadie."

"What doesn't she like?"

Trent pulled a long swallow of beer, leaned forward, and rested his forearms on the table. He considered Joscelyn. "It's just hard. When Sadie's mom took off, Sadie came to live with us until Cade came home. Gran thinks Sadie should still live with us because Cade... well, he has a hard time most days. That's all. He'll figure things out."

"It must have been upsetting for him to come home and face all of that." Joscelyn said, her voice low and filled with compassion.

Trent remained silent. Joscelyn noticed he excused his brother's behavior and had high hopes Cade would be able to pull it together soon. Trent never said a negative word about him.

Finally, Trent answered. "He was having a hard-enough time dealing with being in the war. Knowing his wife abandoned his daughter when he was so far away crushed him."

"Has he gotten any help?"

Anger flashed across Trent's face. "You therapists are all the same. You think if you can get someone to talk about their feelings, they'll be cured."

Joscelyn's brows shot up. "Wow. That's a broad statement."

"I'm sorry." He said, contrite. "It's just that Gran is always trying to get him to '*go to a therapist*.' But he'll be fine. He's strong and with a little more time, he'll settle in."

A picture of the family situation came into focus for Joscelyn. "He might need more than time, Trent. It's common for combat vets to struggle with coming home. There are a lot of reasons for that and it isn't anything to be embarrassed about. If he had a broken leg you'd make sure he went to a doctor, wouldn't you?"

"Of course, but this is different."

"Only because you can't see the break, yet his wounds are still debilitating."

The waitress brought their meals, and they ate in silence for a time, both deep in their own thoughts.

"The thing is, Trent, your brother's issues have become Sadie's issues, and I know for a fact *she* needs help."

He looked up at her and sighed. "I suppose you're right. I really thought Cade would have worked through this stuff by now."

Trent's phone rang and he pulled it out of his back pocket to check the screen. One of his delicious smiles spread across his face and he looked up at Joscelyn. "I have to take this. Excuse me for a minute." He slid out of the booth and stepped into the lobby.

Joscelyn watched him talking and laughing. He ran a hand through his wavy hair. *What am I doing here with this guy?*

CHAPTER 11

After dinner, Trent walked Joscelyn down the street to the library. She took her keys from her purse, stepped up into the inset to unlock the door.

"Thanks for dinner, Trent."

He stepped up behind her into the doorway. "Can I come in?"

"Not tonight. I'm tired and sore. I think I'm going to have a hot shower."

His eyes gleamed and he offered her his crooked smile, his intention clear.

He's crazy if he thinks he can spend all evening on the phone with someone else and then come home with me. "Alone," she said, irritation creeping into her tone.

He let out a breath that might have been a laugh and bent to kiss her. She ended it quickly, against the vibrating demands of her body which didn't seem to care about his roving attention. She placed a hand on his chest and gave him a gentle push.

"Good night, Trent," she said, not bothering to hide her annoyance.

His eyes assessed hers before he stepped back out of the entrance landing. "Good night, Joscelyn."

She turned to let herself inside. Joscelyn flipped on the light and watched from the window as Trent pulled out his phone, held it to his ear, and walked toward his truck. He wouldn't spend the night alone. She wrapped her arms around herself and closed her eyes against the familiar pull of loneliness.

Joscelyn made herself a cup of herbal tea and breathed in minty steam as she climbed the stairs to her apartment. She stopped short, a sensation like ice water splashed her in the face and squeal shot up her throat. Joscelyn almost stepped on a dead mouse laying in the center of the third stair. There was no trap and she never used poison. Her heart thumped and she shivered. *Oh, for heaven's sake. It's just a dead mouse. Mice die all the time.* Irritated with how easily she was frightened, Joscelyn swept the tiny corpse into the trash bin by the back door. She peered out the window at the patio and slid the chain into its slot on the door. On her way back upstairs she stopped at the front door, double-checked the lock, and with a shiver, threw the dead bolt.

~*~

For the final session with the teenage girls, Joscelyn built two long half-walls out of hay bales creating an alley in the center of the arena where she set up several obstacles. She turned a barrel on end and placed a pan of oats on top. There were ground-poles propped up six inches high that spanned the walkway and posts sticking straight up out of the bales. Joscelyn filled a feed bucket with horse treats and set it on a bale of sweet alfalfa in the middle of the alley. There were right-angle turns and in some areas the passage was only wide enough for one person, or horse, at a time. She placed bales perpendicular to the walls on the outside, stacking them too high to easily step over. All along the top of the walls, she laid out sweet carrots, tangy apple slices, and handfuls of butterscotch candies—Onyx's favorite.

Even though Onyx and Fargo were experienced with this game, Joscelyn brought them out and showed them where all the treats were, to be sure they knew ahead of time.

Joscelyn invited all the parents to attend and take part in the day's session. Three cars pulled into the ranch and parked on the soft, spring grass. Lisa came with both of her parents. Dakota and Tracy each brought their moms. Sadie came in Dakota's car—her dad noticeably absent.

"Welcome, everybody." Nervous bubbles tickled Joscelyn's stomach as she approached the group but went flat when she realized Sadie's dad hadn't come. *How could he neglect this day, of all days?* She stifled a groan and moved ahead. "Today is our last day. I'm going to miss getting together with you. So, let's have fun today and show your parents what kind of learning we've been up to." She gestured to a row of folding camp chairs. "Parents, you're welcome to sit over there and watch the first round. Then it will be your turn."

Joscelyn and the girls approached the hay bale alley. "This represents the path of your life. As you can see, all along the path are temptations." She laughed, "In this case, these are temptations for the horses. The objective is to guide the horse through the pathway without letting them sneak a bite of anything. Who would like to go first?"

The girls glanced sideways at each other and no one made eye contact with Joscelyn. Instead, they seemed to find the toes of their boots fascinating.

After an uncomfortable few moments, Lisa tilted her head and studied the course. She shrugged. "I'll try it."

Our little leader. Joscelyn smiled and said, "Great. Who do you want to try it with? Nyx or Fargo?"

An electric energy shot through Lisa's eyes and she said, "Nyx." She took Onyx by the lead rope and led him safely, the way Joscelyn taught her. When Lisa got to the opening, she hesitated, considering her strategy. She stepped into the alley first and pulled him in behind her. The path was narrow and when she went past the oats, expecting him to follow, he stopped and grabbed a mouthful.

"No, Nyx," she said. Lisa pulled him away and stepped over the ground-poles. While she concentrated on not tripping, Onyx snatched up a butterscotch and crunched it between his big, yellow teeth.

"Nyx!" Frustration edged Lisa's voice. At the turn, she moved around the bale of alfalfa, but

Onyx was too big. He would have to hop over it. She pulled hard but he didn't budge. Onyx munched blissfully on the sweet grass. "Come on, Nyx." She pulled again. He grudgingly acquiesced and followed her the rest of the way through the alley.

"Good job, Lisa." Joscelyn clapped for her as she returned to the group. "Was that harder than you thought it'd be?"

Lisa rolled her eyes. "*Yes.* He's such a pig."

Laughing, Joscelyn asked, "Who's next?"

Dakota raised her hand. "I'm doing it with Fargo though. He's easier." Dakota's strategy was to lead from outside the alley, but she soon found that the perpendicular bales forced her to hold the very end of the lead rope. She dropped it once and Fargo moved fast to the bucket of horse cookies. Dakota had to climb over the wall to retrieve the rope. She stayed inside after that.

Tracy was next and had the same challenges. She could not keep Onyx out of the butterscotch. She gave up and laughing, allowed him to sneak another one with her blessing.

Sadie sat on the arena rail, watching. When her turn came, she made no move to try.

"Sadie? Which horse, do you want to use?" asked Joscelyn.

Sadie shrugged and pulled the hood strings of her ever-present coat tighter around her face. It was late May and far too warm for any type of jacket.

"Nyx or Fargo?" Joscelyn tried again, her breath stuck in her lungs. When Sadie didn't move, Joscelyn handed the lead ropes to Dakota and stepped close to Sadie. With a soft voice meant only for her, Joscelyn asked, "What's up? Don't you want to try this?"

"No." Sadie answered from deep within her hood.

"You're a natural with horses." Joscelyn wondered what happened with Sadie over the past week. They had been making progress, but this was a definite step back. "I bet *you* could get through with only two sneaky bites."

Sadie shrugged but made no move.

Joscelyn put a hand on her shoulder. "Will you please push your hood back a little, so I can see your face?"

Sadie still didn't move.

"Please?" Joscelyn hoped she could find a way to reach this hurting girl.

Sadie jumped off the rail and flipped her hood off, glaring at Joscelyn. A dark purple and red bruise marred her pale cheek. Joscelyn drew in a sharp breath, but before she could say anything, Sadie stripped off the coat and threw it at her, then stormed off toward the horses. She grabbed Onyx's lead rope and pulled him off to the side.

Dakota handed Fargo's lead-rope back to Joscelyn. "What happened to Sadie's face?"

"I'm not sure. Is this the first time you've noticed a bruise?" Joscelyn's stomach roiled as she tied her buckskin to the arena rail.

"Yeah. I mean, she had her hood on all day at school today, but that's pretty normal." Dakota looked askance at Tracy and Lisa. The friends shrugged and shook their heads. Dakota's mom wrinkled her brow and flattened her lips. She met

Joscelyn's look, shook her head, and dropped her gaze to the ground.

Stunned by Sadie's bruise and her abrupt actions, Joscelyn silently watched as Sadie did some ground work with the horse. Her dark hair swung as she asked him to move forward and back, then move his hind feet away to the left, then to the right. Sadie asked him to trot in a small circle both ways. When she finished, he was alert and his ears pointed straight toward her.

Holding his lead rope about eight inches down from the halter snap, Sadie led him toward the path. *Where is this confidence coming from?* Joscelyn smiled to herself, pleased to see Sadie taking charge and making decisions. She would address the bruised cheek later.

At every temptation, Sadie guided Onyx through. She finished the course without Onyx sneaking any treats. Everyone clapped and Sadie tried not to smile, but the burgeoning joy in her eyes gave her away.

"Wow, Sadie. Great job." Joscelyn took Onyx from her and tied him to the arena rail next to Fargo. "Tell us what your strategy was, starting with the ground work."

Sadie glanced at her coat draped over the rail. Now that she was the center of attention, Joscelyn wondered if she felt naked without it.

She stirred the sand with the toe of her boot and answered, "I wanted him to know I was in charge, so I made him move his feet in the direction I wanted."

"Looked to me like he decided you were a leader he could trust," Joscelyn interjected.

Sadie nodded. "My uncle taught me that. It's what dominant horses do to get the herd to move. Like when Onyx and Fargo pushed the other horses off the hay on our first day."

"That's right." Joscelyn smiled at the girl. "So, what happened in the course? How did you manage to get him through without eating anything?"

"I showed him I knew where I was going and that I expected him to follow me. When he veered over to a treat, I reminded him to refocus by jiggling his lead. He's a great horse, though, so it was easy."

Dakota slung her arm around Sadie's shoulders. "I've been around horses my whole life and I couldn't do that." Sadie grinned and her eyes flitted downward.

Joscelyn addressed the group. "We'll talk more about our experiences in a few minutes, but first let's give the parents a try." She untied Fargo, clipped the lead rope to one of the cheek rings and clipped a second rope to the other side. "This time, two parents will go at a time. One on each side of the course walls. Together, you must try to get through the obstacles."

The two moms went first. They didn't get past the oats. Each mom pulled sideways in a tug-of-war against the other, and Fargo stood still between them, munching away. As they continued through the course, their frustration grew. The women were so intent on each getting their own way that Fargo was free to choose his vice. Joscelyn figured he would not be hungry for his supper.

Next, Lisa's parents tried the maze with Onyx. When they got to the opening, Lisa's dad pulled hard. Onyx moved toward the man and pulled his tiny wife into the hay bale wall. Lisa's mom tripped on the ground-poles sticking out. She fell and yanked on Onyx's head. Startled he pulled back, and both parents lost their grip on the ropes. They rushed to catch him, startling him further.

Frustrated, the parents stopped talking and wouldn't look at each other. As they came to the end, Lisa's mom shouted, "Watch out for the horse cookies." She leaned toward the bucket as she spoke. Her husband peered inside too, giving Onyx plenty of rope and opportunity to go for it. He had a mouthful before they could pull him out of the alley.

"That was much harder than it looked." Lisa's dad snickered, as his cheeks reddened.

"Good work, parents. Girls, let's give the older generation a hand." They clapped and the girls laughed, obviously pleased to be more accomplished at something than their parents.

Joscelyn tied the horses and directed everyone to pull the chairs into a circle and sit.

"When we started today's session, I told you girls that this obstacle course symbolized the path of your lives. You tried to guide the horses past several of their greatest temptations. What are some of the temptations you face?"

No one answered.

"Don't be shy about talking in front of your parents. They're going to have to talk in front of you in a few minutes. Let me name the elephant in the room. You all were tempted to smoke weed. It's why you were in detention. Your parents already know that." The girls stifled giggles and fidgeted. "What else?"

Joscelyn allowed the silence to sit heavy. Finally, Lisa spoke while staring at her shoes. "A boy at school offered to pay me $20.00 to write an English paper for him." She glanced up at her parents from the corner of her eye and rushed to say, "But I didn't do it."

"Why not?" Joscelyn asked.

Lisa's brows drew together and she narrowed her eyes. "Because it would be wrong. It's cheating."

"How do you know that?"

The girl scrunched her brows together. "I guess from my mom and dad."

"You might say they guided you?" Lisa nodded and Joscelyn continued. "What other temptations have you faced—or might you face?"

"I almost snuck out of the house to go to a party once," Dakota shared.

"Sometimes I think about running away." Sadie looked Joscelyn right in the eye when she spoke as though she was challenging her in some way.

Joscelyn asked, "Do you want to talk about that with the group?"

"No."

Joscelyn nodded knowing she would need to talk with Sadie alone after the session. "Thanks for sharing, girls. I know it's hard. Now, let's look at some things you might have to face in the future. Like drinking, other drugs, and sex."

The girls shared embarrassed glances as though they wished Joscelyn would stop saying things like that in front of their parents.

"Don't worry ladies. These temptations aren't new to your generation. Believe it or not, your parents had to face the same temptations you do. They might even have advice if you're brave enough to talk to them about it." Joscelyn crossed her legs. "How hard was it to keep the horses away from their temptations?"

"Freaking hard." Tracy made a face.

"Why was Sadie so successful?" Joscelyn looked into each face as she posed the question.

Lisa answered, "Because she was a good leader. Nyx trusted her so he followed her."

Joscelyn grinned at another lightbulb moment. It was flickering. She hoped it would go on for everyone. "Right. We learned about choosing reliable leaders to follow at the beginning of our time together, didn't we? What else?"

Dakota's mom cocked her head and smiled. "She had a plan and set clear boundaries. Onyx knew what she expected." The light was dawning.

"And when he faltered, she was quick and clear with her reminder." Tracy's mom added.

Joscelyn nodded and paused for a minute of reflection before she moved on. "Let's think for a little bit about Lisa's mom and dad." Joscelyn focused on them. "Tell us about your experience."

Lisa's dad said, "It was hard. We didn't work together very well."

"Yeah, and when I fell, we lost control of the horse." Lisa's mom added. "Then we got frustrated with each other and stopped communicating. That's when Onyx almost ate the whole bucket of cookies." She grinned and rolled her eyes.

Joscelyn let out a soft laugh, and said, "Right. Another thing I noticed was when you got to the end, all three of you were completely focused on the bucket of cookies. Somehow, that seemed to paralyze you from action which gave Onyx free rein." Lisa's mother opened her mouth in a silent "O".

"Girls, do you think if I got on Onyx right now and rode him around the arena, asking him for gate changes or lead changes that he'd be focused on the temptations in the middle?" They shook their heads.

Dakota said, "No way. He likes to work."

"Are you saying he wouldn't even care about the treats if he had something better to do?" Joscelyn looked at the girls meaningfully, wanting them to get the connection. They returned her stare with sheepish grins and nods.

"Okay, some things I'm hearing are that when guides don't work well together, they can get frustrated with events outside the path. If they stop communicating, they aren't successful. I also heard that success comes from setting clear boundaries and being ready to provide quick but gentle reminders. I think a good guide could only do that if they were engaged and paying attention."

"Are you showing us that this is like parenting?" asked Lisa's dad.

Joscelyn smiled at him, "Did you learn anything that could help with parenting a teen through some tough obstacles?" He nodded and returned her grin.

Dakota's mom leaned forward. "There are a ton of parallels in this exercise for parents. I know we were pretty skeptical about you in the beginning, but this is so cool. Thanks, Joscelyn."

"What about the kids, though? What are their parallels?" asked Tracy's mom.

"What do you think, girls? By now you know how to pull lessons from our time with the horses. What did you learn?"

"I want to be a good leader, like Sadie," Lisa spoke up. "I'm tired of worrying about what other kids think."

"Yeah, and we should hang around friends who care about us," Dakota said. "Like you guys. We've got each other's backs."

Tracy scrunched up her face in thought. "I guess I'm gonna watch for temptations." She smiled at the group and then pursed her lips to one side. "And we need to find something cool to do."

Sadie sat slumped in her chair and remained quiet. Joscelyn bent over a little and tried to catch her eye. "Did anyone consider how hard it was to be the guide? When Lisa's mom fell, everything went a little crazy, even though she had the help of her husband. What if a guide falls and doesn't have any help?"

Sadie glanced at her. Joscelyn continued, her pulse trotting in her ears. "I bet things could get out of control pretty fast. I bet if Lisa's dad wasn't there to hold the other lead rope, Nyx would have run away." Joscelyn rested her hand on Sadie's shoulder. "Do you think?" Sadie nodded, and a tear rolled down her bruised cheek. "Sadie, you know a lot about horses. Do you think Onyx would survive very long out in the wilderness on his own?"

The girl shook her head and broke down in tears. She turned her face into Joscelyn's shoulder and Joscelyn put her arms around her. The others took their cue and gathered their things and quietly went to their cars.

Dakota set Sadie's water bottle in the cup holder on her chair. "I'll call you tonight," she murmured. Lisa rubbed Sadie's shoulder on her way to the car. Tracy's mom held her hand up like she was talking on a phone, indicating that she would call later. Joscelyn nodded and rocked Sadie like a child.

CHAPTER 12

Joscelyn usually wouldn't offer to give a client a ride home. It was important to keep clear boundaries in therapy. This wasn't therapy though, not really. She simply helped a group of girls with some object lessons. And Sadie *was* Mary's great-granddaughter. And Trent's niece. And Sadie needed help—that much was obvious. So, Joscelyn found herself bumping along a gravel road, following Sadie's directions.

"The girls and me want to keep doing stuff with you and the horses," Sadie spoke with her face turned toward the passenger's window. She moved her gaze from outside down to her lap. "We wanted to talk to you today about meeting once a week. Maybe starting a saddle club or something?" She watched Joscelyn's reaction from the corner of her eye.

Joscelyn pursed her lips in consideration.

"We were gonna ask you before I started crying like a baby." Sadie's shoulders slumped, and she looked back out the window.

Joscelyn reached over, nudged Sadie's shoulder, and laughed gently. "You weren't crying like a baby. Babies cry like this, 'Waaa, waaa, waaa'." The girl smiled in spite of herself.

"Seriously though, you were crying like someone whose heart hurts. Sometimes, when you feel like that, the very best thing to do *is* cry. It relieves some of the pressure."

They came to a ranch entrance made of huge logs standing on end, one on either side of the drive. Another massive log was attached to them horizontally across the top, from which hung a wrought-iron sign that read, "Wolf Run".

"Is this your place?" Joscelyn asked.

Sadie unbuckled her seat belt. "Yeah, you can drop me here."

"Nope. I'll drive you in." Joscelyn pressed the gas hard enough to force Sadie back into the seat, but she gripped the armrest and pulled herself forward again.

Panic tinged Sadie's voice and her eyes grew wide. "No, really, Joscelyn. Just let me out here."

Joscelyn didn't slow down, she was determined to meet Sadie's father. When Sadie realized what was happening, she threw herself back against the seat and with a heavy sigh she crossed her arms and glared at Joscelyn.

"Did your dad know about the Parents' Participation day?"

"Yeah," Sadie answered from somewhere deep in her chest.

They rounded the last bend before the house and Joscelyn pushed down the knot of heat forming in her chest. *There is always more to the story than you can see from one angle*, she reminded herself.

The ranch nestled in a golden-green prairie at the base of wooded foothills. A split-rail fence lined the drive and a herd of horses grazed in the pasture. A beautiful log-cabin with a large, front deck overlooking the property stood at the end of the road.

"Wow, this is gorgeous," Joscelyn said in awe.

Sadie shrugged and as soon as Joscelyn stopped the truck, she jumped out the door and ran into the barn, leaving its wood door open behind her. Joscelyn put the truck in park and climbed out. She turned, appreciating the full 360-degree view.

"Who the hell are *you*?" A man's voice, thick with alcohol, came from the shadows of the deck.

Joscelyn startled and then lifting her chin, she took a deep breath. "Mr. Stone?"

"What d'ya want?"

Joscelyn walked toward the steps. She couldn't see more than the dark shape of the man attached to the voice. "I'm Joscelyn Turner—a friend of your brother and grandmother's. I'm also the person Sadie has been doing her detention assignment with for the past four weeks." He didn't respond to that, so Joscelyn started up the stairs. "We missed you today. Parents were invited to see what their daughters were learning."

"That was today?" His tone sounded resigned.

Once Joscelyn stepped into the shade, she could see Cade Stone clearly. His black-brown hair hung in oily cords and was long enough to push behind his ears. The stubble on his face gave him a grizzled look and covered the top edge of a mottled scar that ran up the left side of his neck and onto his jaw.

She cleared her throat. "Yes, it was."

"So, did you teach those girls all about the evils of smoking dope?" He glared at Joscelyn with condescension and she wondered why he was so hostile. *It was a bad idea to come out here by myself.*

She pushed her hands into her jean pockets. "That wasn't really the point. It was more about learning to make good choices in friends, whose lead they choose to follow, and better uses for their time."

Cade stared hard at her before he turned back to studying the barn yard, his eyes alert, roving back and forth.

Joscelyn took a step further and drew in a fortifying breath. "I wanted to ask you about the bruise on Sadie's cheek."

Cade stood so fast, Joscelyn took two steps back and almost fell on the stairs. She grabbed the log rail to catch herself.

A storm raged in his eyes. "You think I hit her?" he yelled as he towered over her.

"I didn't say that," Joscelyn countered, her heart galloping. "I just wondered what happened." *I should just take Sadie and go—but that wouldn't accomplish anything.*

"Well, I didn't." He glared at her and then ran a hand down the length of his face. He sat heavily back down. "It *was* my fault, but I didn't hit her. I would *never* hit her."

Joscelyn, cautious but determined, walked across the deck and propped herself against the railing in front of him. "What happened?" She could smell the alcohol hovering around him like too much cologne. An empty bottle of bourbon lay on its side on the plank floor next to his chair.

"How is it any of your business? I don't even know you," he growled.

The afternoon grew breezy and dissipated some of the alcohol fumes. Joscelyn looked over her shoulder to the barn, her long hair blowing in her face.

"I'm a friend of your family's and I care about Sadie. Anyone would wonder about the bruised cheek. I'm surprised you didn't get a call from the school."

"Hell, I probably did." He glanced up at her, daring her to say more.

At that moment, a sudden gust of wind whipped down the mountainside and blew into the barnyard. The open barn door slammed shut with a loud bang. Cade leapt out of his seat, grabbed Joscelyn and threw her to the floor, covering her with his body. He knocked the breath out of her and it seared her lungs when she tried to draw air.

Terrified, Joscelyn blinked her watering eyes. *What the hell?* When she could focus, she noticed Cade's rapid breathing and his eyes squeezed shut. He gripped her so hard her arms hurt. Joscelyn's heart careened against her rib cage. She couldn't breathe under his weight.

"What happened? What the hell are you doing?" she choked out.

His eyes fluttered open, and he peered at Joscelyn as though trying to make sense out of her being underneath him. His turbulent gray eyes held a deep pain that made Joscelyn want to stroke his cheek and tell him it would be all right.

He blinked several times and then he jumped up, swaying a little when he got to his feet, his left leg refusing to hold his weight. A ruddy shade darkened his cheeks. Cade covered his eyes with a large, square hand and wiped across his damp forehead, then turned his back to Joscelyn.

She coughed, crawled to her feet, and stood facing him. Between breaths she asked, "Are you all right?" Joscelyn realized Cade had thrown her to the floor to cover her from perceived harm.

Without turning back, he sighed, his shoulders sagged, and with a defeated voice, he said, "Will you please just leave?"

Joscelyn stared at his back for what seemed like five minutes but he didn't turn around. "Has it been like this since you came home from the war?"

After another long moment, he shrugged. He reached down for the bourbon bottle and when he realized it was empty, he threw it, with force, off the deck.

"Is this how Sadie got the bruise?" Joscelyn tried again.

Sadie answered from the deck stairs, startling Joscelyn who hadn't heard her footsteps. "No. My dad slammed a cupboard shut, but it bounced back open and I happened to be there. It cracked me in the face but it was just an accident."

"Mr. Stone?" Joscelyn persisted. Finally, he turned, stiff on one leg, and glared at her, holding back angry tears. "Have you talked to anybody about what's going on with you? You can get help to work through these feelings, these... reactions. What you're going through is fairly common for combat vets." She forced her voice to sound calm, and she put an arm around Sadie when the girl stepped next to her. Joscelyn hoped Sadie couldn't feel her heart rattling.

"I asked you to leave," Cade said through clenched teeth.

Joscelyn raised her chin. "I'm worried about Sadie's safety."

This time he yelled, "I would never hurt my daughter."

Joscelyn flinched, then stared into his eyes and waited for him to calm down. "The thing is, you *are* hurting her, even though you don't mean to." Sadie's body shook in silent sobs and tears washed her cheeks.

"I think it would be a good idea for Sadie to spend the night at Mary's tonight. Is that okay?"

Cade's eyes moved to Sadie. The raw love that flooded them broke Joscelyn's heart and softened it toward him even more. He swallowed and nodded a resigned yes. Then without a word, he turned and limped inside.

Sadie took a step toward him. "Dad?"

Cade closed the door without answering.

Joscelyn placed her hands on Sadie's wet cheeks and lifted her face. "We'll get this all figured out. Your dad loves you. He's having a really rough time right now, but neither of you are alone in this. Okay?"

Sadie nodded and wiped her eyes on her sleeve, black kohl smeared her cheeks.

"Do you need to pack anything to go to your great-grandma's?"

"No, I stay there a lot. I have stuff there."

Joscelyn and Sadie got back into the red truck for the long trek back to Stone Ranch. Sadie stared out the window. "He hates me."

"He doesn't hate you." Joscelyn reached over and took Sadie's hand.

"He's mad at me all the time and I don't know what I'm doing wrong."

"Sweetheart, his anger comes from hurts deep inside, probably from things that happened to him or that he saw during the war. They aren't because of you. He needs to work through them and heal and that's going to take time."

"Why won't he tell me what's wrong? Why doesn't he trust me?" Sadie's eyes were bright with tears.

"It's not you, Sadie. I think your dad doesn't trust himself. He feels out of control of his thoughts and emotions. He needs help to get better."

Sadie sniffed, "I hate this. Sometimes he really scares me. I never know which dad is gonna to be here when I come home. His mood changes so fast, I'm scared to say or do anything. The littlest stuff pisses him off."

Joscelyn squeezed her hand. "You're in a tough situation and I know it's hard. Together, we can all try to help your dad but for now, you have a place to go when it gets too difficult."

When they got to Stone Ranch, it was almost dark. Mary came out the front door to meet them. She opened her arms to her great-granddaughter and Sadie fell into them. Mary met Joscelyn's eyes over the top of the girl's head.

"Sadie is going to spend the night here tonight, if that's okay." Joscelyn kept her tone light.

"Of course, it's all right." Mary squeezed Sadie and closed her eyes. "I love having you." She turned and keeping her arm around Sadie, she walked toward the house. "There is a big pot of soup on the stove. How does that sound?"

Joscelyn stayed for supper and when Sadie was settled in for the night, the two women sat on the porch, sipping cups of tea. The breeze died down and the stars were bright.

Mary whispered into the silence, "I think Cade has that PTSD I've heard about on the news." Joscelyn nodded. "It's not just that though, his wife up and left him, ya know. She drove Sadie over here one night and dropped her off. We haven't seen or heard from her since. That selfish little... well, she left Cade while he was away, fighting in the war. She didn't even tell him herself. And when he came home, it was to an empty house and an eleven-year-old daughter he hardly knew." She stared out into the darkness. "He hasn't been the same. Cade used to love animals, especially horses. He was a hard worker, and he used to be funny and kind. Cade was a good dad, and I thought he and Sadie's mom loved each other." The silence drew out before Mary caught Joscelyn's eye. "Did he give Sadie that bruise on her face? Is that why you brought her here?"

"They both said it was an accident, but it *did* happen because of his anger." Joscelyn took a sip of her Sleepytime tea. "Sadie's having a real hard time. She doesn't understand any of this and thinks it's her fault on some level."

"Poor darlin'. I try to be here for her."

"She's lucky to have you." Joscelyn squeezed Mary's hand. "Have you talked with Cade about any of this?"

Mary ducked her chin. "Not much. He's hard to talk to. We all walk on egg-shells around him." She shifted in her seat to face Joscelyn but couldn't quite meet her eye. "And that's when he's sober."

Joscelyn rolled her lips inward and bit down before she spoke. "He was drinking when I got there today and he was emotional. I thought it would be better for Sadie to stay here for a couple of days. I'd like to try to talk to him but I never see him in town.

"He'll be at church on Sunday," said Mary.

Joscelyn nodded and took a deep breath. I hope he doesn't explode at me in front of the congregation.

CHAPTER 13

Church started ten minutes before Joscelyn arrived. She slipped into a wooden pew in the back during a hymn. Glancing around, Joscelyn noticed Cade also standing in the back, on the opposite side of the small sanctuary. He'd had a fresh haircut and shave for the service. Even though his scarred neck and cheek testified to the cost of battle, Cade was alluringly handsome with his cleaned up, military bearing. He stood tall, staring straight ahead. She couldn't catch his eye, so Joscelyn panned her gaze across the congregation and recognized several familiar faces. She saw Trent in the second row with Mary and Sadie.

During the service, Cade stood when the people stood and sat when they sat, but he did not sing hymns or utter any prayers. To Joscelyn, he seemed present in body though not in spirit, and she wondered why he didn't sit with his family.

After the final song, the pastor dismissed the congregation for coffee, lemonade, and cookies out on the lawn in front of the little white church. Joscelyn allowed herself to be swept along with the crowd. She shook hands with the pastor who stood by the front door greeting parishioners.

He held her hand with both of his. "Welcome. It's always a pleasure to have visitors. I hope you'll consider this your church home as long as you're here in Flint River."

"Thank you, Pastor. I'll definitely be back. Please excuse me, I need to speak with someone." Joscelyn stepped outside to look for Cade. She found him standing alone in the shade of an ancient cottonwood tree.

Joscelyn clasped her hands together and let out a long breath as she approached him. "Hello."

His eyes narrowed at her when she stood before him. He said nothing.

"It sure is a beautiful morning, don't you think?" She tried again.

Cade stared across the lawn and said, "Yeah." He shifted his weight and stretched out his stiff leg. He cleared his throat and his attention dropped to his boots. "Look, I'm sorry about what happened last week."

Joscelyn nodded. "You don't need to be sorry about that. I know you were protecting me."

He scrunched his brow and looked confused. "I acted like an idiot. I hope you weren't hurt."

Reflexively, she reached a hand toward him. "You didn't act like an idiot." When his eyes flew to her hand, she dropped it to her side. "You may have *over* reacted, but I can understand that. In any event, I wasn't hurt," Joscelyn watched Cade's face, his eyes darted back and forth across the churchyard. He avoided her scrutiny and didn't respond.

She stepped into his view and he gave her an irritated glare. "I wanted to ask you a favor."

That jarred him. "What?"

"I want to ask you a favor," Joscelyn repeated. "The girls—Sadie and her friends—asked me to sponsor a new saddle club they want to start up. I wondered if you would let us meet at your ranch and use your arena once a week on Sunday afternoons?"

"Why the hell can't you meet at Trent's place, where you met before?" He scowled at her.

Joscelyn gave him her sweetest smile. "Would you be willing to trailer Sadie's horse over to Trent's every Sunday?" She figured he wouldn't since he hadn't bothered to come to the parent's day. If they met at Cade's, Sadie would always have her horse available, whether or not her dad was able and willing.

"I don't want any 'My Little Pony' club at my barn," he scoffed.

Joscelyn tilted her head. "Why not?"

"Look, lady..."

"Joscelyn."

A small muscle bunched in Cade's jaw. "Look, *Joscelyn,* have you ever been involved with a saddle club before?"

She bit the corner of her bottom lip. "No, not exactly. I belonged to 4H for a couple of years when I was a kid."

"The moms get crazy competitive. I don't want to have all that nonsense at my place."

"It's only three hours, once a week. I promise to keep the drama to a minimum. It will mostly be the girls learning about horsemanship and riding, and I figured it would be easier for you if you didn't have to haul Sadie's horse." Joscelyn's chest was buoyant as she waited for his answer.

Cade regarded her. "What's in it for you?" He sounded skeptical.

Joscelyn's smile broadened. "There is a $100.00 membership fee for the saddle club, but I propose that Sadie's fee be waived and in return, I could board my horses at your ranch during the saddle club season—for free. It would be a trade, of sorts."

He let a derisive burst of air out through his nose. Joscelyn waited.

"How many horses do you have?"

"Just two."

"I guess we could give it a try, but I reserve the right to change my mind if it becomes a pain in my ass."

Joscelyn clasped her hands together. "Thank you, Mr. Stone."

"Call me Cade."

Joscelyn nodded and after a moment of silence, she spoke. "It'll give us a chance to talk too." Her voice lowered and filled with compassion. "I've heard you've had a pretty rough time since you came home from Afghanistan."

A tempest stormed in his eyes and he raised his voice. "You don't know anything about me and it's none of your damn business." He worked hard to swallow his anger. "Why do you care, anyway?"

Several congregants cast concerned glances their way. Joscelyn took a step toward Cade and lowered her voice. "You are your daughter's hero."

Cade swallowed hard and blinked his eyes against a flash of rebellious tears. His jaw hardened.

Joscelyn continued, "I know because my father was also a Marine and he was *my* hero. I care because I'm thankful for the sacrifice you made for our country—for all of us."

Cade visibly wrestled with his emotions for several minutes, opening and closing his fists. Joscelyn didn't interrupt his process. He glared at her before he said, "I'm not a 'lay on the couch and cry about my problems' type of guy."

"That's a relief, because I'm not a 'listen to a man lying on a couch crying about his problems' type of gal." She grinned at him and settled for a smirk in return. "How about we just take our horses out for a ride sometime?"

Cade considered her for a long moment and then gave her a slight nod. "Sure, I guess." He scanned the perimeter another time before returning his eyes to Joscelyn. "How about this afternoon?"

~*~

Joscelyn hauled her horses over to Wolf Run. Cade showed her where to settle her buckskin in a stall and then she tacked up her black horse for their trail ride. Cade's horse was a big, beautiful, sorrel quarter-horse he called Sherman. He led the way out the back of his property and up into the National Forest. The afternoon was warm, but it was cool in the shady woods. He noticed Joscelyn rub the chill out of her arms and was glad she wore a long-sleeved shirt.

They rode several miles enjoying the peacefulness of the scenery when Joscelyn broke the silence. "The trees here are different from those in Colorado."

"How so?"

"Montana pines seem taller with thinner trunks and shorter, lacier needles." A slight breeze gave the great pines a voice with which to whisper their pine-scented secrets. Blue-jays called out to their mates. Cade's breath came easy and his muscles loosened in the rhythm of Sherman's gait. He adjusted the gun he wore holstered to his hip. He never left home without it. You never knew what might jump out at you up in the high-country. When the trail widened enough to ride side by side, Joscelyn closed the gap between them.

"I appreciated your apology today," she said.

Cade nodded.

"Why do you suppose you had such a strong reaction to the barn door slamming last week?"

Cade remained quiet, so she continued, her voice softening, "You know—PTSD is a lot more common than you might think. It's simply a normal response to an abnormal event, but the suffering that follows can indicate a need for help."

Cade narrowed his eyes at Joscelyn, sarcasm sharpened his retort. "And I suppose you think you're the person to help me? I don't need a therapist."

She ignored his tone. "No, but I might be able to help point you in the right direction. I'm just trying to be a friend."

"I don't need any help. I came home from Afghanistan with all my body parts. Hell, I'm alive. A lot of guys have it a whole lot worse than me."

"That may be true, but it doesn't diminish what you're going through."

Cade brought his horse to a halt. "What do *you* know about it?"

Joscelyn stopped next to him, stroked her horse's neck, and answered, "You remind me a lot of my dad, that's all. When he came home from deployments to Iraq, he sometimes exploded with anger I couldn't understand." She stared far off in the distance a while before continuing. "I don't have to know the specifics of your situation to know that what you experienced caused trauma to your brain. When someone gets shot, you can see the wound and you respond accordingly, without questioning whether or not he needs help. When people are traumatized by horrific events, we can't see their wounds, but they're still there. Trauma *is* a wound."

Cade scanned the surrounding woods, his eyes darting toward every sound. "I don't want to talk about the war." he murmured. Sherman shifted his weight, pawed the ground, and tossed his head. "Steady," Cade commanded.

"Okay—can I ask how you're sleeping?"

Cade gave his head a slight shake. "Not great."

"Do you have nightmares?"

Cade nudged Sherman to move on up the trail. "Sometimes, but I never remember them when I wake up."

The trail narrowed and forced Joscelyn to fall behind Cade's lead again. "Traumatic memories aren't filed away in regular long-term memory, instead they remain active and can repeatedly intrude as dreams and flashbacks."

Cade's back stiffened. He reined Sherman in and turned. Uncertain how much he should share. "The thing is, I don't remember. I don't know why that loud noise made me tackle you. It's like there's something, just at the edge of my mind, but I can't get ahold of it." Frustration clogged his throat. Sherman side-stepped. "Whoa, Sherman." Cade's angry tone and abruptness caused the horse to toss his head.

Joscelyn leaned forward in her saddle. "That's probably your brain trying to protect you. Whatever caused it, your reaction to the barn door slamming would be normal during war, but now that you're home, it's a little extreme."

Cade nodded, turned, and rode on. Joscelyn followed him, her words hovering in the natural song of the forest. Eventually, they came to a clearing near a small creek. Sherman balked at Cade's asking him to cross the water. He backed up and spun away from the bank. "Damn it, Sherman. Get-up." Cade growled as he pressed his heels into his horse's sides and slapped his hindquarters with the ends of his reins. Sherman leapt forward, into the water. Once they were on the other side, the horse kicked out in complaint.

"Sherman's only responding to your agitation. It's a great thing about horses—they reflect our emotions, even when we aren't fully aware of them ourselves."

Cade pulled back on his horse's reins and Sherman pranced.

"Try to relax and remember to breathe."

Cade took a deep breath. "Steady, Sherm." He breathed out. After a few minutes Sherman calmed down.

"Horses are awesome." Joscelyn laughed.

Cade raised his eyebrows.

"Seriously, they can help people with their emotions because they give bio-feedback. Sherman will show you with his own behavior that your emotions are ramping up even before you notice it. Then you can do something about it before things escalate."

"Yeah, I get it." Cade patted Sherman's neck. He had the uneasy sense that Joscelyn was analyzing him again and turned up the corner of his mouth. "That'll be helpful when I'm *on* my horse, but what about the other times?"

"Whenever you're with him, if you concentrate on it, you'll notice how you feel inside as Sherman reacts to your emotions spooling up. You can learn from his cues and begin to sense it too. When you're aware, you'll have more control."

Cade stared at Joscelyn in thought awhile before moving on. He inclined his chin to the right. "Let's ride up the crick another mile, then we should probably turn back."

Water, tumbling and splashing over stones, lulled his tension. Cade sighed with contentment and listened, thankful for its musical balm. The golden-white reflection of the late afternoon sun on the stream was dazzling. On their way back down the path toward the ranch, Cade spoke only once to point out a moose standing in a bog. The bull lifted his colossal head from the water and regarded them while water dripped from limp grasses caught on his massive, scooping antlers. At the end of their ride, Cade felt more at peace than he had in a long time.

At the barn, they took off their tack and brushed their horses. Joscelyn said, "I'd like to do some arena work with you next week, after the saddle club meeting. Would you be willing to try something with me?"

Cade didn't answer. Instead, he led Sherman to his stall. He'd had a nice time with Joscelyn today and didn't want her to see any more of his weak crap. He did, however, want to see more of her. On his way out of the barn, he passed Joscelyn and said, "We'll see." He turned and walked backward, "You're feeding tonight, right?" He asked with an impish grin.

Joscelyn smiled and shook her head. "Yeah, I got it."

The front door of the cabin swung open and Sadie ran out, followed by Teddy and Cade's dog, Max. Together, they spilled down the steps.

"I'll help, Josce," Sadie called. She was no longer wearing the large coat, and the pure shine of hope that beamed from her eyes when she looked at him pierced Cade's heart. More than anything he didn't want to let her down. If he could only help it.

Still walking backwards and facing Joscelyn, Cade said, "Ya know, I haven't gone on a trail ride since before I deployed. Haven't felt like it. I forgot how much I love to ride." He cocked his head to the side. "Thanks."

CHAPTER 14

Joscelyn pulled her truck into a parking spot in front of the library. A light glowed from the back of the shop near the kitchenette. She didn't remember leaving it on but was relieved she had. Coming home to a dark house always emphasized her loneliness. She hopped down from her truck and held the door for Teddy to follow.

When she got to the door, it was unlocked and ajar. Joscelyn hesitated, holding her breath, her stomach clenched hard. She pushed open the door but didn't follow it in.

"Hello?" she called. Teddy ran inside and disappeared behind the bookshelves. "Teddy?" Joscelyn took a wary step inside. "Teddy, come here." When he didn't immediately appear, her chest tightened as her apprehension grew. She drew an umbrella out of the antique stand in the entry and brandished it like a baseball bat. "Teddy?"

"I wondered when you'd get home." A man's voice echoed from the shadows of the bookshop, near the fireplace.

Joscelyn jumped at the sound, screamed, and swung the umbrella, knocking over a stack of books waiting to be shelved. Her heart clamored against her ribs as she tried to focus on the form behind the voice.

"Whoa, girl. You're gonna to hurt somebody with that thing," Trent chuckled as he stepped forward and commandeered the waterproof weapon. "Most likely yourself." He dumped the umbrella back in the holder.

"Trent!" Joscelyn raced from fear to fury in half a second. "What are you doing here?" Teddy barked and wagged his tail. "Quiet, Teddy. You could have barked before now, you know." Joscelyn hugged herself and turned away from her friend and her dog. "How did you get in?"

"I'm sorry, Josce. The door was unlocked. Nothing unusual about that—nobody locks doors around here."

Anger creased the edges of her voice, "*I* do. In fact, I am certain I locked the door when I left."

"Well, maybe the lock just didn't quite catch. Anyway, it's just me. Why are you so mad?" Trent touched her arm, and she pulled away from him. She squeezed her eyes closed trying to keep the tears inside. "Joscelyn, what's going on?" He grasped her arm again and this time didn't let her pull away. Instead he drew her into his chest and held her until she stopped trembling.

Joscelyn sniffed. "I'm sorry. You frightened me, that's all."

"I had the light on and Teddy came right to me for a scratch. Why were you so scared?" He lifted her chin to look in her eyes. "Startled, I get, but you were ready to beat somebody to death and then you burst into tears. Why are you so upset?"

Joscelyn blinked at him a couple of times and pulled her chin out of his hand. "I thought you were someone else." She took a big gulp of air and asked, "You have time for a cup of tea?"

Trent lifted one shoulder. "I'd rather have a beer if you've got one."

She nodded and flipped on her electric teapot before reaching into the mini-fridge. Joscelyn opened a bottle of beer and handed it to him, then brewed her tea while she considered what to tell him. She'd never been comfortable sharing her private affairs, and she didn't want to do anything that would make it easier for Lenny to find her. When her tea was ready, she sat in the chair opposite his, in front of the darkened hearth.

"I never told you why I left Colorado," she began. "The fact is, I'm avoiding an ex-client who threatened me." Joscelyn blew the steam from her cup.

"Threatened you how?" Trent's brows gathered and he frowned. He sat forward, his fist flexed around his beer bottle.

"He was stalking me, so I loaded my horses and Teddy and we drove to Montana. I'm taking a hiatus until things cool down." She left out the gory details, not wanting Trent to worry about her.

Trent stood and moved to the counter. "You thought I was him? Your stalker?"

"No—I don't know. You just scared me. He's definitely why I lock my doors though." Joscelyn took a sip of tea and let the warmth comfort her nerves.

"Do you think he'll try to find you all the way up here in Montana?"

"I don't know." Joscelyn thought back to her last phone call from Lenny. "I doubt he'd come up here. He couldn't find me even if he did."

"I'm sorry I scared you. I had no idea." Trent ran a hand through his hair.

"You didn't mean to. I'm obviously over-sensitive." Joscelyn tried to laugh at herself but it came out more like a sputter. "Please keep this between us, though, okay? I don't want my business spread around town."

"No one'll hear it from me. Do you think you should tell the sheriff though?"

"There's no need. I'm just lying low for a while until it all blows over."

"Okay, but you better call me if anything happens."

"I will, thanks."

"I guess that explains why you're not planning on staying?"

"Yeah." Joscelyn sipped her tea. "By the way, why *are* you here?"

Trent tilted his head and offered Joscelyn his most engaging smile. "I wanted to see you, maybe take you out for dinner?"

"That's nice of you, but if it's okay, I'd like to have a raincheck. I'm tired and want to turn in early."

"Sure, I get it. Let me check all around to make sure you're safe and sound before I go though, so you'll sleep easy." Trent drained his beer and dropped the bottle into the recycle bin with a clink. He checked the lock on the back door before he ran up the steps with Teddy on his heels. Their footsteps clattered overhead.

When he came back down, Trent carried a dead bird in a paper towel. "You're all locked up and secure and I left the lamp on by your bed." He held up the bird. "I'm not sure how this guy got inside, but I think he committed suicide. He must have broken his neck trying to fly out through the glass. Poor little fella. Do you have something I can wrap him in? I'll throw it away outside."

Joscelyn grimaced when she peered at the robin with his head wrenched backwards. She shuddered as a chill ran through her body. When Trent left, she closed and locked the door, throwing the deadbolt and checked to be sure it caught correctly. Trent put on his cowboy hat and touched the brim. He nodded at her from the other side of the glass. She gave him a weak smile before she turned to climb the stairs, rubbing away the gooseflesh on her arms. *Will I ever be free from this constant fear?*

~*~

The following Sunday after church, Joscelyn met Cade and Sadie in the arena at Wolf Run. "Today we'll try an exercise that's designed to improve communication. We'll only work with one horse. Sadie, would you please go get Fargo?"

"Sure." Sadie skipped off. She seemed excited to be doing something with her dad.

While they waited for her, Joscelyn built a small jump in the center of the arena. She glanced up at Cade and asked, "How was your week?"

Cade's eyes darted across the horizon before he answered. "Lots of nightmares and I still can't remember them when I wake up. It sucks." He helped Joscelyn by picking up the other end of a ground pole. They set it across two bales of hay.

"What about when you're awake? Any difficult memories?"

"I haven't tackled anyone, if that's what you mean." Cade tried for humor. When Joscelyn smiled, he answered, "Sometimes, when I'm out here working, I flashback. How can I make it stop?"

Joscelyn was pleased to see he was interested in getting better. "Do you notice any specific triggers?"

Cade shook his head, thinking. "Sometimes a loud noise or a flash of light. They come out of nowhere and take over."

"Don't feel bad about not being able to control them. That's normal at first. As a general rule, traumatic memories will continue to intrude until they make sense, until you can process them to the point where your brain can file them into your long-term memory."

Cade rested his hands on his hips. "How do I do that?"

"Talking about it helps."

Cade rolled his eyes and turned away.

"I know you don't want to hear that, but our memory system is built on language. So, when you put words to your memories it helps you process them."

Sadie came out of the barn leading Fargo. In the arena, there were a couple of ground-poles pushed off to the side next to a stack of orange traffic cones. Joscelyn removed Fargo's halter, and he wandered to the rail, trying to reach the grass growing on the other side.

"Sadie, you've done this type of exercise before." Joscelyn winked at her. "Today, the goal for you two, as a team, is to get Fargo to go over the jump. There are four rules." Joscelyn held up her index finger. "No one can touch Fargo. You may not use halters or lead ropes in any fashion. You may not bribe him with any food or simulate bribing, and you may use only what is in the arena."

Joscelyn clapped her hands together. "Okay, we'll try this for five minutes and then if Fargo hasn't gone over the jump yet, we'll take a break. Ready... set... go." She glanced at her watch.

Cade expertly herded the horse toward the jump. Sadie tried to help, but Cade ignored her. It looked like Fargo headed straight for the jump, but at the last minute he veered off and moved around it. Cade shook his head and sent an exasperated look to Joscelyn. She flattened her lips and raised her eyebrows to acknowledge him, but she didn't say anything.

"Dad, you have to let me help. We're supposed to do this *together*," Sadie complained.

He sighed. "Okay, let's try it again. You stand there and raise your arms if he tries to avoid the jump on your side."

"But–"

Cade cut Sadie off. "This won't work with only two people."

"Dad—"

"Just stand where I said." Cade herded Fargo back toward the jump. The horse walked toward it, but when he got close, Sadie raised her arms and Fargo trotted the other direction, avoiding the jump on the opposite side.

"Time," Joscelyn called. "Come on over here and let's talk about what's happening."

Cade strode toward Joscelyn "This is AFU. Have you ever done this with only two people before?" Frustration flooded his voice.

Joscelyn smiled at the familiar acronym. Her dad used to say it all the time when he thought something was screwed up. "Yes, I have, but it looks like you two aren't having a lot of luck."

"A horse always takes the path of least resistance. He's not going to jump over the pole for no reason." Cade looked at Joscelyn like she was a simpleton.

Joscelyn nodded but refused to be baited and faced Sadie. "It seemed like you were trying to say something out there. What was it?"

Sadie gave her dad a sideways glance. "I was *trying* to say we should work together. If we both herd Fargo, one of us on each side, he might go over the jump."

"What do you think about Sadie's idea, Cade?" Joscelyn asked.

"Still won't work."

Joscelyn changed the subject. "Who's the leader on your team?"

Sadie narrowed her eyes and pursed her lips. "My dad, *obviously*."

"That makes sense, *I'm* the dad. *And* I have more horse experience." A serrated edge of irritation sawed at Cade's tone.

"I'm sure you do have more experience than Sadie but does that mean that her ideas are invalid?" Joscelyn let the rhetorical question resound in the air. Cade shrugged one shoulder.

"I have another idea, too," Sadie ventured. "There are some ground-poles and cones at the side of the arena. Joscelyn said we could only use what is *in* the arena, and those things are."

Cade sighed. "So, are we doing this again?"

"Are you finished with the team discussion?" asked Joscelyn.

Cade clenched his jaw and let out an irritated sigh. He turned and walked toward the jump.

Joscelyn shrugged and held her wrist out to see the minute hand. "Okay. Ready… go."

Father and daughter started back toward the center of the arena. Cade carried two ground-poles back to the jump. He returned for the cones. Sadie stood to the side and watched him as he made an alley with the poles and cones for Fargo to enter before facing the jump. Then he herded the buckskin into the alley. Fargo stopped at the jump and seemed to think about it. He tossed his head up and down before he turned and stepped over the ground-pole alley and walked away. Sadie smirked.

Cade tore off his camo-colored baseball cap and threw it in the dirt.

"Is there anything that's working?" Joscelyn asked.

"No." A storm hovered in Cade's eyes.

Undeterred, Joscelyn asked, "What isn't working?"

"The whole damn thing," Cade grumbled.

"Sadie?"

Sadie crossed her arms over her chest. "I never got to tell my Dad my idea."

"I noticed that too." Joscelyn's voice was soft. "Cade, you listened to the first part of Sadie's idea and then shut her down. You took her idea, but tried to do it all on your own. You didn't include her."

Cade looked chagrined. "I guess you're right." He set his hands on his hips and cast his gaze to the ground. "Sorry, Sadie. I'm just getting frustrated."

Joscelyn continued. "Sadie, you didn't assert yourself. Do you believe in your idea?"

"Yeah."

"You let your dad take over without speaking up for an idea you believe in. I noticed you stood off to the side. What were you thinking?" asked Joscelyn.

Sadie swallowed. "That he would fail again."

"Was it all right with you that your team member was going to fail?"

Sadie's cheeks flushed. "No."

"It seems like you guys are supposed to be a team, yet each of you does your own thing. Cade, you make decisions and push them through without listening to any input. Sadie, when you aren't heard, you step aside and allow your teammate to fail." Joscelyn paused, letting that sink in. "You guys are a family. A family is a team. What can you work on that will make your team more successful?"

Sadie gave her dad a half smile. "I could try to speak up and help a little more."

Cade drew his hand across his mouth. "I'll try to listen better, Sadie. I guess I'm used to giving an order and having it followed."

"I get that, Cade," Joscelyn said, "but one sign of a good leader is that he listens to other's ideas before deciding on the best course of action. Right?"

"True. I guess I think of Sadie as just a kid."

"*Dad!*" Sadie frowned. "I'm not a kid anymore. I'm almost thirteen."

The hard glint in his eye softened a bit and gave Joscelyn hope for their future. "Let's let this percolate for a while. We'll try this again next week and see if things improve."

CHAPTER 15

During saddle club, the girls practiced basic equitation and then, after putting their horses up, they met in the tack-room. Joscelyn leaned against the door and rested her eyes on Sadie who stood in the back of the room, cleaning and oiling her bridle.

Dakota reached in her bag and pulled out some bright green papers. "What do you guys think about going to a gymkhana?" She passed out the fliers advertising an upcoming event. "This one's over in Silver Bow County in July."

Lisa studied the information. "What's a gymkhana?"

Dakota leaned against a saddle rack. "It's a bunch of speed games on horseback like barrel racing and pole bending," Dakota answered. "There's lots of other cool stuff too, like trying to balance an egg in a spoon while you ride."

"You can win ribbons." Tracy pulled her phone from her back pocket and opened her photos. "These are some of mine." Lisa and Dakota leaned in to see.

"Oh, yeah. I remember seeing those in your room," Lisa said. "If we go to this, will you guys help me?"

Nodding, the three girls chattered with excitement. Joscelyn noticed a haunted contemplation hovering in Sadie's dark eyes as the girl slumped down onto a bale of hay.

Parents arrived at six o'clock. Dakota and Tracy loaded their horses and waved as they left. Lisa gave the horse she'd borrowed one last cookie.

"Bye, Sadie," she said and got into the van with her mom. Sadie waved from her spot on the bale and watched her friends leave.

"Everything okay?" Joscelyn asked, sitting next to her. Sadie shrugged. "You've been pretty quiet all afternoon."

Sadie spoke so low Joscelyn barely heard her. "My dad's drinking again."

"Are you all right?"

"Yeah. I just hate it when he drinks."

Joscelyn draped her arm around Sadie's shoulders. "I know." She paused, "I think he hates it too."

Sadie peered at her with a skeptical expression.

"Your Dad has some awful memories of the war. Memories he wants to escape and never think of again, but they keep coming back."

"So he drinks?" Sadie searched Joscelyn's face, looking confused.

"Maybe he's trying to drown out the images. Your dad's trying to get better, but it takes time."

Sadie considered this and nodded. She wiped her face with the back of her sleeve. "I want to help him but I don't know how. I try to stay out of his way, cuz I just make him mad."

Joscelyn's senses went on alert. "Are you afraid of him?"

"What?" Sadie sat up and faced Joscelyn, her brows drawn together. "*No.*" Sadie looked at Joscelyn like she'd just asked her if she believed in Godzilla. "I'm not afraid of him. My dad would *never* hurt me, but I'm sometimes afraid of what he might do."

Relief slid through Joscelyn at Sadie's response. "I'm glad to hear that." She sat back against the wall. "Did you learn anything during the exercise with your dad that might apply here?"

Sadie stared off into the distance while she thought. "I guess I could talk to him about it, tell him how I feel. But it's impossible to talk to him when he's been drinking."

"It would definitely be better to talk to him when he's sober." Joscelyn squeezed her shoulder. "Do you want me to drive you to your great-grandma Mary's?"

"No. Dad smashed his last bottle of whiskey on a rock out back. He doesn't have anything else to drink now."

Joscelyn wondered if he had done that so he wouldn't drink it. "Well, that's good." Sadie nodded. "Let's go check on him. Maybe we can make you two something for dinner and he'll be ready to talk to you for dessert."

"Maybe." Sadie gave half a smile.

~*~

At the end of May, Jocelyn contacted her landlord in Colorado. He refused to hold her rental property until she could return, and so with a heavy heart, she called a moving company and had her belongings packed and moved into storage. As of yet, neither the Sheriff's Department nor the Police in Castle Rock found any trace of Leonard Perkins. Joscelyn emailed her boss and requested an extension on her leave of absence. The mere thought of Lenny caused the skin on her arms and neck to pucker. She wouldn't be fully at ease until he was in custody. A blue-hot flame burned deep in her belly when she thought of the loss of her home, her job, and her normal life. All of it gone because of Leonard Perkins.

June swept into Montana on a warm breeze, and the townspeople prepared for the Founder's Day Celebration. All the shops along Main Street decorated their windows for the event. The day began with a parade that started at the Courthouse and proceeded down Main Street, ending at the town park. Floats depicting the town's history trundled by, and folks costumed in nineteenth century clothing waved from them. They threw candy to the children who watched from the curb. Joscelyn smiled, knowing only small towns still allowed candy-tossing during parades.

Mayor Smithers sat in the back of a 1965, Arcadian blue Mustang convertible and nodded to the crowd. Riding their horses side by side, the Saddle Club girls followed him down the street, waving. They all wore matching pink and black, bedazzled western shirts that Tracy's mom bought them for the event. Behind the girls, thirteen high-school band members marched by in their orange and white uniforms playing the national anthem while feathered plumes bobbed on top of their caps.

A hand settled on Joscelyn's shoulder and she turned. Margaret Bell stood behind her wearing a pioneer bonnet and a skirt with an apron.

"You've done a good thing with those girls."

Joscelyn smiled and nodded at the costume. "Were you in the parade?"

"Me? No. I just like to get into the spirit of things." Margaret smoothed her apron and chuckled at herself. "Joscelyn, I understand you're working at the library but I want you to know we sure could use a school counselor at the high school next year. I'd love to talk to you about it."

"Thanks, Margaret. I really appreciate that but I'm only staying in Flint River through the summer."

"Oh, that's a shame. I thought you were making a home here." Margaret patted Joscelyn's shoulder. "Well, you chose a lovely time to visit. Summers in Montana can't be beat." She picked up the hem of her skirt to turn down the walk. "See you at the picnic?"

"I'll be there." Joscelyn waved.

Many of the shops set up booths in the park. Artists and craftspeople spread their homemade wares on tables next to booths. Food and drink vendors provided for people who didn't bring their own picnics. Snaking through the crowd stood a long line of folks waiting for ice cream.

The kids from the marching band removed their hats, took seats in the park's gazebo, and played big band and patriotic music to entertain the crowd for a couple of hours. Families brought blankets and sat themselves on the grass in the park next to an open area set aside for games. Joscelyn wandered through the crowd with Teddy on his leash and watched children race in the three-legged race, toss eggs back and forth, and pull with fierce determination to win the tug-of-war.

She scouted out Mary's picnic spot and joined her. "Here you are."

"I'm glad you found us. Have a seat." Mary rummaged in a large, wicker picnic-basket. "I brought fried chicken, potato salad, and coleslaw."

Strong hands grabbed Joscelyn by her waist. She jumped, pin pricks shooting through her scalp and causing her heart to leap into her throat. Trent leaned around and kissed her cheek. Turning to Mary, he said, "Hope you brought your apple pie for dessert, Gran. It's the only reason I come." A sly smile slid onto his face and he snuggled Joscelyn close, bumping her cheek with the wide brim of his hat. "Well, it *used* to be the only reason I came."

Joscelyn wriggled out of his grasp. "Knock it off, Trent."

"Leave that poor woman alone and sit down for lunch." Mary shook her head. Joscelyn pressed her lips into a stiff smile. She hated it when Trent acted as though they were a couple in public. Joscelyn didn't like being seen as another Trent Stone fan-girl. She knelt next to the basket, taking care to hold her denim skirt down, and helped Mary unpack.

"Sadie said she'd be here as soon as they got the horses set up with hay and water at the trailer." Joscelyn glanced across the park to the back of the parking lot to see if the girls were coming. She saw them standing together, laughing with a blond-headed boy. "It might be a few minutes. Looks like they found an admirer."

Mary followed her line of sight. "That's the new boy. Sadie told me he just moved here and will start his senior year in the fall."

Joscelyn opened the cooler and pulled out three cans of Pepsi. She handed one to Trent and set one by Mary. "Thanks for sharing your picnic with me. It's nice to feel like part of a family."

Mary eyes softened, and she smiled. "We're awful glad to have you." She patted Joscelyn's knee.

"That's good, because it looks like I'll be here for longer than I planned." Joscelyn snapped open her soda and took a sip. "I thought I'd be headed home by now, but it looks like I'll be here through August." *Or until the cops catch Lenny.*

Trent laid back, propped on his elbows. "That's great news." He grinned.

"Not really. I lost my rental in Colorado so I don't have a home to return to. I'll have to start looking for another place."

"Will you go home as soon as you find one, then?" Mary asked as she rummaged in the basket.

Joscelyn set out the paper-plates, napkins, and plasticware. "That's my plan."

Mary studied Joscelyn with a speculative gaze and said, "Good. That still gives us a few months together." Joscelyn remembered Mary suspected she was running from something and she looked away.

Mary handed Trent a jar of pickles she couldn't open and asked him, "Did you talk to Cade?" She set crispy pieces of fried chicken on three plates and passed the potato salad to Joscelyn. "Were you able to convince him to come?"

"I asked him," Trent said as he twisted the lid. "But he wouldn't commit, said he had stuff to do."

As though the mention of his name conjured him, Cade arrived. The bill of his USMC hat pulled low over his eyes. He lifted it in a nod toward Trent and leaned against a tree several feet from the blanket.

"Glad to see you, Cade." Mary took the plate meant for Trent and handed it to his brother.

Trent grunted and reached for an empty one. He held it toward Mary. "He always *was* your favorite," Trent teased.

"Where's Sadie?" Cade's ever-watchful eyes scanned the crowd.

"She's putting her horse up and talking with friends over by the trailer. She'll be here soon," Joscelyn answered. Cade's eyes settled on her like a bright overcast sky and his mouth hinted at a smile.

A microphone crackled and whistled out of several large speakers set up throughout the park. The crowed groaned at the painful squeal.

"Good afternoon, Flint River Folk. Welcome to our 150th Annual Founder's Day Celebration." The Mayor waited for the applause. "I hope everyone is enjoying themselves on this beautiful June day. There's plenty of food and drink along with games. Be sure to support our local businesses.

I hope everyone will stay for the chili supper, dancing, and fireworks this evening." Several hoots and shrill whistles sounded from the crowd. "In a few minutes, I'll be announcing the winner of this year's annual Quilt Contest. Will all the participants please find their way up to the stage?"

Trent laughed, "Hopefully no one will notice any sun-faded spots." He nudged Joscelyn.

She grimaced. "No kidding. Who do you suppose will win?"

"Hard to say," Mary answered. "All those quilters do a fine job." She ran a hand over her own home-spun quilt they were picnicking on. "Not like my rough work."

"Sure, but none of those quilts will ever be used," said Trent. "They'll just hang on walls or lay on guest beds where no one actually sleeps."

Joscelyn glanced at Cade. His eyes continued their constant scan. She wished he could relax and enjoy himself.

"Who are Sadie and the girls talking to?" he asked.

Everyone turned to look. The kids were too far away to make out facial details, but Joscelyn saw the girls waving at the boy they had been talking with. "I don't know, but it looks like they're on their way over to the picnic now."

Tonya's voice came from behind Joscelyn and startled her. "That's David. He's new to town."

Mary brushed crumbs from her hands. "Hello, Tonya. Would you like to join our picnic?"

Tonya's eyes settled on Joscelyn from underneath the net veil of her white, pill-box hat. She smoothed the full skirt of her 1950s style shirt-dress. Her gaze bounced to Mary. "No, thank you. I just stopped by to say hi." She looked down. "Hello, Trent," she murmured.

Trent touched the brim of his cowboy hat. "Tonya."

Cade asked, "How well do you know that kid, Tonya?"

"Not well. I just met him coming out of the library the other day." She pursed her red lips and gave Joscelyn a pointed look. "He said he knew you."

"Really?" Joscelyn cocked her head trying to remember. She drew the corners of her mouth down. "I don't remember him."

Tonya stood at the edge of the blanket in an uncomfortable silence before she finally said, "Well... I just wanted to say hello."

Mary gave the woman a kind smile. "I'm glad you did. It's good to see you."

Tonya acknowledged the kind words with flattened lips and after a lingering glance at Trent, she nodded and floated away into the sea of picnickers.

A minute later, Deputy Brown walked by, his eyes on Tonya. He stopped, surveyed their picnic spot, and then dipped his cavalry-style deputy hat toward Mary. "Afternoon, Ms. Stone."

"Wayne." Mary smiled.

His large head looked too heavy for his skinny neck as his eyes moved to Joscelyn. "Ms. Turner."

Joscelyn held up her hand to shade her eyes from the sun. "Hi Wayne."

The deputy nodded and glared over at Trent. "Stone," he said with an icy tone. "Just so you know, I'm keeping an eye on you."

"Of course you are, Wayne." Trent laughed without mirth. "You never could keep your eyes off me."

"You're such an ass," Deputy Brown said under his breath. Louder he said, "I'm sorry, ladies. Have a nice day." He touched the brim of his hat, nodded at Cade, and ignoring Trent, he followed in the direction Tonya went.

Joscelyn gave Trent a quizzical look. "What's up with the two of you?"

"He's just a little worm." Trent shook his head. "Wayne's always hated me, ever since high school football when I tackled him and broke his arm in practice. He's always had a thing for Tonya, too." Trent barked a short, derisive laugh. "Like that would ever happen."

Joscelyn sat with the Stone family all afternoon. Using Teddy as a pillow, she dozed in the warmth of the sun, or at least she tried to. It was hard to relax while Cade kept his persistent vigil for an unseen enemy and refused to sit. When dusk fell, the Rotary Club served a chili supper. After dinner, a dance-band from Missoula began playing and couples took to the dance floor in front of the gazebo.

Trent leaned in and whispered in Joscelyn's ear. "Want to dance?" His hot breath tickled.

Joscelyn nodded as she scrunched her shoulder up against the sensation. "Okay, but just one."

Trent stood and pulled her to her feet. She told Teddy to stay, slipped on her sandals, and followed

Trent to the dance floor. He twisted and turned her to the rhythm of the music and when the song changed to a slower one, Trent pulled Joscelyn in close. She gave in to the second dance and closed her eyes. For a moment, she let her head rest against Trent's chest. Joscelyn could hear his heart's tempo and felt his muscles hard against her cheek. She liked the idea of being part of a couple, but she was realizing that Trent probably wasn't the guy for her.

Halfway through the song, a tall, willowy woman Joscelyn had never seen before, tapped her on the shoulder. "Can I cut in?" The woman's eyes never acknowledged Joscelyn, they were focused on Trent.

"Uh, sure." Joscelyn stepped back, and the woman slid into Trent's arms. He gave the new woman a wicked grin and said something in her ear that made her laugh. Joscelyn felt foolish standing alone on the floor as the woman swayed off with Trent, so she turned and made her way back to the picnic blanket. Mary left before it grew dark, and thinking she was alone, Joscelyn slid down next to her dog on the quilt.

A voice shot out from the shadows of the tree. "That's my little brother for you." Cade's voice conveyed derision as he maintained his night watch.

Joscelyn drew in a sharp breath. "You startled me. I didn't see you there."

"Sorry." Cade crossed his arms. "Don't feel bad about Trent though. He never could focus on one woman at a time." He pushed himself away from the tree he'd been leaning on. "I'm gonna round up Sadie and head for home."

"Aren't you two staying for the fireworks?"

"Heh," Cade scoffed. "Not really my thing anymore, ya know?"

Joscelyn looked at her lap. "I suppose not. I wasn't thinking." She stood, lifted the blanket, and shook it out. "Here, grab the other end."

Cade took one edge of the blanket. "Don't feel like *you* have to leave."

"I don't want to sit here by myself, and I'm tired, anyway. I'll help you find Sadie and then call it a night."

They folded the blanket together and on the last crease their hands met. Cade held her gaze for several long seconds. Joscelyn's pulse surged, and she blinked her eyes. Disconcerted, she pulled away and set the blanket next to Teddy. She cleared her throat and said, "Thanks. I'll return this to Mary tomorrow at church."

Cade stood silent, watching her. Joscelyn pressed her palm over the fluttering in her belly and chewed the bottom corner of her lip. *Did something just happen between us?* She shook her head. *Oh, for heaven's sake, loneliness is now causing me to imagine things.*

Sadie's voice broke through the tension as she walked toward them and called back to her friends. "See you guys tomorrow." She turned to her dad. "I'm ready, Dad. The horses are loaded in the trailer." Teddy licked Sadie's hand, and she patted his head. "Good night, Teddy. Night, Josce."

"Good night, you two."

~*~

175

On Wednesday, Joscelyn sat at the counter in Alice's Diner and ordered the chicken-fried steak with mashed potatoes and gravy. Down-home, comfort food was exactly what she needed and Alice didn't disappoint. Joscelyn scooped the last bite of gravy-drenched mash onto her fork and savored the rich flavor.

"Room for huckleberry pie for dessert?" the waitress asked.

Joscelyn had never heard of that. "Huckleberries? What do they taste like?"

The girl topped Joscelyn's coffee off. "I think they taste like purple." She smiled. "A cross between blackberries and blueberries."

"I'll have to try that."

"They're only around in the summer months, so now's the time."

Joscelyn rinsed down the last tangy bite of pie with a swallow of coffee, paid her bill, and stepped out the door onto the walk. The sun hung low in the sky and beamed straight down Main Street as Joscelyn looked west. People and cars on the street were dark shapes rimmed in gold. A silhouetted couple stood together across the street from the library. The boy leaned back against a car, dangling a cigarette in his hand. He spoke with a girl who stood in front of him. Every once in a while, he reached his free hand forward and ran it down the girl's arm.

Joscelyn walked toward the library and as the sun sank, the shadows grew longer. The young man seemed to be looking up and down the street. When his outline looked toward Joscelyn, he stood, said something to the girl, and got into the car. He revved his engine and pulled away from the curb, turning right at the first corner.

The shadow girl crossed the street and waved. Joscelyn could now make out her features. The mystery silhouette turned out to be Sadie.

"Hi Josce," she called.

"Well, hello. What are you doing in town? Are you here with your dad?" Joscelyn glanced around for him.

"No. I went to Lisa's after school. I thought I'd visit you at the library 'til my dad could come get me."

"Sorry I wasn't here. I went down to the diner for a quick bite of supper. Come on in." Joscelyn turned the key in the lock and opened the door. As Sadie passed her to enter the library, Joscelyn noticed her hair smelled like cigarette smoke. She wrinkled her nose. "Sadie, you're not smoking now, are you? Who was that guy you were with?"

CHAPTER 16

S adie ignored the question and studied with great interest a stack of books on the counter.

"Sadie?" Joscelyn waited for her to look up. "Who was that?"

Sadie turned away. "Just a guy."

"Is he the guy you were with at the picnic? Does he live around here?" Joscelyn kept her voice casual. Sometimes talking to teenagers was like playing chess.

Sadie shrugged a shoulder and sighed. "He just moved here. He's cool."

"It looked like you knew each other pretty well." Joscelyn set her purse on an end table.

Red blotches stained Sadie's cheeks. Her eyes flashed under scrunched brows. "Were you spying on me or something? Jeez."

"No, I was just walking up the street when I saw you talking to some guy. I wondered who he was, that's all."

Sadie rolled her eyes, hefted a huge sigh, and tossed herself into one of the overstuffed chairs. She peered at the screen on her phone.

"Call your dad." Joscelyn tapped the top of Sadie's cell. "I'll be right back, I need to let Teddy in from the patio. Then we can have a cup of tea while we wait."

Joscelyn unlocked the old door that led to the small fenced-in area behind the bookshop. "Come on, Teddy. Sadie's here," she called. Teddy laid in the corner on the dirt and whimpered. He lifted his head and thumped his tail once but didn't get up. "Teddy, come." Joscelyn patted her leg. She watched her dog struggle to pull his feet underneath his body. He strained and fell back. A chilled alarm raced through Joscelyn's brain and she shivered. Teddy tried again and stood but wheezed a high-pitched whine with each slow limp he took.

"Teddy, what's the matter, boy?" She ran out back and dropped to her knees next to her friend. Joscelyn supported him as he collapsed back to the ground.

Sadie followed Joscelyn out the door. "What's wrong?"

Joscelyn stroked the long black, brown, and white fur from head to tail. Teddy laid his head on the dirt. He bared his teeth when she ran her fingers down his side, then whimpered, and licked frantically at her hand. A tight fist gripped Joscelyn's heart and tears blurred her vision.

Joscelyn turned to blinking eyes to Sadie. "He's in a lot of pain. Do you know who the local vet is?"

"Yeah, Doc Taylor. He's friends with my dad."

"Do you have his number?"

179

"No, but my dad will be here soon. I'm sure he has it." Sadie bent over and stroked Teddy's satin ears.

Cade called out when he entered the library.

Joscelyn's voice broke when she answered, "We're out back." She was weak with a sense of helplessness but relief warmed her when Cade stepped through the back door. "Teddy's hurt," The dog's tail slapped once on the ground in greeting. "Sadie said you know the vet?"

Cade rushed down the step as he pulled out his phone and dialed. He knelt next to Joscelyn while he spoke and then slid his phone into his back pocket. "Doc Taylor's on his way."

The vet arrived ten minutes later and gave Teddy a preliminary once-over. "We need to get him inside. Cade, help me lift him, but be careful. He might have a broken rib or two. Any idea what happened?" Dr. Taylor asked, glancing around the patio for clues. Cade slid his hands under the dog's shoulders and the vet stabilized his hips. "Ready, lift." Teddy's yelp wrung Joscelyn's heart.

She and Sadie followed the men inside. "I have no idea what happened. I put him out here about two hours ago. He was perfectly fine then. I went to dinner and came right back. I can't imagine how he could have hurt himself." Joscelyn looked back at the small space trying to make sense out of it. She scanned the cracked cement pad that served as a patio. Then her eyes moved to the rickety gate in the privacy fence that opened to the alley behind the shops. A dark sense of foreboding crept up her spine, kick-starting her pulse.

Sadie spread an afghan in front of the fireplace and the men laid Teddy down. Cade moved to Joscelyn and rested his hand on her shoulder. "It's too dark to see anything now. We'll look again tomorrow."

Doc Taylor set his vet bag next to Teddy. He took out his stethoscope and listened to different spots on the dog's body. "It sounds like he's breathing okay. He can get up and down and walk fairly well even though it's painful for him. At this point, I'm guessing several of his ribs are cracked but hopefully not broken." He put the stethoscope back into the bag and pulled out some rolled cloth bandages. "I'll wrap his torso with these for support and give him something for the pain. If he gets any worse during the night, I want you to call me right away. If not, bring him by the clinic tomorrow and I'll give him a complete exam."

"Thank you, so much, for coming to see him tonight." Joscelyn offered her hand.

The vet shook it. "No problem. He seems like a sweet dog."

Cade knelt next to Teddy. "He'll be fine here for the night." He brushed the dog's nose with his thumb. "I don't think he'll want to try those stairs."

Joscelyn carried his food and water bowls over and set them near Teddy's head. "Thanks for your help, guys."

Cade nodded. "Come on Sadie, it's time we got you home."

Unable to shake the dark shadows lurking in the back of her mind, Joscelyn reached for Sadie's arm as they walked toward the door. "What did you say the name of that boy you were talking to was?"

Sadie's eyes popped wide at the question and her eyes darted to her dad to see if he heard, but Cade was already outside on the way to his old truck. "His name is David, if you must know. I just met him the other day and ran into him again tonight. It's seriously, no big deal."

Cade's back and shoulders tensed as if he heard the cock of a shot-gun behind him. Joscelyn's question fired through his brain again. "What guy?" he turned and asked his daughter as she stepped out of the library.

Before Sadie could answer, Trent shouted to him from down Main Street. He was getting out of his truck in front of the brewery. "Cade!"

Sadie's face brightened at the interruption. "Hi, Uncle Trent." She waved. "Haven't seen you in a while."

Trent set a dove-white cowboy hat on his head and adjusted it before he crossed the street to them. He winked at his niece and turned piercing eyes on Cade. "Never thought of you as a library type, but here you are—after hours." The edge in his voice held a clear challenge. "You here to see Joscelyn?"

Cade wondered at his brother's jealous tone. His muscles braced in response. Joscelyn was too good a person to have to put up with Trent's womanizing. "I've found a new love of reading," he goaded.

"Ever heard of Amazon? Maybe you should check it out—order your books from there." Trent stepped up to Cade.

Without warning, blood rushed behind Cade's eyes. Heat flared in his head and his heart rate surged. "Back off, Trent. I'll get my books wherever

I want." Cade sucked in a breath and tried to slow his pulse. He clenched and unclenched his fists.

"You're the one who needs to back off." Trent pushed Cade's chest with his fingers.

Before either of them knew what happened, Cade reacted. He grabbed Trent's wrist and wrenched his arm behind his back as he spun him up against the side of the truck, smashing Trent's face against the window.

"Don't ever push me again." Cade's voice was low and menacing. "You don't have any claim on Joscelyn." His breath came fast, and he squeezed his eyes against the unwarranted rage bursting behind them.

Trent grunted and struggled to get loose.

"Dad!" Sadie screamed. Joscelyn heard the ruckus and ran out the front door. Cade released his brother, wishing Joscelyn wasn't there to see him losing his shit... again.

Trent faced Cade and pushed his arms away. "And you think *you* do? You don't even know her." Trent cocked his arm and took a swing at his brother's chin.

Cade stepped back, the blow barely grazing his jaw. He grabbed Trent's arm, and using his brother's own momentum, shoved him back into the truck and held him against the bed. "Don't make me hurt you, little brother. This isn't a fight you're gonna win."

"What the *hell* is going on?" Joscelyn rushed over to Sadie and gathered the girl into her arms, her angry eyes darting between Trent and Cade.

"Damn it." Cade said under his breath. "Nothing," he said louder. "Just a family disagreement." He released Trent again and received a shove followed by a fierce icy-blue glare. "We're done here, aren't we Trent?"

Trent shook Cade off. "Yeah, we are. *You* were just leaving." He turned to Joscelyn and smoothed his voice. "I came over to ask you out for a drink." His usually charming grin was brittle.

Cade swung his gaze to the beautiful woman holding Sadie. Joscelyn glared at both he and Trent in turn.

"I can't believe you two are fighting in front of Sadie. You're supposed to be the adults." Joscelyn walked Sadie to the passenger door and helped her into the truck. She leaned in and gave Cade's daughter a hug. "Call me if you need anything. Otherwise, I'll see you soon." Joscelyn smiled at Sadie and closed the door. "Good night, Cade." She pressed her lips together and stared at him over the hood. Her expression was one of sympathy or worse, pity. Heat flared up the back of his neck. She walked to the library door and turned to Trent. "Teddy is hurt and I need to spend the evening with him, but thanks for the offer."

Unexpectedly relieved that Joscelyn wasn't going out with Trent, Cade opened the truck door. "Good night, Joscelyn. I'll call you tomorrow. I was thinking we could go for another ride."

She tilted her head and raised her eyebrows, obviously still concerned. "I think that would be a good idea."

In five long strides, Trent was behind Joscelyn, following her into the library. "I'll hang out with you and Teddy for a while. What happened to him?" He held the door for Joscelyn and just before he stepped inside he looked over his shoulder and gave Cade a satisfied smirk.

Cade gunned his truck engine but closed his eyes and calmed his breathing before he shifted into reverse. Strong feelings threatened to push him over the edge. He wanted a drink. Bad. Cade glanced at Sadie and clenched his jaw, waiting for the roiling emotions to subside.

"Dad, are you okay?" Sadie asked. Her voice sounded small.

"I'm fine."

"Why are you and Uncle Trent mad at each other?"

Cade didn't know how to answer that. He was as surprised as she was. If he were honest, he'd have to admit he thought about Joscelyn in the dark hours of the night, but the heat of his jealousy over Trent shocked him. He had no understanding with Joscelyn. She only spent time with him because she felt sorry for him. But damn, he didn't want Trent seeing her. Trent never stayed with any woman other than Tonya for longer than three months. Joscelyn deserved better than that. Besides, Trent and Tonya were on and off again ever since grade school. Yet, Trent *did* try to punch him in the face over the new librarian.

"We're not mad at each other... exactly," Cade said as he backed his truck out of the parking spot.

A few minutes down the road, Sadie asked, "Do you like Joscelyn?" His daughter's voice was quiet but her eyes held hope.

Cade glanced at her and couldn't prevent the grin that tugged at the corner of his mouth. "I guess, maybe I do." He shifted gears and drove out of town. Trying to sound casual, he asked, "Is she dating your uncle?"

Sadie smiled wide at his question. "I think they've gone to dinner a couple of times, but she never talks about him. I'm pretty sure they're just friends. Josce is friends with Grandma Mary, too."

Cade nodded at her answer. He didn't trust himself with any more words. Shit, he couldn't trust his emotions right now at all. Trent wasn't any good for Joscelyn, but Cade knew, sure as hell, that he was even worse. He had nothing to offer such a bright and caring woman. Which was too bad, because Joscelyn certainly was good for Sadie. Cade wished things could be different, wished that he wasn't broken.

~*~

The next morning, Teddy was sore but able to get around. On her way out to Wolf Run, Joscelyn took him to the vet clinic. Dr. Taylor confirmed that Teddy's ribs weren't broken but were badly bruised. He left the support bandages on and prescribed pain killers and rest. Joscelyn was relieved, but the fact that Teddy got hurt that badly in his own little back yard frightened her. The memory of her animals being attacked in Colorado terrified Joscelyn and she refused to leave Teddy alone. She took him with her out to Cade's ranch, knowing Sadie would be happy to care for him while she and Cade went on their therapeutic ride.

Joscelyn and Cade rode together up a steep trail through the forest and she listened quietly as he told his story. He spoke as thoughts came to him and were often random and somewhat confused.

"I grew up on Stone Ranch. My grandparents raised me and my brothers after our folks were killed in a car wreck. My grandma's plan was to leave the ranch to all three of us, but I was determined to make it on my own. I bought Wolf Run with some money my folks left me and built the house during my summer breaks from college." He stopped, pulled out a canteen, and took a swig of water.

"I'm sorry to hear about your parents. How old were you?" Joscelyn put the pieces together in her mind of a young boy who had to grow up fast. She figured he felt the weight of responsibility for his younger brothers.

"We were little. I was six, Trent was four, and Jack was only a baby."

"Where's Jack now?"

"He left home when I was in college. Jack and Trent got into a big argument over running Stone Ranch. Now we hardly ever hear from him." Joscelyn heard sorrow lurking in his tone.

She nodded. "Where'd you go to college?"

Cade glanced at her and pulled the bill of his camouflage USMC cap down. "Missoula State. My degree's in Agricultural Business, but I always wanted to be a Marine." He nudged Sherman, and they moved on up the trail.

"Is that where you met your wife?"

Cade looked back at her with hard charcoal eyes. "It's where I met my *ex-wife*. We dated for a couple of months and she got pregnant. Sadie was born in 2004." The smile that passed over his lips when he spoke of Sadie triggered a warm broadening sensation inside Joscelyn.

"Sadie's a terrific kid." Joscelyn reached down and patted Onyx's shoulder.

"Yep. I wish I was a better dad. She doesn't deserve this shit."

"That's what we're working on." Her heart swelled.

Cade's turbulent eyes appraised her before he continued. "Anyway, after graduation I went to The Basic School and became a 2nd Lieutenant in the United States Marine Corps. Oorah!"

Joscelyn smiled at his pride. She remembered her dad shouting the same guttural cheer.

"What was your job—your MOS?"

"0301—Basic Infantry Officer. Louanne and Sadie followed me around from The Basic School in Quantico, to my duty station at Camp Lejeune. When I deployed the first time, Louanne brought Sadie home to Montana. It was during my second deployment that Louanne took off, leaving Sadie with my grandmother. She sent me divorce papers while I was still in Helmand—in Afghanistan." His tone turned bitter.

"That must have been horrible."

"It sure as hell wasn't the worst thing that happened there, but it totally sucked." Cade grew quiet as he guided Sherman through a rock-filled stream. "It wasn't like Louanne and I had a great marriage or anything, but I couldn't do anything to help Sadie from overseas. I wasn't able to talk to her very often, and I worried that something might happen to me. She'd be alone. I still can't believe that bitch up and left our daughter like that. She couldn't even wait till I got home." Cade bunched his hands into fists. Sherman pranced sideways and tossed his head.

"Cade, try not to resist the strength of the emotions you're feeling. Just breathe through them. Focus on your breath. They'll subside in a few minutes." Joscelyn stopped her horse and watched Cade struggle. He swallowed several times and slowed his breaths. "Try to relax your jaw." She yearned to help him and caught herself breathing slowly, in and out... in and out, in sympathy.

Cade regulated his breathing and ran his hand down Sherman's mane. "Steady, Sherman. Steady." The phrase became a mantra. Eventually, the tension dissipated.

"Well done, Cade. Strong emotions can trigger you, even if the emotion itself is a positive one, like the love you have for Sadie."

Without meeting her eye, Cade pointed his chin up the trail. "I'm good, let's keep riding."

Joscelyn knew he wasn't good, but he was doing better. They rode in silence for about a mile. Joscelyn felt Cade was close to a break through, so she pressed further. "You were in Helmand?"

"Yeah."

"Will you tell me about it?"

Cade was quiet a long time. "Teddy seemed much better today. Did you ever figure out how he got hurt?"

Joscelyn rocked back and stopped Onyx. "Cade..."

He glanced back at her. "I don't talk about it, Josce."

Joscelyn swallowed the nerves that jiggled up from her belly. "Do you remember what I told you about memory, and about what happens when someone suffers from trauma?"

He didn't answer.

"It might help you get control over your intrusive memories if you can talk about them. Kind of like sacking out or desensitizing your horse. Same theory—the more you can verbalize your memories, the less power they'll have over you."

Still, the silence hovered.

Finally, Cade released a great sigh and spoke, his voice sounded detached. "It was brutal there. Hundreds of Marines were killed." Joscelyn rode next to Cade. They came to the edge of the trees and upon a meadow before he went on, his eyes seemed to be looking far away at something she couldn't see. "My unit was on a mission outside the wire when several IEDs went off simultaneously." Joscelyn noticed the cords in Cade's neck strain. His biceps bulged and his knuckles whitened in their grip on Sherman's reins. "It was chaos. We got separated. My unit. There was gunfire everywhere." Cade's eyes glazed but Sherman's grew wide and rolled backward.

"Cade," Joscelyn said loud and firm. "Keep breathing. We need to dismount now, before you tell me the rest."

"I can't see. I don't know where it's coming from!" In a flash, Cade was mentally and emotionally back in Afghanistan. Joscelyn realized he was no longer aware of her. He couldn't hear her. One of his arms flew up as if he was blocking his head from something. "I—God—I can't tell.

My men. They're falling. Christ! J.T., you're hit! J.T.!" Cade curled over the saddle horn, his arms reached forward to a friend only he could see. His legs gripped tight on the sides of his horse.

Joscelyn's heart pummeled her sternum as she reached for his reins but the leather whipped through her fingers, burning her skin. Sherman reacted to Cade's extreme stress and bolted like a rifle-shot across the meadow.

"Cade!"

CHAPTER 17

Blood fled from Joscelyn's extremities and she took chase across the meadow at a full gallop. Afraid she'd pushed Cade too far, she prayed he and his horse wouldn't get hurt. Cade pulled up at the far edge of the open space. Sherman reared up, his eyes wild. Cade fell backward to the hard ground and curled up into a ball, covering his head with his arms.

"Cade!" Joscelyn leapt from her saddle and ran to him, her pulse cartwheeling. "It's okay." She threw her arms around his hunched form. "You're home now. You're at Wolf Run."

He rocked back and forth before he spoke. "I'm home," his voice broke into his knees. "*I'm* home, but my men aren't! They're dead because *I* failed them." He lifted tumultuous eyes that bore into hers. Tears smeared across his face. He grabbed Joscelyn's shoulders, his fingers digging into her skin. She fought against a rising panic. "Why? Why did *I* have to survive? So many men died. Better men than me." He scrunched his eyes closed and covered his face with his hands. Cade's body shook with silent sobs.

Joscelyn rubbed his shoulders and drew him tight into her arms. She bit down hard on her own swirling emotions and her sense of being in over her head, out in the wilderness. She knew she needed to stabilize the situation as quickly as possible but didn't want to diminish what Cade was going through.

"I'm here Cade." Joscelyn steadied her breath. "I can't imagine what you lived through and what you're feeling, but I can see it was horrible." She ran her hand the length of his shoulder blade, up and down, in a soothing rhythm. "I want to help."

They sat there together, crouched at the edge of the meadow for a half hour or more. The sun began its descent. At last, Cade's muscles eased, and he sat up.

"I can't believe I lost my shit, in front of you. Again." Cade let a gust of air out of his lungs. "I'm such an ass."

"In no way are you an ass. After what you've been through, I'm amazed you're doing as well as you are. You didn't fall apart, Cade. You remembered, and you felt, and it was difficult."

Cade raised his eyes to the western sky. "We should head back. We gotta get home before dark." He avoided Joscelyn's eyes as he gathered Onyx and Sherman and handed her the reins. Joscelyn swallowed against the swelling ache in her throat as they mounted their horses.

Again, they didn't speak at all on the ride back, each grappling with their own thoughts, and

Joscelyn giving Cade space to work through his memories. She watched his broad back and his natural balance as he rode in front of her on the path. Back at the ranch-yard, they dismounted at the hitching post, and went about the business of putting their tack away and brushing down their horses. They were comfortable in their silence. Joscelyn watched the muscles in Cade's arms flex as he stroked his horse and she found herself appreciating the view when he bent over to check Sherman's hooves. A powerful magnetic pull drew her toward him and Joscelyn wound her fingers in Onyx's mane to keep herself from acquiescing to it. *What is it about these brothers? I need to keep my mind right. I'm supposed to be helping Cade—trying to be a friend, not… well, not anything else. It's unethical.* Joscelyn chewed the inside of her cheek, irritated at herself for having any kind of feelings for Cade. The last thing he needed was more emotional complication. Joscelyn chalked up her attraction to an over-reaction to the heavy emotions of the afternoon. She turned her thoughts to Cade's brother. *I should be thinking about Trent, he gets me every time with that good-old-boy charm,* Joscelyn frowned to herself. *Too bad I can't trust him..*

"Do you need something?" Cade's gruff voice broke into her musing.

Joscelyn jumped and heat rushed into her face. "No, why?"

"You're staring at me." His eyes warmed with a knowing humor.

"I *am* not," she snapped. Joscelyn turned away to hide her embarrassment. She wrung her hands together and looked for something useful for them to do. "I, uh... must have been in a trance," Joscelyn stammered. "I don't even remember what I was thinking about." She bent to rummage in the grooming bucket, as much to stop talking as to hide her flaming cheeks.

Cade shrugged, untied Sherman, and turned toward the barn. "I'll start feeding while you finish up then."

Joscelyn buried her face in her horse's neck and groaned. "I'm such an idiot. I ought to stay away from both those men. As soon as the police find Lenny, we're going home." Onyx nickered at her.

The big black horse followed Joscelyn into his stall. She checked his feed and water, gave him a pat, and closed his stall door. She turned to look for Cade and ran straight into his chest.

"Oops." Joscelyn's heart sprang to her throat and pummeled her tonsils. "I didn't realize you were right there." She looked up at him. He didn't move back, and the air thickened and pressed in on them, like the atmosphere before an electrical storm. After a long, uncomfortable moment, Joscelyn stepped sideways toward the tack room for some space. "I wanted to talk to you about an idea I have that might help you move forward." She hung Onyx's halter and lead-rope on a hook by the door and turned back to Cade. He followed her into the tack room but this time allowed for a little more space when he stood before her.

"What idea?"

"Have you ever considered visiting any of the families of the Marines from your unit?" Joscelyn breathed in Cade's scent, a mixture of leather, horse sweat, and a musk that was simply Cade. Distracted, she missed the typhoon forming in his eyes. "You mentioned a name—J.T.?"

Cade's eyes turned black. The heel of his fist slammed into the wall, inches from Joscelyn's head. Her eyes flew open, every nerve snapping. She opened her mouth to scream and Cade's hand flew up to cover the sound. Joscelyn's pulse slammed inside her skull, throbbing behind her eyes.

"Don't move. Don't make a sound." He spit the words into her ear. Joscelyn thought her chest might explode. She stared wide-eyed at Cade and then realized he wasn't present. She watched, in terrified fascination, as he gradually came back to himself. Breathing hard, he blinked his eyes several times, drew his brows together, and stared at her. He pulled his hand off her mouth and moved it to the side of her face, cupping her cheek. Joscelyn was certain, in that moment, Cade was going to kiss her but he seemed to get ahold of himself and stepped back.

"I'm sorry, Josce. I—" His face grew ruddy.

"You have nothing to apologize for." Joscelyn's throat stuck to itself when she tried to swallow. She breathed in through her nose. "You've already had an emotional day and I pushed a hot button. Are you okay?" Joscelyn reached her hand toward him.

He took another step back and shoved his hands into his jean pockets. "This is my life. This is who I am now." He released a heavy sigh. "The question is, are you okay?" He looked down at the dirt, shame radiating from him.

"You don't need to worry about me. I'm fine." Joscelyn brushed some loose hair out of her face. "Cade, listen, this may be your life right *now*, and that's to be expected—but it isn't who you are. Next time you feel something like this coming on, try to keep yourself in the present moment. Take notice of your body. Ground yourself in your surroundings." She swept her hand toward rakes and buckets lined up on the barn wall. "Try naming four or five things that you see like the stall door, the hay rake, or the wheel-barrow. Then secure yourself in the present time by looking at the date on your phone or looking at your driver's license, to remind yourself where you are and what the date is."

"How will that help?"

"Hopefully, it'll remind you that you are not in Afghanistan anymore, but home—that your flashback is not actually happening but is only a memory. You can work through this and gain control. Cade, you're amazing and you have a family that loves you. You have friends who care about you and want to help."

"I don't deserve that." His voice was so low Joscelyn barely heard him.

"You deserve that, and so much more." She resisted an urge to touch him, to comfort him.

Cade considered her words. "Look, I know I need help, but I can't officially see a therapist because having mental health issues gets stamped into your permanent record."

Joscelyn balled her hands into fists, a lump of icy-heat formed in her gut. "Getting the help you need should *never* create a stigma. Every combat veteran should be debriefed and given time to heal—as a matter of course." She tried to slow her breathing. This was an old anger she carried deep inside. "That kind of crap just pisses me off. It's not like PTSD is an uncommon problem." Joscelyn knew that her dad never sought help for the same reason and because of that, she lost her connection to him way before he was actually killed.

She stepped out of the tack room and faced Cade. "It just makes no sense that we have the best trained and best outfitted armed forces in the world, as prepared as they can possibly be, but when they're discharged, they're given no preparation to re-enter civilian life. It is infuriating." Joscelyn turned and stomped toward the barn door, but halfway there she had an idea and swung around to face Cade.

"What do you think about going to one of the VFW spaghetti dinners with me?"

He drew his brows together and pulled his chin back. "What?—No."

"Why not?"

"I'm not some doddering old man who wants to relive his war-time glory days."

"Oh. So, you think those old guys loved their war days? You don't think they struggle with their memories?"

Cade rewarded her challenge with a blustery glare.

CHAPTER 18

"**B**ob never told you we have a summer art fair?" Kathy Kinney bustled in with a four-by-four-foot oil-painting of a bowl of apples on a lace-covered table.

"Oh for heaven's sake." Joscelyn clenched her jaw and stepped back, out of Kathy's way. "Is this like the quilt contest?"

The woman, who looked to be in her mid-forties, swished her patchwork skirt over the top of her moccasins and tightened the macramé belt around a painter's smock smeared with color. Long brown hair touched with a few strands of gray, hung loose down her back. "I have no idea. I don't quilt." She leaned her painting against one of the overstuffed chairs in the book shop. "Why?"

"Bob surprised me with the fact that the library hosts the annual quilt contest *last* month." Joscelyn raised her hands to her hips and narrowed her eyes. "Why don't you have the art fair at the Opera House? Don't you run the place?"

Kathy pressed her lips together and then spoke in a patronizing tone, "First of all, that would be a conflict of interest, since I am a participant. Second, I cannot take down the show posters or the headshots of the actors to put up paintings that have nothing to do with the play we have running. Besides, the art fair has always been here." She turned toward the door. "I have two more pieces to bring over. I'll be back soon. Too-loo."

Joscelyn shook her head and indulged in a low throaty grumble. *There's no fighting tradition.* She needed to borrow Bob's ladder again, and when she did, she would give him a piece of her mind. The least he could have done was warn her about the art fair.

The bell on the library door tinkled. "Hey." Trent took off his cowboy hat as he entered. The allure of his smile pulled a responding one from Joscelyn.

"Good morning. What are you doing here so early?"

Trent made himself at home, and strode to the back counter to pour himself a cup of coffee. "I had to stop at the feed store, so I took the opportunity to visit Flint River's sexy librarian."

"That's a little over the top. Do you need something?"

"Actually, I really did want to see you, and," he winked, "I didn't want to pay three dollars for a cup of coffee from the Kaffee Klatch."

Joscelyn laughed. "Help yourself... oh—I see you already did."

Trent leaned his hip against the counter and took a sip. "Do you mind?" His eyes roamed over her.

Joscelyn turned away from him. "No. Actually, I'm glad for the company. Have a seat." She wondered at herself. It wasn't long ago she welcomed Trent's flirting, but lately she felt uncomfortable with it.

They moved to the chairs. "Did you ever figure out how Teddy got hurt?" Trent rubbed the dog's head and was rewarded with a wet lick.

"No, but he seems to be getting better." An errant chill popped goose bumps up on her arms and she rubbed them away.

Trent shifted and his brows drew together. "Where'd this painting come from?" Realization dawned on his face. "Oh, yeah. It's that time of year again. The art-fair." He chuckled. "You have the distinct opportunity to *enjoy* the creative expressions of Flint River's finest artists. Want help hanging?"

Local artists dropped off all kinds of art throughout the day, not only paintings. There were drawings, pottery pieces, stained glass, fiber art, and jewelry. Joscelyn worked all afternoon to find just the right spots to display the wares. While Trent hung paintings on the walls around the shop, Joscelyn made cards with the artist's name and the title of their piece.

A little after three, Kathy returned with two other women who also entered paintings in the fair. "We thought we would preview the art display," she said as she sailed into the library.

"We're just about finished hanging everything," Joscelyn said, straightened a painting behind the cash register.

Kathy and her friends stood before the fireplace and looked up. She gasped. "Why did you hang this monstrosity above the mantel?" She glared at Joscelyn. "My paintings are *always* hung there. I left my apples right here for you."

"Oh... I didn't know there were assigned hanging positions. You should have told me." Joscelyn dropped a book onto a stack with a loud clap and willed the flint out of her voice. These surprise displays, where she was expected to do all the work, were getting on her nerves "I hung your apples back here." She gestured to the wall space above the coffee counter. "I think the light here compliments your work, and it seems like a nice place for a food painting."

"The painting isn't of *food*. It's a study of light, shining on the apples, and how realistic they look." Kathy peered at the artist's name-card in the corner of the stunning landscape depicting a mountain meadow. "I've never even heard of this person. I knew I should have asked Tonya to hang the paintings. She has such an artistic flair." Joscelyn forced her eyes down rather than allow them to roll skyward.

Trent stepped down from the ladder. "Your apple painting is awful nice, Kathy."

Kathy spun around, not having seen Trent in the room. Her cheeks flushed. "Trent Stone, I didn't see you there."

"Well, I sure saw you," he flirted and Kathy fluttered her lashes. Her color deepened. "It's mighty gracious of you to give up your prime painting spot to an undiscovered artist this year. Takes a fine person to do such a thing." His smile was lazy under his blue sparkling gaze. Joscelyn's eyes widened, and she opened her mouth in astonishment. She quickly covered it with her hand.

"Oh." Kathy glanced up into his face. "Oh. I… yes, well, it's the least I can do. You know, we *are* trying to promote art here in our little town."

Joscelyn joined Trent in his ploy. Stepping forward, she hooked her arm through Kathy's and turned to appreciate the landscape. "It's especially wonderful of you, because this artist is in high-school. Which is probably why you didn't recognize the name."

"What?" Kathy's face looked stricken. She was indignant but recovered herself. "My goodness, isn't that something," she said in a less-than-convincing tone.

"That young artist is certainly lucky to have you as a mentor." Trent put his arm around Kathy's shoulders. Joscelyn felt the woman sway a little and she coughed to cover a smirk.

"Thank you, Trent. I *do* try to be there for the younger artists."

"It's something I've always admired about you." He said as he turned Kathy toward the door. "You'll have to introduce yourself to the young lady at the reception in a couple of weeks." He opened the door for her to leave.

"Will *you* be coming to the party?" Kathy had the look of a lovesick teen at an Elvis concert.

"I wouldn't miss it. See you there." Trent's voice was low and smooth as he shut the door.

"It is so thick in here, I'm having trouble breathing." Joscelyn faked gagging.

Trent laughed. "I got you out of a sticky mess and I got myself out of re-hanging all the paintings to Kathy's specifications."

"You are shameless."

Trent held his hands out. "I say, 'use it if you've got it.'" One corner of his mouth curled up as he strode toward Joscelyn. He reached for her cheek and brushed it with his thumb before he pushed his hand into her hair and leaned toward her. "You weren't jealous, were you?"

Joscelyn clenched her jaw and pulled away from him. "Don't flatter yourself." She moved behind the counter. His smooth self-assurance scraped at her nerves. He was obviously used to women swooning into his arms.

Undeterred, Trent leaned his forearms on the counter across from her. "Can I take you to dinner when you close up here? Or, if you want, we could drive up to Missoula and see a movie?"

Joscelyn kept her eyes on the spine of the book she was checking back into the library. "Thanks for the offer, but I already have plans."

"You do?" He straightened. "With who?"

She shrugged and went to slide the book onto its shelf. "I'm meeting Sadie and Cade at the diner."

"What the hell, Joscelyn? When did you and Cade become so friendly?" He crossed his arms in front of his chest.

"You know I worked with Sadie and the girls when they got into trouble, and that I board my horses out at Wolf Run now.

"Yeah, so?"

"Well, I'm leading their new saddle club and we meet out there on Sunday afternoons. Plus, Cade was at the Founder's Day Picnic, remember?"

"Still trying to figure out how any of that has to do with you having dinner with him." Trent set his jaw and his eyes hardened.

Joscelyn sighed, releasing some of her frustration. "Let's sit down, you want some tea?" She walked down the hall from the library to the shop and switched on her electric kettle.

Trent followed her but didn't sit. He braced his hands on his hips. "So?"

Joscelyn sighed. "I've been spending a lot of time with Cade."

"So now you two are best friends?"

Joscelyn scrunched her brows together. "What's the matter with you?"

"Nothing." His tight jaw gave away the truth. "Finish your story."

"The times I was out at Wolf Run, I noticed that Sadie and Cade had some trouble... communicating." Joscelyn looked to see if there was any acknowledgement of what she was talking about in Trent's eyes, but they remained cold blue ice. Her voice rose as she tried to explain. "Listen, Cade is suffering from PTSD. He's having a really hard time assimilating back into civilian life. He needs a little help."

"And, of course, *you're* the one who can save him, is that it?" Trent spun around and strode to the back sink. He propped his hands against the counter and stared out the window. "I've told you, Cade is fine. He just needs a little more time."

Joscelyn ground her teeth. She went to Trent, placing a hand on his shoulder. "He's not fine, but he *will* get better. He refuses to go to a therapist, so I'm trying to help him out—*as a friend*." She took a deep breath and gentled her voice. "Trent, he needs your support, not your denial." Joscelyn watched the muscles in Trent's jaw ripple.

He turned and took her by the shoulders. "I'm not in denial. He just needs some more time. He's had a rough go, I know that." His grip tightened. "I also know he can be dangerous. You need to stay away from him."

Joscelyn assessed the intensity in Trent's eyes for a few seconds before she responded. "What about Sadie? Do we leave her to deal with his outbursts until he has had enough *time*? I'm not willing to do that. I'm also not willing to leave Cade to suffer on his own after all he sacrificed for our country."

Trent dropped his hands from her shoulders and ran his long fingers across his eyes. He leaned back against the sink. "Do you think I haven't tried to help him? He won't talk to me about what's going on in his mind." He pushed himself up and paced to the front window and back. "I took care of Cade's ranch while he was gone, after his psycho ex-wife abandoned them. My grandma took Sadie in. I've rounded up his herd and sent them to market. I even did that this year because Cade couldn't be bothered. Damn it! I *am* helping. What else do you expect me to do?"

"I didn't mean to imply you haven't done anything. What I mean is, we all have to accept that he's having a hard time learning to live in the regular world again. PTSD is a real thing and it can cause a change in normal brain function. Constant vigilance and adrenaline flooding into his blood stream has changed the chemistry in his brain. He needs help to heal from his horrific memories." Joscelyn reached out and squeezed Trent's forearm, wanting him to understand. "He'll eventually be able to function normally in society, but you should know up front, he'll never be the Cade who left here all those years ago. Life as a combat Marine has changed him."

Defiant tears flashed in Trent's eyes and he turned away. "We used to be so close," he choked on his words. "Now he won't even talk to me."

Joscelyn moved up behind him and rested her palm between his shoulder blades. "I know. Right now, he needs all of us to accept that he has trouble dealing with life. We don't want him to get stuck at this stage." She tugged on Trent's arm to get him to go to the chair and sit down. Once seated, they leaned forward, facing each other. "Cade was drinking a lot to escape his nightmares, but he's realized that only makes his outbursts worse, so he's trying to quit. He wants help, but he doesn't think he deserves it. He still hasn't told me much about what happened to him in Afghanistan, but he's definitely suffering from survivor's guilt."

"So, what's going on between you two then? Are you his therapist?" He swallowed. "Or do you have feelings for him?"

Joscelyn wasn't sure what her feelings for Cade were. She was attracted to him, but any healthy woman would be—to both brothers, for that matter. "I'm simply trying to be his friend. I have some experience with PTSD, but I'm too close to the situation and to Sadie, Mary, and you, to act as his therapist." Joscelyn briefly closed her eyes against painful memories of her Dad struggling with the same disorder. "I'm trying to help Cade understand what he's going through is a natural brain defense mechanism. We've gone riding together and I think spending time with his horse is helping. I want to help him any way I can, but he will need to find a therapist who specializes in PTSD."

Trent thought about all of that for a while before he asked, "So, there's nothing going on between you two?"

Joscelyn avoided his eyes. "Not really, no."

"Not *really*?"

"No."

CHAPTER 19

Cade stood as Joscelyn approached the table. Sadie waved at her. Joscelyn wiggled her fingers and smiled. "Sorry I'm late."

"You're not late, we're early. Dad had an errand at the hardware store," said Sadie.

Cade pulled out her chair and Joscelyn smelled a subtle cologne—fresh with a hint of spice. She breathed it in. "Thanks," she said and met his eyes. Joscelyn sat when he pushed in her chair and her skin tingled as his hand brushed the back of her shoulder. *This is ridiculous. The man simply pulled out my chair. He has manners. So, what? Get a grip.* "The hardware store, huh? Do you have a project you're working on?"

He sat back in his chair facing the door and grinned. "Well, I do live on a ranch. There's always a project."

"True." Her obvious question embarrassed her but she was glad Cade was starting to be productive. That was a good sign.

Cade continued, "I picked up posts and wire for mending fences—a constant chore. I also needed some lumber to fix up a section of the barn that's falling apart. I'm thinking of expanding the tack room." The pride shining in his eyes stirred something deep inside Joscelyn.

Sadie sat forward in her chair. "He's going to make me my own space for all my saddle club stuff." She sounded like a little girl in her excitement.

"That's great, sweetie." Joscelyn's gaze went from the girl to her dad. "It's wonderful, how you're supporting Sadie in her riding."

"She's good at it." He winked at his daughter.

"Cuz I learned from you." Sadie gushed.

Joscelyn was happy to see this improvement, but knew it wasn't an end to the struggle. Her heart ached for Sadie. She knew from her own experience the ups and downs of Cade's disorder would be difficult for his daughter to navigate without giving up hope.

"What are you guys having?" Joscelyn picked up her menu.

The waitress took their order and brought drinks. Joscelyn told them about the art-fair. They talked about school, horses, and the ranch.

"Have you decided which events you will compete in at the gymkhana?" Joscelyn asked Sadie.

Sadie's eyes lit up as she drew soda through her straw. "Pole-bending for sure, and barrel-racing too. I'm too scared to enter the Western Trail Class though. I don't want some judge staring at me while I ride. What if I screw up?"

Joscelyn laughed. "What if? Would that be the end of the world?"

Sadie glared at her and then dropped her eyes to her plate.

"I'm sorry, Sadie. I shouldn't tease, but I think you should do it. Push yourself—you never know."

Cade nudged Sadie's arm. "You're a good rider. I'm sure you're competitive."

"You really think so?" Sadie beamed at her father's praise.

He nodded and winked at her. "I sure do."

Sadie turned back to Joscelyn and lifted her shoulders. "Then I guess I'll try it." She took another long pull on her straw. "Dakota's competing in all the events but I think Tracy's only barrel-racing."

"What about Lisa? Is she braving any of the events?" Joscelyn set her glass down and wiped the condensation on her napkin.

"She's scared because she's never been to a gymkhana before. I told her some kids enter just to try it and not compete. I said she should try the key-hole race and barrel racing. She hasn't decided."

Joscelyn touched Sadie's forearm. "It's nice of you to encourage her. We'll talk about it more at our next meeting and we can practice all the events you girls want to go for."

After dinner, Cade and Sadie shared a slice of huckleberry pie and Joscelyn sipped chamomile tea.

She looked Cade in the eye. "Things seem to be going well."

"Yeah, I think so." He nodded.

"It's good to be here with you two, having such a fun time together," Joscelyn said. Sadie nodded and took another bite of pie. Cade's eyes were calm like an overcast day as he rested them on Joscelyn. She asked, "Have you thought any more about joining a therapy group?"

In an instant, his eyes changed from high overcast-gray to thunderstorm-slate. "I can handle it on my own."

Joscelyn didn't read the warning in his eyes and pressed on. "There are so many combat vets who face the same struggles you do. It might help you to hear about their experiences and learn from their successes."

Sadie looked from her dad to Joscelyn and she set down her fork.

Other diners turned to stare when Cade shouted, "I don't need a fucking support group!" He threw his napkin on his plate and his fork clattered to the floor.

Joscelyn felt the blood drain from her face, helpless to shield Sadie who stood, her eyes the size of golf balls and her cheeks a deep red. The girl glanced around the diner at the staring faces and pulled the hood of her sweatshirt up over her head. She ran out the door. Cade closed his eyes, swallowed hard, and dropped his head into his hands. Joscelyn was torn between chasing after Sadie and staying to help Cade pick up his pieces.

"I shouldn't have brought that up tonight. We were having such a nice time." She rested her hand on Cade's arm and felt his muscles flex under his shirt sleeve.

Cade stared at the table. "It isn't your fault. It isn't anybody's fault but mine." He looked at

Joscelyn, with tortured eyes. "Can you go after Sadie while I pay the bill?"

"Of course, but—"

"Just go. We can talk about it in the truck." He turned away from her.

Joscelyn went outside and looked left, up the street but didn't see Sadie. She looked right, down the other way toward the park. Sadie was there sitting on a swing, but she was not alone. The boy from the other night sat in the swing next to her. At least Joscelyn thought it was him. It was hard to see them in the evening twilight. Joscelyn stepped off in their direction and walked about a block when she saw the boy reach over, pull Sadie's swing toward his, and kiss her.

That same odd sense of foreboding washed over Joscelyn and her heart raced. "Sadie!" she called out. But Sadie was too far away to hear her. Joscelyn picked up a jog. The boy stood and pulled Sadie with him and the two walked together into the pines edging the side of the park. "Sadie!" Joscelyn screamed and broke into a run.

Cade's truck pulled up beside her. "What's wrong? Where's Sadie?" He asked through the open window.

"She was with that boy she met the other night. I called to her, but she couldn't hear me. They walked together up through those trees."

"Get in."

Joscelyn opened the door and climbed onto the bench seat of Cade's old Ford. He drove to the park and onto the road that circled it.

"Where did you last see them?" he asked.

"About thirty feet, up there." Joscelyn pointed to a break in the pines. "They walked from the swings up through those trees." She couldn't slow her heart rate. Her breath came fast.

"There's a path." Cade stopped the truck and reached across Joscelyn to the glove compartment for a flashlight. "Let's go."

Joscelyn noticed the butt end of a handgun under the flashlight. She was certain Cade knew how to use the weapon but wasn't sure he should always have it with him at this stage in his recovery. She shook the thought from her mind and leapt from the truck to follow Cade.

The path led up an incline, about fifty feet, before it ended at a gravel parking lot. The parking lot was empty.

"Who did you say was she with?" Cade's voice was strained.

"I'm not sure. I think she's with the boy she met the other night, when you came to pick her up at the library." Joscelyn's voice shook.

"Josce, what's wrong? What aren't you telling me?" Cade stopped and faced Joscelyn in the dusk. Even in the dark, Joscelyn thought he could see right into her soul. "Why are you shaking?"

"I'm not sure. I have a bad feeling about that boy. He reminds me of someone that's all." Joscelyn closed her eyes.

Cade flashed the light around the gravel looking for tracks. He stared down the road for several seconds before he commanded, "Come on." He ran back to his truck and Joscelyn pushed hard to keep up. "Do you know what kind of car he has?"

Joscelyn pushed down sudden nausea. "No. I think it's small, like a Toyota or something." She crossed her arms and gripped her biceps as Cade spun the truck around and sped out of the park. He turned right up Main Street and slowed down, taking time to look into each shop that was still open.

"There she is!" A cold shower of relief flushed through Joscelyn. She pointed ahead to the left side of the street. "Coming out of the drug store."

Cade swerved over to the left side of the road, taking up several of the angled parking spots by pulling up parallel to the curb. He rolled down his window. "Sadie, get in the truck." She gave him a petulant glare. "Now."

Joscelyn leaned over to talk to the girl out of Cade's window. "Sadie, thank God you're all right. We've been looking for you. Please get in the truck."

Sadie took her time crossing over in front of the hood, sucking on a straw in a cup and holding a lily. She climbed in on Joscelyn's side after Joscelyn opened the door and slid over to the middle.

"I don't know what the big deal is," Sadie said as she slammed the door. "It's not like Flint River is a giant metropolis or something."

"I thought I saw you in the park." Joscelyn put her hand on Sadie's knee. "Are you all right?

Sadie looked at Joscelyn sideways. "Yes. Why wouldn't I be? Gawd, you'd think I robbed a bank or something."

"Were you with that boy from the other night?" Joscelyn asked.

Sadie rolled her eyes and stared out the window. "What if I was? At least he doesn't yell at me in public." She turned to glare at her father.

Ignoring the jab, Cade rested his gaze on his daughter for several seconds. "You were in the park with him, and then what? He brought you to the drug store?"

Sadie sighed long and loud, revving up the teenage drama. "I can't *believe* you two. I left the diner and went to the park to think. David was there and so I said hello. He brought me here for a soda and he bought me a flower to cheer me up." She held up the saccharine bloom and the to-go cup as evidence. Her dark eyes rolled again as she shook her head.

"David?" Joscelyn stared at Sadie. "His name is David? David what?"

"Stop interrogating me!" Sadie turned her body to face the door, putting an end to the questioning.

Cade pulled the truck away from the curb and crossed the street, parking one block down, in front of the library. "I'll drop you here and take Sadie home." He got out of the truck and helped Joscelyn down from the driver's side. He closed the door and walked her to the library.

Joscelyn turned to thank him for dinner and to say good night when she saw Trent come out of the brewery across the street. He was walking with Tonya. Joscelyn watched as he draped his arm around the woman's shoulders. She stopped and said something to him, then Trent caressed her cheek.

"What's wrong?" Cade looked concerned and Joscelyn realized her expression must reflect her sense of confusion and betrayal.

She tried shaking her head to forget it, but Cade followed the direction of her eyes. He made a scoffing noise. "I'm sorry, Josce. I don't know what's going on between you and Trent, if anything, but those two have been on and off again since they were kids. Someday, Trent will give in and marry her. But for now, seems he'd rather torture her and every other woman he sets his sights on."

Joscelyn thought about Cade's comment while she watched Trent and Tonya walk arm and arm up the street to Tonya's place. Seconds later a light blinked on in Tonya's apartment above her salon. A weak laugh coughed up Joscelyn's throat. "I shouldn't be surprised." Her eyes met Cade's, "Thanks for dinner."

"Sorry it was such a crazy night."

"Don't worry about it and the stuff with Sadie—pretty normal for a teenager, I think." Joscelyn winked and turned to unlock the door.

Cade touched her elbow. "Would it be okay if I call you later? After Sadie's in bed?" Joscelyn smiled at him over her shoulder.

I'd like that." She realized in that moment she would like it indeed.

CHAPTER 20

Joscelyn sat on a picnic table outside the round pen at Cade's place and watched him work, first with Sherman and then with Fargo. She kept silent for the most part, occasionally stating an observation or asking a reflective question. "You look peaceful. How're you feeling?"

"Peaceful is exactly how I feel. How'd I forget that working with horses gives so much satisfaction?"

Joscelyn stood and leaned on the rail. She admired his skill and intuition with the gentle giants. "Wasn't it Winston Churchill who said, 'There's something about the outside of a horse that's good for the inside of a man'?"

"I thought it was Ronald Reagan." Cade grinned. "Either way, they were both good horsemen." Joscelyn nodded.

"Cade, have you changed your mind at all about visiting the family of your friend who died in Helmand?" As soon as she asked the question she could see his emotions transmit themselves to Fargo. Her horse's ears twitched and his head shot up. He moved away from Cade and turned to face him, his eyes alert. Joscelyn steeled herself to deal with Cade's emotions.

"I'm *not* doing that."

"Why not?"

"I've told you, there's no way I could ever face his parents—tell them how I failed their son and how because of me, he's dead." Cade's hands flew to his head. He pressed the heels of his hands into his temples. His knees buckled, and he landed on the dirt. Joscelyn grabbed the halter and lead-rope hanging on the gate and ran into the round-pen. She caught Fargo and tied him outside the pen, then went back to Cade.

She put her arm over his shoulders. "I'm here. It's okay. Breathe and concentrate on relaxing your muscles. Go loose as possible and let your thoughts and emotions come." Joscelyn rubbed his back. "Lean into the flash of emotion. It'll last five or ten minutes, but it *will* pass."

Cade shook his head from side to side, but he drew a big breath and let it out. Joscelyn watched him try to relax his hands. She continued, "Breathe. Imagine yourself floating on a cloud or on a lake. Release any struggle. Don't strive for anything. Just accept your feelings, without judging them." Joscelyn rubbed his broad back in a steady rhythm. After several minutes she asked, "Can you tell me what you're seeing or give a name to your feelings?"

A shuddering emotional surge coursed through Cade like a lightning bolt. He pushed away from her, inadvertently knocking her backward onto the sand. Joscelyn landed on her back and elbows. She waited, her heart hammered knowing this could turn into an emotional explosion. After about five minutes, Cade's muscles relaxed, and he turned tormented eyes to Joscelyn.

She moved to her knees and brushed sand from her jeans. "Do you want to talk about it?"

"No. I don't even want to *think* about it, but I can't seem to stop it. I feel like I'm going crazy."

"You're not crazy. What's happening inside you is a physiological issue. It's going to take time to heal your sensitized nervous system. It's a chemical readjustment."

He sat with his forearms draped over his knees. "I feel so angry all the time. I mean I feel sad and ashamed, but anger always seems to take over." His shoulders sagged.

Joscelyn scooted closer and placed a hand on his arm. "Anger's not as painful as sadness, shame, or fear. It's often a secondary emotion and you might be letting it take over because it feels more powerful. Anger is often focused away from ourselves." She let her hand drop to her lap. "What do you think you might be getting out of your anger?"

"What do you mean?"

Joscelyn peered up at him, squinting in the sun. "What are the effects of your anger?"

Cade shrugged. "It scares people, I guess."

"Pushes people away?"

He gave her a level look.

"What positive effects might there be if you were less angry?"

"I'd probably have a better relationship with Sadie." He looked down. "With other people, too. Maybe my wife wouldn't have left us."

"It seems like that's a separate issue. She left before you came home."

"I guess." Cade pulled a stray clump of grass growing up in the sand.

"Do you know what triggered your anger? Did you have any physical sensations?"

Cade reflected for a while. "When I pictured meeting J.T.'s mom and dad, my heart started pounding." Angry tears flashed in his eyes. "I can't face their pain."

Joscelyn's heart wrenched, but she maintained her even tone. "Remember, anger is a secondary emotion. Underneath it is the primary emotion. It might be pain or the fear of being hurt. Anger can help you avoid those painful feelings but won't make them go away, it only masks them. Can you identify the primary emotion and put it into words?"

Cade braced his elbows on his knees and rested his face in his hands. "It hurts and I hate myself. I can't stand this anymore." His words filtered through his fingers.

Cade worked to even out his breathing and as it slowed, his muscles released.

In a soft voice, Joscelyn asked. "You said you feel responsible for not saving J.T.?"

He closed his eyes. "Yeah."

"One hundred percent responsible?" Joscelyn took a handful of sand and let it filter through her fingers back to the ground.

Cade's eyes narrowed to slits as he watched her hands. "Well, ninety-five percent, at least."

Joscelyn smoothed the pile of sand and repeated the action. "Ninety-five percent your responsibility? Not more? Not less?"

His eyes darkened to slate. "Yeah. The other five percent would go to the rag-heads who triggered the IEDs and fired on us." Cade shifted his position to face the drive and his eyes made a rapid sweep of the ranch.

"Was it your responsibility to determine your unit's objective?" Joscelyn kept a close eye on his face and hands, watching for increasing tension. Her own pulse ramped up.

"No, we were under orders from the CO."

"What percentage of responsibility would you assign your commanding officer for his decision?"

Cade's gaze returned to Joscelyn's face and he shrugged. "I suppose five percent."

Joscelyn nodded. "So, he's five percent responsible for your unit's location and the enemy is five percent responsible for the gunfire and exploding and IEDs that killed your friend and others in your unit, and you're ninety-five percent responsible?"

The corner of Cade's mouth pulled back, and he looked at Joscelyn out of the corner of his eye. "Well, when you put it that way, I guess the rag-heads are more like twenty percent responsible."

"Do you think that's a fair percentage?"

Cade shrugged.

Joscelyn continued. "Do you take responsibility for J.T. becoming a Marine? Or his assignment to your unit?" Cade shook his head.

"What about his location at the time of the attack?" She paused, not expecting him to answer but hoping her point would sink in. "Were there any other survivors?"

He swallowed. "Yeah, three."

"What percentage of the blame would you give to them?"

His eyes flashed and he glared at her. "None. It wasn't *their* fault."

Joscelyn nodded. She walked the tight-rope of Cade's emotions and decided to give him a few minutes break. Pushing herself up, she stood before Cade and offered him a hand. "Let's sit in the shade." He took her hand, pulled himself up, and followed her, stopping to pull out a couple of water bottles from the cooler next to the picnic table.

Joscelyn sat on the bench at the table. "Let's talk about the enemy. Are they good at what they do?" She opened the plastic lid and chugged the icy drink.

Cade followed suit and then sat on top of the table with his boots resting on the bench. He arched his brow. "If you mean hiding like snakes in the rocks and striking out with no concern about who they hit and kill, including women and children, then yes, they're excellent at what they do." His neck muscles flexed causing his tendons to stand out.

Joscelyn grimaced and shook her head. "How about your men? Were they performing their duties to the best of their abilities that day? Could their skill have prevented the explosions?" She twisted the lid back on her bottle.

Cade shook his head.

"When you really look at it, don't you think the enemy deserves more than twenty percent?"

Cade slammed down the rest of his water and crushed the bottle with his hands. "I guess. Maybe thirty or forty percent."

"Wait, is that too much? For the last couple of years, you've only ascribed maybe five percent to them." Joscelyn moved to sit next to Cade on the table. "By the way, you've assigned far more than a total of one-hundred percent responsibility for the Marines who were killed. Let's recalculate. Is your responsibility still ninety-five percent? If so, then all the others share the remaining five percent."

Cade kept silent but gave his head a slight shake.

"What about senior military staff? The ones who strategize and plan your maneuvers? Do they deserve any responsibility?

"They're just doing their job."

"What about the politicians who send the military to war? How about them?"

His frustration grew more obvious and Cade slid off the table and paced its length, loosening up the tightness in his leg. "No one forced me to sign up."

"True." Joscelyn undid the lid of her bottle and finished her water. She gathered both bottles and put them back inside the cooler. "So, let's look at you again. How much responsibility did you have for being there that day and for what you did or did not do? Because it's true, you were there, and you reacted to your situation." She stepped in front of Cade's path causing him to stop. Her heart knocked against her ribs. She hoped she wasn't pushing him beyond his limits. "Look, I'm not trying to explain away any of the responsibility you truly believe you deserve for what happened—once you've *fully* reflected upon all the others who share in that responsibility as well. Considering all the factors and people involved in J.T.'s death, what percentage of the responsibility do you realistically believe is yours?"

Cade placed his hands on his hips and let out a deep sigh. "I guess, doing the math, it's more like thirty to thirty-five percent."

Joscelyn looked up into his face. "Do you think maybe you've punished yourself and suffered over your assumed ninety-five percent responsibility long enough?"

"Not a day goes by that I don't re-live that attack."

She reached out and clasped his shoulder. "But how much punishment do you think you deserve?"

Cade pulled away. "Well... I'm alive. J.T. is dead."

"What could you have done differently that would absolve you?"

He gritted his teeth. A twitch pulsed at the corner of one eye and he pressed them both closed. "I could have been in front of the bullet that he took in his chest!" He spun around setting his back to Joscelyn.

"Cade, if you could go back and change that, what would the outcome be?"

He was quiet for so long, Joscelyn almost gave up, when he said, "We'd probably both be dead."

"So, there was really no way you could have saved him?" Joscelyn stepped closer and placed her hand on his back. She could feel the steel-like tautness in his frame. "Since that's the case, what percentage of guilt would his parents assign you, do you think?"

He didn't respond, but she felt his muscles give.

"Do you think you've punished yourself enough?" She moved her thumb back and forth over the fabric of his shirt.

"Maybe."

"What else do you think needs to happen before you can forgive yourself?"

Cade turned his face to her. His eyes held the pain of the ages. "I don't know if I ever can."

"Sometimes it helps to say you're sorry."

His brow creased, and he dropped his chin to his chest. "How could I ever do that? J.T. is dead."

Joscelyn took a deep breath, her stomach taut. "You could visit his parents and tell them how much J.T. meant to you. You could tell them what you wish you could have done and that you're sorry."

Cade moved past Joscelyn and walked into the barn. Giving him time to be with his thoughts, she gathered the grooming tools into the bucket and scooping up a few random piles of manure. Eventually, Cade came back outside.

"Would you go with me?"

"To Texas?" Joscelyn propped the manure fork against the barn wall, but it slipped and fell in a clatter.

Cade gave a half smile. "Yeah, I think I should go... but I don't think I can do it alone."

CHAPTER 21

Sadie walked up the drive after being dropped off by the school bus. "Let me grab something to eat and I'll be right out," she hollered to Joscelyn and Cade on her way to the house.

Joscelyn waved. "I'll get the arena set up." She untied Fargo and led him to the barn, switching him out for Onyx.

"Same game?" asked Cade.

"Yep, would you mind setting up the jump?"

When Cade finished, Joscelyn asked, "Any new ideas for success?"

Cade shrugged and took a brush from the grooming bucket. He applied long strokes to Onyx's back and sides.

When the exercise began, Cade and Sadie fell into their usual pattern. Cade told Sadie what to do and didn't listen to her suggestions. Joscelyn could see the disappointment and frustration in Sadie's face.

"You guys seem to be falling into the same patterns you tried last time, even though they weren't successful. You know the definition of insanity, right?" Joscelyn teased, trying to keep it light to diffuse the tension. "Why don't you two take a couple of minutes and come up with a new strategy."

Cade grumbled, "This is pointless."

Sadie stood next to her dad. "Remember, Josce said we could use whatever is in the arena."

"Sadie, if you would do what I tell you to do, we could accomplish our objective and move on."

"But…"

"Don't answer back. Just do what you're told."

Sadie clenched her teeth and balled her fists. She turned and stomped several paces toward the gate before she spun back to face Cade. "I am not one of your Marines, you know," she screamed at him. "You can't just order me around and expect me to jump to attention and march."

"Don't you dare storm off. I deserve more respect than that, and so does Joscelyn." Cade's voice boomed. Sadie ran into the barn. Cade's breath came fast and heavy. Joscelyn was concerned he might lose the battle to intrusive thoughts, so she gently clasped his forearm.

"Cade, keep breathing. Look at me."

He glowered at her. "I'm not losing it, I'm just pissed." He shook her hand off his arm. "She's right, when I give an order to one of my Marines, it's followed without question. I guess I expect the same respect from my own daughter."

"I agree that you deserve her respect, but she's right too. She isn't a Marine. You're her father, not her commanding officer. She might have some good ideas. If her ideas don't work, she'll learn from that, too."

Cade rested his hands on his hips and stared at the ground. He kicked the sand and then called out, "Sadie, come on back. I'm sorry. Let's try again." Sadie peered out from the shadows of the barn. "Let's try one more time, okay?"

Joscelyn gestured for her to come out. Sadie came, but she took her time and spent her energy on crafting the most defiant facial expression she could muster. She crossed her arms with a huff.

Once they were standing next to each other, Joscelyn said, "Cade, I know you believe this whole thing is pointless, but actually the objective is to learn to communicate better, build trust, and strengthen your relationship."

"How? Clearly Sadie doesn't trust my instructions."

Joscelyn cocked her head to the side. "I don't know… I think she trusts you enough to try your suggestions, but do you trust her enough to try hers?"

He popped his chin up as though she struck it and clenched his jaw. "I get your point."

"Good. Now, I'm going to add a new feature." Joscelyn pulled a red bandana from her back pocket. She shook it out and folded it from corner to corner.

Sadie's mouth fell slack. "You're blindfolding one of us?"

Joscelyn laughed. "No, but in a similar way as blindfolding someone can help them learn to trust their partner, I am going to gag each of you in turn."

"Gag us?" Cade looked at her like she was crazy. "What good will *that* do?"

"Come here and bend down so I can reach you." Joscelyn tied the bandana over Cade's mouth. "I'm not really gagging you, but the bandana will remind you that in this turn, you may not speak. You can communicate in other ways, but no speaking." She turned to Sadie. "Sadie, you don't have any new limitations, but all the original rules still apply. Ready," Joscelyn looked at her watch, "begin."

Sadie giggled at the sight of her dad with the bandana on his face. "You look like a bank robber." He rolled his eyes, but Joscelyn could see his smile peeking out.

"Don't laugh too hard, Sadie, you're next." Joscelyn moved out of their way.

"Okay, Dad. What I was trying to say is that we can use anything in the arena. So, let's build an alleyway with those ground-poles. We can prop them up on those buckets to make the ground pole alley as high as the jump. Then when we drive Nyx into the alley, his only way out is to jump."

A muffled sound came from under the bandana. Joscelyn was quick to remind Cade he could not speak. He shrugged and went with Sadie to collect the items they would need to build her idea. When the alley was set up, the father-daughter team worked together to herd Onyx into the space and toward the jump. The black horse went into the alley, but when he got to the jump, he balked and tried to back out. Sadie shouted and waved her arms. Onyx ran through the post wall, knocked it down, and trotted away.

"Ugh!" Sadie groaned. Cade looked at Joscelyn and pointed at the bandana.

"Yes, you both can talk now. Take one minute to discuss what happened. Then, Cade, tie the bandana over Sadie's mouth.

Cade bent down, bracing his hands on his knees so he was on eye level with his daughter. "Your idea was solid. I think it broke down when Nyx was in the alley and he felt trapped. Let's make the alley wider so it doesn't feel like a box so much as a suggestion." They went to work on the tweaked plan. When Onyx approached the jump, Cade walked at his flank encouraging him to go forward, but Sadie walked up next to him. She faced forward and held her hand up as though she carried an invisible lead rope. Then she stepped over the jump and without turning to look at the horse, she took a step forward and stood still. Cade held his arms out and waved them trying to get Onyx to move forward. The horse flapped his lips several times and bobbed his head up and down before he shifted his weight back to his haunches and hefted himself over the jump.

Sadie pulled the fabric from her mouth and threw her arms around Onyx's neck. "You did it! Good boy!" Then she ran to her dad and jumped into his arms. He twirled her around, they laughed and cheered.

"Way to go you two!" Joscelyn clapped her hands. "Let's get a cold drink and talk about what happened."

They sat at the picnic table with bottles of water. "How was it for you not to be able to share your thoughts, Cade?"

"Honestly? Damn hard. But, Sadie's idea was actually a really good one." He smiled at his daughter.

"How about you, Sadie?" Joscelyn asked.

"It wasn't too hard because we had a little time before it was my turn. Mostly, I wanted to talk to Nyx, to call him."

"Before we forced the issue with the bandana, what was your communication like?"

Sadie pursed her lips and looked at her dad out of the side of her eyes. He chuckled. "Okay, so I had a hard time listening when I was trying to give the orders," he said.

Joscelyn was relieved that Cade was able to laugh at himself. That was growth. "How did you feel about that Sadie?"

"It's frustrating when you can't share your ideas."

Joscelyn nodded and took a long gulp of her water. "It's hard not to be listened to. Also, a team loses out if only one voice gets to be heard. When you two were forced to listen, it helped you to trust one another. I also think you proved that two heads really are better than one." Their success encouraged Joscelyn.

"Sadie, you're right. I have kinda been treating you like one of my Marines. I'm sorry." He reached for her and ruffled her hair. "You're a smart kid with good ideas. There is a good purpose behind Marines following orders without questioning, but that's for the battlefield, not home." Cade looked at

Joscelyn. "I'm working on remembering I'm home now."

Sadie smiled at him with a mischievous sparkle, then aimed her bottle at him and shook it, splashing his face, neck and chest.

"Oh! You will regret that." He laughed as he leapt up and grabbed her. He poured icy water from his bottle onto her head. Sadie screamed and tried to get away. Then they both turned on Joscelyn and lunged.

"No, you don't!" Joscelyn jumped up and tried to run. "I'm not a part of this."

"You're the instigator." Cade grabbed her arm and drew her back into a bear hug while Sadie splashed her in the face and chest with the rest of her water. Joscelyn aimed her water back at Cade's head and escaped when he tried to grab it out of her hand. By the time the bottles were empty, the three of them were soaked.

Still laughing, Joscelyn held her wet shirt away from her skin. "Well, that's one way to cool off." She reveled in the game and wished she could have stayed in Cade's arms a little longer.

"Hey, Sadie," Cade said, "will you take Onyx to his stall and start feeding?"

"Sure." She went to catch Joscelyn's horse.

When Sadie moved out of ear shot, Cade moved up close to Joscelyn and said, "I want you to know, I've looked into getting help but a big reason I don't want to make an appointment is because I don't want to take someone else's spot at the VA. So many guys need the help more than me. It takes weeks, even months to get in."

Joscelyn flexed her jaw and shook her head in frustration. This was a sore topic with her. The country owed their veterans more than this. She followed Sadie into the barn to help give the horses their hay and some grain. When they were done, she strode back outside and asked Cade, "So, will you at least go with me to the VFW spaghetti dinner then?"

Cade narrowed his eyes at her but they held a spark.

CHAPTER 22

The following Thursday night, Joscelyn met Cade outside the old VFW Post. "I'm proud of you, Cade. I know this is hard, but I really think it'll be helpful."

"I wouldn't be here if you weren't making me." Cade stuffed his hands in his jean pockets. Joscelyn willfully kept herself from rolling her eyes. She couldn't force Cade Stone to do anything he didn't want to do.

Inside the VFW building, the air was filled with the scent of garlic and marinara. Joscelyn pushed her palm against her stomach as it gnawed in anticipation. She and Cade were greeted by a few VFW members and shown to their seats.

"We'll have dinner following the Table Ceremony." An older gentleman wearing a red garrison cap and matching vest, covered with his old unit patches pulled out a chair for Joscelyn. "It's in memory of all POWs and MIAs."

Joscelyn thanked the man. Cade's jaw tightened, and he said nothing as he pulled out his own chair and sat.

Arranged at the front of the darkened room was a small, round table, covered in a white cloth, set for one. Behind the table stood an American flag, glowing from the light of a single candle. Next to Old Glory was the black and white POW flag.

Silence blanketed the room and the VFW Chaplain, a balding man of slight stature but strong military bearing, approached the side of the table and presided over the ceremony.

"We are here to remember and honor our fallen and missing brothers- and sisters-in-arms." He made a sweeping motion with his hand, drawing everyone's focus to the table. "This table is round, demonstrating our everlasting concern for those who are missing from our presence. It is draped in white to symbolize purity. This single red rose stands for the blood that was shed and for the families waiting for their loved ones to return." The chaplain touched the flower vase. "This red ribbon, tied to the vase, symbolizes our determination to account for each missing service member. The lighted candle illuminates our hope and exemplifies the unconquerable spirit of our missing service members." He clasped his hands together and remained silent for a moment. Joscelyn thought of her father and a deep loneliness shifted in her soul.

"The slice of lemon on the bread plate reminds us of their bitter fate. Salt symbolizes the countless tears of their families. This empty wine glass stands inverted because those missing cannot toast with us, and the chair remains empty because they are not here." The chaplain completed the ceremony with a prayer for the missing and deceased service members then he blessed the food.

Lights flooded the room and conversations chased the solemnity away. Joscelyn leaned toward Cade. "I grew up in the Marine Corps and I never saw this ceremony before. It's powerful," she whispered. He gave her a slight nod and his Adam's apple bobbed up and down.

The MC dismissed tables, one at a time, to go through the Italian buffet. Pans of cheesy lasagna and bowls of spaghetti promised no one would leave hungry. Joscelyn filled her plate with Caesar salad and pasta, topping the food with two pieces of garlic bread. People of all ages attended the event. Many of the veterans seemed to know each other even though they wore different colored hats and vests. It was a light-hearted evening and Cade relaxed by the time dessert was served. Kids passed out slices of frozen tiramisu served with coffee.

When the evening came to a close, Joscelyn and Cade stood to leave. The man who greeted them in the beginning came to the door. "I hope you two had a nice time."

"It was a lot of fun and the food was delicious." Joscelyn rubbed her full belly. "Thanks for having us."

The man smiled and his kind gaze rested on Cade. "I'm glad you came, son, and I hope you come back." The old man clasped Cade's hand with both of his. "These men are our brothers. No one understands the way they do. I couldn't have made it through without them." The men shook hands.

Cade couldn't speak. His eyes glistened and he tossed his head back to ward off the unwelcome emotion.

"I know, son. You come by anytime. I'm Daniel and I'm here most always."

Cade gave him a curt nod, took Joscelyn's arm and rushed her out the door. He didn't speak on the way home, but he didn't break down either. Joscelyn was sure this was a solid step toward his healing.

Sunday dawned a beautiful day. The temperature was in the low eighties and a soft breeze made it perfect. Joscelyn sat next to Mary and Trent in church as had become their habit. Sadie pulled Cade up from the back to sit with the family. The sermon was on forgiveness which pleased Joscelyn because the topic would give her a nice segue to talk to Cade about visiting J.T.'s family.

Refreshments were served outside on the front lawn of the white clapboard church. Large, ancient trees blessed the gathering with shade. Joscelyn wanted Cade to find peace, and she had a strong feeling that facing his friend's family would help. He also needed to forgive himself. The death of the Marines in his unit was not his fault, but Cade didn't see it that way.

"You look deep in thought." Joscelyn turned at Cade's voice.

"In fact, I was thinking about you."

Cade smiled in a way that reminded her of Trent's charming grin. "That so?"

Something warm uncoiled in her belly and she returned his smile. She nibbled on her bottom lip, knowing she was about to change the mood. She answered, "Yeah. I was wondering what plans you've made for visiting J.T.'s family in Texas?" Joscelyn was sorry to see the handsome smile drop from his face.

"I know I said I'd go, Josce, but I changed my mind. I don't think I can do it."

"Why not?

Cade stared at the dirt. "Truthfully? I can't stand the thought of causing them more grief than they've already had to cope with." He covered his eyes with his hand and lowered his voice. "What if I have an *episode* and lose control? They shouldn't have to deal with that." When he looked at Joscelyn again, his eyes had clouded over with pain and fear.

"I've decided to go with you." Joscelyn reached forward and squeezed his arm. "Does that help?"

"This looks serious." Trent strode up and put an arm around Joscelyn's waist. "I'm not interrupting anything, am I?" She tried to step sideways, but he held his grasp.

Cade narrowed his eyes. "As a matter of fact, you are."

"Sorry." Trent smirked as though sorry was the last thing he felt. "I just wanted to say hello to my girl." He bent to kiss Joscelyn on the cheek.

"I'm not your girl, Trent." Joscelyn pushed him away.

"No?" He ran the back of his fingers down her bare arm. "That's not how it seemed when we kissed on the porch." One side of his mouth tilted into a teasing smile.

"Leave her alone, Trent." Cade's voice was low and his jaw bulged.

Trent laughed. "Now why would I want to do that?"

Joscelyn snapped, "Don't you think *Tonya* might be looking for you?" As soon as the words were out, she felt shamed by the eighth-grade tone in her voice.

Trent caught her up in an arm again. "Now, honey, don't be jealous. You know there isn't anything going on between me and Tonya anymore. We're just friends, that's all."

Cade stepped up and grabbed his brother's arm, yanking him backward. "I said—leave her alone."

Joscelyn heard the warning in Cade's voice, even if Trent didn't. "Cade, it's okay." She stepped between the brothers. "Cade, listen to me. Look at me." Cade's eyes flickered down to her. "Breathe. Focus on where you are. Focus on me."

Trent finally seemed to grasp how close Cade was to losing control and becoming violent. "I didn't mean any trouble, Cade." His gaze moved to Joscelyn. "I'll call you later." He doffed his hat and strode to his big truck.

Cade watched his brother drive away, and without taking his eyes off Trent's tailgate he said. "Okay, I'll go. If you're going with me."

CHAPTER 23

The following weekend, Joscelyn put a 'Closed until Tuesday' sign in the Library/Book Shop window. Cade picked her up after dropping Sadie and the dogs off at Mary's house.

Joscelyn buckled her seatbelt and asked, "How long does it take to get to Missoula?"

Cade grinned, "Depends on how fast you drive."

Joscelyn glanced at him from the corner of her eye and flattened her lips.

He chuckled. "I'm serious. The speed limit is 80, but it's just a suggestion."

She shook her head. "Drive safely, will you?"

He laughed.

They arrived at the Missoula airport in plenty of time to catch their plane to Houston. There were no lines at the small airport's security station. Once through TSA, they stopped at a place called *Jedidiah's* for lunch.

After he finished his Philly-cheesesteak, Cade took a drink from his beer bottle and said, "Thanks for coming with me. If you weren't here, I'd turn back for home right now." He wiped his mouth on a napkin.

Joscelyn glanced down at her half-eaten burger. "You're stuck now, because I'm going to need help squeezing into my seat on the plane. I'm stuffed." She dabbed her napkin on her lips. "Want the rest of my burger and fries?"

Cade smiled, traded her plate with his, and washed the remainder of Joscelyn's lunch down with a second bottle of beer.

After take-off, Cade selected a movie but Joscelyn noticed he wasn't watching it. Instead, his stare hovered about six inches above the screen. He sat deep in thought. She placed her hand on top of his and gave it a reassuring squeeze. Cade glanced at her and smiled. He returned the squeeze and kept her hand in his. Joscelyn's skin tingled at his touch.

When they arrived in Houston, they rented a car and drove north-east, to the small town of Paris. On the drive, Joscelyn asked Cade to tell her more about J.T.

"He was a great guy. Always pulling pranks and making guys laugh." His gaze grew distant as he remembered. "One time he covered his naked-assed body with shaving cream and ran through the barracks." Cade chuckled and then grew serious. His eyebrows drew together.

"J.T. was shot in the chest. It bled like crazy. I tried to cover the wound, you know? Put pressure on it. I told him to hold on—we'd get help. I *promised* to get him out of there." Cade closed his eyes and Joscelyn put her hand on the steering wheel to keep them in their lane. He blinked them open and glanced at her. "There was an explosion and the next thing I can remember is waking up in a hospital in Germany. Three other men and I were the only survivors from my unit. That was it. When I was well enough to travel, they sent me Stateside, handed me my DD214—my discharge papers—and, wham-bam-thank you-ma'am, I was released. When I got back to Montana, my wife was gone, my daughter didn't know me, and was scared of me. Hell, I was scared of me, too."

Joscelyn swallowed to moisten her dry throat. She moved her hand to Cade's arm and closed her fingers around it. "I'm so sorry you had to go through all of that." Cade stared straight ahead, his grip tight on the wheel.

The sign for Paris welcomed them and Cade found their motel. He parked the car, turned off the engine and they sat in the quiet. Finally, he spoke, "I promised J.T. I would get him out of there. I broke that promise. Now he's dead."

"Cade, you didn't willfully break that promise. You were in an explosion. Your options were taken away from you." Joscelyn's heart constricted and a stone lodged in her throat. Cade's pain was so raw, it emanated from him like waves of heat.

He sat quiet for a long time. Joscelyn finally said, "Let's go to our rooms and get freshened up."

Cade nodded, then studied the Google Map on his phone. "I think I should call the Millers first. Let 'em know I'm coming."

"That's a good idea."

"Maybe they're traveling and not even in town?" He sounded hopeful.

Joscelyn shook her head. "No such luck. I called them last week and told them we would be coming through town. They're looking forward to meeting you."

Cade frowned. "How'd you get their number?"

"You can find almost anything on Google. It wasn't that hard. I thought it might be kind to give them a little heads-up."

"I guess there's no backing out now," Cade grumbled.

"Exactly." She winked at him and patted his hand.

They went to their rooms to unpack. Joscelyn hung up a few things and changed to go for dinner. Cade knocked on her door an hour later.

"I called the Millers to set a time to meet at their house tomorrow. Mr. Miller seemed... stoic. I couldn't get a read on him over the phone," Cade said when Joscelyn stepped out of her room. "I hate more than anything to do this to him. Maybe we shouldn't go."

"What do you mean?"

"I can't put him through the pain of losing J.T. all over again."

Joscelyn studied his face. "You aren't doing that. You'll be helping to give them some closure. I'm sure they'll be glad to meet you."

"If you say so."

~*~

The following morning, Cade pulled up to the curb in front of a tidy, brick, ranch-style home with light-blue trim. Bright-pink azaleas hedged the house which sat on a perfectly trimmed lawn. Cade glanced at Joscelyn, turned off the engine, and sat unmoving. His stomach churned. His chest felt tight and perspiration dampened his collar.

"Are you ready?" Joscelyn asked him.

He couldn't speak so he gave a short nod. Side by side, they walked up the path and rang the doorbell. Cade shifted his weight from foot to foot and shook out his stiff leg. It seemed to hurt more here, on the threshold of J.T.'s childhood home. He straightened his tie and smoothed his suit coat. Humidity and nerves worked together to bead sweat across his forehead. The scar on his neck and jaw itched from his fresh shave.

"It's going to be all right. Just remember to breathe." Joscelyn clasped his hand and held it tight. Cade nodded and swallowed.

The front door opened and a petite woman with a dark, puffy, Texas-style hairdo greeted them. "Hello." She reached out a hand in greeting. "You must be Captain Caedon Stone." She smiled up at him with kind eyes, her Texan drawl stretching out her sentence like pulled taffy.

Cade cleared his throat. "Just Cade, ma'am." He took her hand. It felt as fragile and delicate as a bird's wing.

"I'm Patricia Miller, J.T.'s mom," she smiled then turned her attention to Joscelyn. "And, you must be Joscelyn. Thank you both for coming to visit. Please, come in."

Behind her stood a tall rigid man who looked to be in his late 50s. Close-cropped gray hair stood stiff above steel-blue eyes—J.T.'s eyes. The man stared hard at Cade. "Captain Stone, I'm Richard Miller."

A cold rock seemed to lodge itself in Cade's chest as he shook the man's hand. "Please sir, call me Cade. Your son and I were good friends."

"He told us about you in his letters." Mr. Miller offered a vague gesture for them to enter the living room but tension held everyone in their place.

Finally, Mrs. Miller tried to move the group past their awkwardness. "*Please*, have a seat. I made a pecan pie."

Cade hesitated. He wasn't sure he could chat about J.T. over pie. His stomach tightened into a ball. He fought the urge to retreat to the car and race away. Joscelyn gripped his elbow in what felt like solidarity and she guided him into the room. She pulled him down next to her on the sofa. The Miller's both took chairs facing them.

J.T.'s mom sliced the pie and dished it up on china plates. "I hope y'all like pecans. I know not everyone does, but this was J.T.'s favorite. I take it to all the church potlucks. Most folks seem to like it." She prattled on and it was painfully obvious she wanted to fill the strained silence.

"I love pecan pie. There's nothing better with a nice cup of coffee. Don't you think, Cade?" Joscelyn joined forces with Mrs. Miller.

After they were all served, the silence still refused to be chased off and hung like a black-out drape in the room. It seemed no one knew who should talk first or what to say.

Finally, Cade swallowed and began. "I'm so sorry I couldn't bring J.T. home to you." He lowered his head and to his mortification, a tear fell to the floor.

Mr. Miller stood and turned away from them, bracing his hand on the fireplace mantle. His chin lowered to his chest.

Patricia Miller rushed to Cade and dropped to her knees on the carpet before him. "Oh, Cade, it wasn't your fault. We knew you were in the hospital." She took his large hand in her two tiny ones. "We were told how you threw yourself on top of J.T., trying to save him from the explosion. You tried to shield him with your own body. We know that, and I am so grateful. The report said that he...that he was..." she stumbled over her words and cleared her throat. "He died from the gunshot wound before the explosion. There was nothing anyone could do." She wept as she put her arms around Cade. He strained every muscle in his body against breaking down but he couldn't keep his shoulders from shaking.

Mr. Miller cleared his throat and returned to his chair. He leaned forward, his arms on his knees and his gaze cast to the floor. "It was a brave thing you did, son." His voice thick with restrained emotion. "I don't know how to thank you."

Cade's eyes shot up to the man. He drew his brows together and leaned his head to the side. "Thank me?" He stared at Mr. Miller, swinging his head from side to side, not understanding.

"Cade, you couldn't have saved J.T.'s life. There was nothing you could do. But, you were a friend to him when he was scared and lonely. He treasured your friendship and he wrote about your times together. He said you were like the brother he never had. Patty and I are broken hearted but also eternally thankful that J.T. had you for a friend in his last days and to know he didn't die alone. It brings us tremendous comfort."

Cade kept shaking his head. "But, I didn't protect him. I didn't *save* him." His heart pounded against his ribs. It was hard to breathe. Cade's vision narrowed into a tunnel view, his breath rapid and shallow. "I was in a hospital in Germany when they flew him home." His words came out in a whisper.

Joscelyn touched his knee. "Cade?" She moved closer to him on the couch and put her arm around his shoulders and spoke low, only to him. "Cade? Slow down your breathing."

She breathed deliberately along with him, her breath soft on his cheek. Cade focused on her and tried to comply. Mr. Miller approached and touched Joscelyn's shoulder. She moved out of his way, so he could sit next to Cade on the couch. She wrung her hands and moved to the picture window. Cade knew she must feel like an outsider in this intense personal moment, but he was glad she was there.

"Son, listen to me," Mr. Miller said as he sat down. "J.T. was proud to be a Marine. He'd wanted to be a Marine and serve his country since he was a little boy. We all knew the risks involved. I am certain he's looking down at us now, not wanting us to be sad, but rather to be proud of the sacrifice he made." Richard Miller put an arm across Cade's shoulders and reached for his wife's hand. The three huddled together sharing the ache in their souls.

Eventually, Mr. Miller cleared his throat and wiped his eyes. "I have something for you." He rose and left the room. Cade looked at Joscelyn in bewilderment. She smiled and nodded, reassuring him.

Mrs. Miller cupped Cade's cheek in her hand, her eyes swimming in tears. "I'm so glad you came to see us, Cade. It means the world."

"I worried it would cause you more pain." Cade's voice was rough and his throat ached.

"Oh, sweetheart, nothing could be less true. It's a comfort to meet you. You, Richard, and I share memories of J.T. and that's a wonderful thing." She patted his knee and pushed herself up off the floor and sat back in her chair.

Mr. Miller came in with a set of dog tags hanging from a chain. "We have a set too, so don't hesitate to take these. I want you to have them, to remember J.T. by."

Cade's heart constricted in pain but he stood to receive J.T.'s tags. "Thank you, sir. I can't tell you what they mean to me."

"You don't have to." Mr. Miller grasped Cade's shoulder and looked directly into his eyes.

"I'd like to visit his grave, if that's all right?" Cade's breaths were short, he couldn't draw much air past the wad of misery in his chest.

Mrs. Miller stood. "Of course. Let me write out directions to the cemetery." She went into the kitchen and returned with a pad of paper. "When you're finished there, we hope you'll both come back here for supper. We would love to hear more of your memories of our boy."

"Of course." Cade choked on the words.

Cade placed his hand on the small of Joscelyn's back and as they left for the cemetery, Mrs. Miller touched Joscelyn's elbow. "Thank you for bringing Cade to see us, sweetheart. I know it is hard for him, but I hope he will find some peace."

Joscelyn put her hand over the top of Mrs. Miller's. "I hope so too. Thank you for being so gracious to him."

Cade gave the Miller's a curt nod. "We'll be back by five."

CHAPTER 24

From the top of a green, grassy hill in the Paris Cemetery, J.T.'s grave overlooked a pond to the south. Joscelyn walked through the trees with Cade to the gravestone but hung back as he knelt down. She sat on a cement bench under a live oak tree, giving him privacy and the time he needed talk to his friend and shed a few tears. A half hour went by in the sticky Texan heat before Cade stood up and looked for Joscelyn. He held his hand out to her and she went to him.

Loosening his tie, he opened his collar and pulled out his own dog tags hanging from their chain. He removed one of them and added it to J.T.'s chain. Then he took one of J.T.'s tags and hung it with his own. Cade draped J.T.'s chain on the small cross at the top of his friend's tombstone and tucked his back inside his shirt. He stared at the stone engraved with 2nd Lieutenant Jonathan Thomas Miller, USMC. Beloved Son and Brave Patriot.

"Thanks, Joscelyn," Cade murmured before pulling her into his arms and resting his chin on the top of her head.

She returned his embrace and reveled in the feeling of being in his arms. "Of course." They held on to each other for a long time ignoring the blazing, humid heat.

~*~

Over a dinner of BBQ ribs, roasted corn, a leafy green salad, and sweet-tea, Cade and the Miller's shared their stories about J.T. Cade's arm automatically flexed when Joscelyn laid her hand on it. He covered it with his other hand, holding hers in place.

She gave him a gentle squeeze. "After tonight, I feel as though I knew J.T. too. I know for sure I wished I had. I love the comradery of the Marine Corps." Joscelyn stood, slipping away from him to stack the plates. "My dad was a Marine too. I grew up in that world and I have to admit I miss it."

Richard nodded. "I was in the Corps and so was my father. He served in Vietnam and was gone most of my early childhood. Where'd your dad serve?"

"He was in the first Gulf War." Joscelyn's voice grew thick. "He was killed in Baghdad." Her gaze dropped to the dishes in her hands and Cade thought he saw her tremble. "My mom and I wrote him letters every day." Joscelyn shook her head and smiled. "It's so nice that service members can talk to their families more often on Skype, email, and even text now."

Cade sat up, his heart aching for Joscelyn. "You never told me your dad was killed in the Gulf War."

"I told you he was a Marine."

"Yeah, but...you never said he was killed. Is he why you know so much about PTSD?"

"I guess. The struggles he had between deployments definitely inspired me to study psychology." Joscelyn gave him a sad smile.

"I'm sorry to hear that, Joscelyn." Richard rested back in his chair. "I know my dad had a tough time coming home after 'Nam." He regarded Cade. "You struggling too?" Cade snapped his eyes up to meet Richard's, but he couldn't answer. "I bet you are. There's no way you can go through something like that and just shake it off." Richard sipped his after-dinner whiskey. "At least we have a better understanding about PTSD now. Back then, they just thought guys were crazy. Now they have all sorts of programs to help vets. I've heard of groups that fly fish, hunt, and even ski together."

Cade nodded. "Joscelyn works with me using horse therapy, but I admit, mostly I still just feel crazy," Cade fought the tightness in his lungs and pulled in a deep breath.

Richard considered him for a time and then said, "I bet you do. Listen, Cade. You get help. It would be a shame to live the rest of your life looking back at the war." Cade couldn't meet Richard's eyes and instead, stared at his hands. "Will you promise me that you'll get help?" Richard set down his glass, the ice clinked. "The world already lost J.T. It would be a sorry waste for it to lose you, too." Cade still couldn't look up, blood pounded in his ears. "Cade, I want you to promise me, for J.T.'s sake."

At that, Cade looked the man straight in the eye and said, "I promise."

~*~

Joscelyn and Cade didn't get back to their motel until after midnight. He walked her to her door and hugged her tight to his chest. "Thanks, Josce."

She slid her arms around him letting her fingers explore the strong muscles of his back. After such an emotional day Joscelyn felt a deeper connection to Cade. She hoped he found some forgiveness and peace. Joscelyn had allowed him to see her deepest sorrow and was amazed that she wanted to share even more of herself with him.

He nuzzled his face in her hair, then released her. "It's an early call tomorrow, best get some sleep."

Joscelyn kept her hands on his waist, bereft at the loss of his embrace. His eyes darkened as he regarded her in the moonlight. She wondered what he was thinking, wondered if he, too, felt the powerful draw.

"Good night." He pushed his hands into her hair, held her head, and kissed her. The kiss came quick and was hungry and possessive. His mouth was at once demanding and gentle. A surge of electric energy swelled up inside of her. Engulfed in heat, Joscelyn pressed herself into Cade to assuage it. Cade drew in a sharp breath and pulled back. In a hoarse whisper he said, "I'll see you in the morning." He ran his fingers down her cheek. "Lock the door behind you."

"I will." Joscelyn whispered back but instead of letting him go, her grip instinctively tightened. With an urgent hunger, she pulled him back toward her, her mouth reached up for his, desire overriding all sense.

"Joscelyn," Cade gasped against her lips, the roughness of his evening beard burned her skin and sent a thrill through her core.

"Yes," she breathed. His mouth took command of hers, the sharp taste of whiskey on his tongue.

Cade took the key card from her hand and swiped it in the lock. He pulled her through the door as he stepped in. Once inside, overwhelmed by need, he pushed her up against the wall and crushed her mouth with his. Joscelyn raked her fingers through his hair and met his intensity with her own, driving him wild.

Cade kissed and nibbled her ear and neck. She smelled of lavender and something bright, like cedar. Joscelyn's fingers moved to his neck and she smoothed them over the slick and puckered skin of his scar. She pressed her lips to it. His body strained to take her there against the wall, but he wanted to love her, please her. She gripped him tight as he lifted her, carrying her to the bed. He set her down on her feet and undid the buttons of her blouse. Her pale skin glowed in the darkness.

"You're beautiful, Josce." He cupped her breast with his calloused hand.

Joscelyn pulled Cade's tie loose and undid his shirt buttons. Impatiently, he tore his shirt off. She traced his scar from his neck down his side to his waist. When she looked up into his eyes they were almost black with desire, but he grabbed her wrist and pulled her hand away from his side.

"What's wrong?"

He swallowed and shifted away from her touch. Joscelyn moved forward and kissed Cade's shoulder, slowly running her lips down along the scar on his ribs. She stopped to kiss each place where his skin puckered. With each kiss her heart expanded for him.

"You're incredible, Cade" she breathed. "I want you." She did want him, but not just to fill a void or to distract her from her loneliness. This was more than that. She wanted Cade—all that he was and all that came with him. Her mouth found his and he lowered her to the bed.

Joscelyn felt Cade's heart careening against her chest. She breathed in his particular scent and her nerves hummed. Her body pressed up against his, begging for him wantonly.

He was fierce and gentle, warrior and captive, greedy and generous. Joscelyn couldn't contain all her sensations and she burst with light and heat, her body its own primitive entity. She heard Cade groan her name as she slowly settled back to earth. Overwhelmed with a collage of emotion, Joscelyn felt two tears spill down her cheeks and into her hair. Her soul cried with the joy of pure connection, a lonely sojourn come to an end. She smiled and snuggled deep into Cade's arms. He kissed her temple.

~*~

Morning sun hit Cade's eyelids and he woke bewildered, at first unsure of where he was. Then the reality of last night struck him. Joscelyn lay in his arms and they were tangled in sheets. She stirred and he held her close. While she was unaware, he studied her face, memorizing her in this perfect moment. A smile flashed across her lips and her cheek plumped against his chest.

"Good morning."

Joscelyn opened one eye. It was the moment of truth. *Will she regret me?*

"Morning." She grinned and kissed his chest.

Cade's body surged to life. Overcome with fresh desire he pressed his mouth against her forehead and said, "We have an hour before we have to go."

"Mm."

Cade pushed her back and kissed her deeply. He felt hopeful for the first time in years and with a grateful heart, he reminded her why they woke so happy.

~*~

An hour later, Cade was back in his room, packing, and Joscelyn stood in the shower. A delicious shudder coursed through her body as she thought of him and their night and morning together.

They left for the airport after breakfast and it was long past dark when Cade pulled his truck up outside the Flint River Library.

"Thanks again, Josce." He took her hand and kissed her palm. "If you hadn't pushed me into this trip, I never would have gone."

"I'm glad you did. The Millers were so happy to get to know you. They're thrilled to have someone to share their memories of J.T. with."

Cade reached over and took her face in his hands. He kissed her. "I have to go get Sadie. I wish…" He didn't finish his thought.

Warmth spread through Joscelyn's chest and she gave him a soft smile. "Me too. Tell Mary I'll pick Teddy up in the morning. Will you call me when you get home?"

"Sure." Cade got out to open Joscelyn's door. "Can I see you tomorrow?"

"I'd like that."

He lifted her luggage and walked Joscelyn to the library door. She unlocked it and turned back. Cade's eyes were like swirling smoke. He touched Joscelyn's cheek with his fingertips before he gripped her jaw bringing her mouth to his. Her whole body tingled with the electricity. She slid her arms around his neck and opened her mouth to his. Their bodies pressed together, demanding. He pulled back, breathing hard, and stared down into her eyes, wanting.

Joscelyn breathed. "You're definitely going to have to find someone else for your therapy, you know."

A rugged chuckle emanated from his throat. "I'll start looking first thing." He kissed her again. "I better go." His forehead rested against hers for a few seconds. "Sadie will be wondering."

"Okay." The tilt-a-whirl of sensations leveled and slowed. She wanted to stay in his arms. Now that she found the place where she belonged, she never wanted to leave. "I'll see you tomorrow." Joscelyn gave him a last quick kiss and let herself inside. She locked the door and waved to him through the glass as he drove away.

Joscelyn swayed slightly as she walked through the entrance hall. Her heart hummed, she hadn't responded to a man like this since she thought she was in love in college. Joscelyn closed her eyes and smiled. She shivered at the arousing memory and promise of Cade. Giggling at herself, Joscelyn flicked the light switch at the bottom of the stairs.

Nothing.

The overhead light didn't turn on. She flicked the switch again, up and down. Nothing but complete darkness.

A cold tremor shimmied up her neck. Joscelyn shrugged off her momentary fear. *I'll get more lightbulbs in the morning.* Joscelyn felt her way up the stairs to the bend at the landing and then fumbled the rest of the way up to her apartment. Her fingers searched for the light switch in the loft.

Flick. Flick. Darkness.

Joscelyn's nerve endings fired hot. Her lungs pulled in a sudden breath. "Calm down," she said out loud to herself. "It's probably just the breaker box." *Crap, where's the breaker box?* Joscelyn rummaged through her nightstand drawer for a flashlight. Her fingers brushed over the cold steel of her gun which gave her a certain sense of reassurance. She found the flashlight, clicked it on and swept the beam around the loft. No breaker-box. Downstairs, Joscelyn searched the walls in the library, then the shop and the kitchenette. For good measure, she shined the light down each aisle to be sure she was alone. Joscelyn peered out the back door wondering if the breakers were out there when she heard rattling behind her. She spun around, her heart pounding in the silence. Why had she left her gun in the drawer?

A knock followed the rattle. "Joscelyn, are you still up?" Cade called out.

A cold sheet of perspiration swept over her as the wave of adrenaline dissipated. "Yes, hold on a minute," she called out. Joscelyn felt her way to the front door and pulled it open. "What are you doing here?"

Cade held up Teddy's leash and her dog wagged his tail. "I thought I'd bring Teddy home tonight, since it was on my way. Sadie's asleep in the truck."

Joscelyn opened the door wider for Teddy to come through. "Thanks," she said and smiled up at Cade.

"Why don't you have any lights on?"

"I think I tripped the breaker. The lights aren't working." She unhooked the leash and Teddy walked gingerly to his water bowl, careful of his still tender ribs. "I have no idea where the breaker-box is though, so I thought I'd just wait until morning."

"Want me to find it?"

Joscelyn gave him a long, penetrating look and said, "I *would* want you to if Sadie wasn't waiting for you."

The corner of his mouth tilted up. "Settle for another goodnight kiss?"

CHAPTER 25

A week later, on their way home from the saddle club's first gymkhana, country music accompanied the easy silence in the cab. Joscelyn, Cade, and Sadie had an early, pre-dawn morning loading horses and all the tack and gear into the trailer. After a long day of horse games and competitions, everyone was exhausted. The languid sun hung like an overripe peach dripping in the western sky and Joscelyn was glad to be driving home. Cade sat in the front with her and Sadie sprawled out in the backseat with Teddy and Max.

"What'd you think of your first gymkhana, Sadie?" Joscelyn glanced at the girl in her rearview mirror.

Stretching, Sadie answered, "It was really fun. Thanks for taking us."

"What was your favorite part?"

Sadie leaned her head back on the seat and closed her eyes. "The timed races. They were a blast. Too bad I sucked at them though."

Cade turned in his seat to look back at his daughter. "Why do you say that?"

"Cuz I lost to Dakota in the pole-bending and I'll never hear the end of losing to Tracy in the barrels." Sadie slouched further down on her seat.

Joscelyn said, "You came in third on the poles and second in barrels. How is that losing?" Her eyes darted to her rear-view mirror in time to catch the adolescent eye-roll.

"You placed third in Trail and, oh-yeah, you took *first* place in the Sit-A-Buck bareback event," Cade added.

"That was just a game, not a race." Sadie huffed. "I mean, I don't really mind losing to Dakota. She's been riding all her life. But Tracy? Her mom just buys her way. She's got like a ten-thousand-dollar horse."

Cade chuckled, "It may be *just a game*, but you have to be able to sit your horse well and have great balance to win. Sloppy riding can be hidden in the speed of racing events."

"That's true," Joscelyn agreed. "In the end, having a solid, independent seat will help you win speed events too, if you keep working at it." She yawned. "What are you going to practice the most before the next gymkhana?"

"I just need a faster horse." Sadie leaned against the door and rested her head on the window.

"Don't go blaming your horse. You two are a team." Cade faced forward and reached for Joscelyn's hand. "Do you want me to drive? You look sleepy.

Joscelyn shook her head and then jolted to full awake when she heard the siren behind her and saw red and blue flashing lights in her side mirror.

"Damn it," she said under her breath. She signaled and pulled her truck and trailer over to the shoulder of the road.

Cade peered at the side mirror out his window. "Were you speeding?"

"I don't think so." Joscelyn turned on the dome light, rolled down her window, and placed her hands on the steering wheel at 10 and 2. "Will you get out my registration and proof of insurance? They're in the black folder in the glove box."

Cade opened the document case and found a note taped to the inside. When she saw it, Joscelyn stared at the note written in a spidery hand. It said:

All around the cobbler's bench, the monkey chased the weasel. The monkey thought 'twas all in good fun, 'til POP! Went the weasel.

"What's this?" Cade pulled the tape loose and glanced at Joscelyn. "Josce, what's the matter? Cade unbuckled his belt and leaned toward her. "Your face is white as ash—you're trembling."

The sharp voice at the window caused a fireball to explode inside her head. Rivulets of sharp flame shot through her veins until they pierced the tips of her fingers and toes.

"Good evening, ma'am." The sheriff pointed the beam of his flashlight around the cab of the truck. "Folks." He nodded, included Cade and Sadie in his greeting. Moving the beam back to Joscelyn he asked, "Do you know why I pulled you over this evening?"

Joscelyn tried to answer, but her voice didn't work. She cleared her throat and tried again, trying to focus on something besides the nursery rhyme. "No, sir, but I need to let you know I have concealed carry permit. I do not have one on me, but there is a shotgun locked underneath the back seat of my truck. How would you like me to proceed?"

"Thanks for letting me know, Ma'am. I pulled you over because there's no license plate on your trailer."

Joscelyn drew her brows together. "What? It was on there when we loaded up. I'm sure of it."

"Well, it's not there now." Skepticism filled the sheriff's voice. "Do you have your registration papers for the trailer?"

"Of course. Right here." Joscelyn fumbled through her papers, but the document she needed was absent. "It *was* right here." Her heart ramped up its pace again.

"Slow down, Josce. Look again." Cade placed a hand on her knee.

"Wait, here's my proof of insurance for my truck *and* my trailer. I wouldn't have that if it wasn't registered." Desperation clawed at Joscelyn's throat as she showed the sheriff her papers.

"May I have your driver's license?" He held out his hand. "I'll take this back to my squad-car and call it in."

When the sheriff left to go to his car, Cade squeezed Joscelyn's thigh. "Hey, are you okay?"

She swallowed and nodded. "It's just—I know the license plate was on my trailer and I *always* keep my paperwork up to date."

"I'm pretty sure I saw it too, but maybe it fell off."

"Yeah, but what about my registration? It didn't just *fall* out of my folder." Joscelyn's tone headed toward hysterical. She took a deep breath.

"What was that note taped inside your case?" Cade reached for it. "When you saw it, you looked like you were gonna be sick." He read the note and lifted his eyes to Joscelyn's.

"I don't know. I've never seen that before." A tremor rippled through her. *Did Lenny leave that there? Has he found me? Is he behind this?*

"Do you think someone's pulling a prank on you?"

Joscelyn closed her eyes. "I hope so." Her body shuddered visibly.

"Joscelyn?" Cade leaned toward her.

"I don't really want to talk about it right now. Okay?"

Cade sat back. "Why not?" He clamped his jaw. "You always want me to share my worst memories and my most depressing thoughts but you never talk to me about anything that's going on with you."

Joscelyn glanced pointedly in the rearview mirror at Sadie. "*Not right now.*"

"Or ever." Cade said under his breath. He chewed on his lip, then said, "Anyway, I'm sure this is just a prank. It was probably one of the girls." He looked over his shoulder. "Sadie, do you know anything about this?" She shrugged and shook her head.

When the sheriff returned, he gave Joscelyn a ticket for not having a license plate or the correct documentation and sent them on their way.

Cade pointed to a gas station half a mile up the road. "Want to stop and get a cup of coffee?"

Joscelyn nodded, "I should get gas too." She signaled the turn and pulled the truck into the outside gas lane and turned off the engine.

"I'll get the coffee. How do you take it?" Cade opened his door and hopped down.

Sadie sat forward. "Can I have a Pepsi?"

Joscelyn met Cade's eyes across the cab and she winked at him. "Just black."

He nodded his head, smiled, and went inside the store. Joscelyn leaned against the cement pillar while she pumped the gas. She closed her eyes and released a sigh. *Cade's probably right, it was just the girls trying to be funny.* She could hear Sadie talking and laughing inside the truck.

When Joscelyn opened the door, and climbed back in she heard Sadie whisper, "I have to go. Call me later."

"Who was that?"

"No one."

Joscelyn turned to face the girl. "No one? Seriously?" She smirked. "You expect me to believe you were talking to no one? Was that about my missing license plate?"

"I told you I don't know anything about that." Sadie sighed with exasperation. "It was just David. No big deal."

"Are you making plans with him?"

"I don't know. We're just friends, so don't freak out."

Joscelyn faced forward and seeing Cade crossing the parking lot, she turned the key. The engine roared to life. Cade opened his door and passed out the drinks.

He climbed in just as Joscelyn said, "I'll try to keep from freaking out, but when can we meet this friend of yours?"

"What friend?" Cade turned to Sadie.

"Ugh! *Joscelyn*." Sadie whined.

"What friend?" This time Cade asked Joscelyn.

Her brows rose, "David, the boy Sadie was with the other night at the park." Joscelyn put the truck in gear and pulled back out onto the highway. "He called while you were in the store."

Cade's eyes shifted from Joscelyn to Sadie and back. "I need to know more about this kid."

"Dad!" Sadie crossed her arms and glared at him. "He's just a friend. Stop being so weird."

"How am I being weird?"

"You're practically interrogating me about him."

Cade's face was incredulous. He drew his brows together and shook his head. "What? I'm not interrogating you, but you're acting like you're hiding something. What's going on? Why don't you want me to know anything about this guy?"

"He told me he doesn't like people talking about him, that's all. Now can we drop it?"

Cade turned confused and worried eyes to Joscelyn. She didn't like the sound of this boy either, but she knew if Cade came down hard about David, it would only drive Sadie toward him.

"I think what your dad is trying to say is, like all your friends, he would like to meet him. That's all and that isn't an interrogation."

Sadie adjusted her crossed arms, restating her irritation, and stared out the window. Toby Keith's *Wish I Didn't Know Now What I Didn't Know Then* strummed into the silence for the remainder of the drive.

CHAPTER 26

Joscelyn typed Amy's name into Google Search. Since she threw her phone into the lake, she lost all of her contact information. Her co-worker's number was easy to find however, and she dialed it.

"Hello, this is Amy Gardner. How can I help you?"

"Amy, hi." Joscelyn closed the Google screen. "It's Joscelyn."

"Joscelyn! How are you? We've been worried about you. You haven't called."

Guilt pinched at Joscelyn's throat, making it dry. "I'm sorry. I've been busy and I don't really have time to explain. I called to check on my two clients that you're supervising. Bonnie and Teresa? They're due to emancipate this month and I wondered how it's going?"

Amy's pause added weight to Joscelyn's guilt. "It's going well so far." Amy's voice sounded resigned. "They've both moved into transition apartments. Teresa's working at Walmart and

Bonnie got a job at a horse-barn in Castle Rock. She's cleaning stalls and doing grunt work, but she seems happy."

Joscelyn smiled. "That's great—really great. Amy, thank you for taking care of them for me. I knew I could count on you."

"Did you? I mean, you trusted me with your clients, I guess, but why won't you tell me where you are? One day you're living in my apartment and the next you're gone. What's going on with you, Joscelyn? Are you all right?"

Joscelyn took a deep breath and decided to share a little of what she knew. "One of my past clients was stalking me. He came to my home and hurt my animals. Which is why I asked to stay with you for those few days, but he found out where I was. I didn't want to put you in danger so I got my horses and Teddy and ran. I don't want to give you any more details over the phone. As soon as the police find the guy and have him behind bars, I'll be able to come home. I'll tell you all about it then."

"But...

"I can't say more now, but I'll be in touch. When I can return home, I'll tell you all about it over a long dinner with lots of wine. Okay?" Her thoughts flashed to Cade and the thought of going home didn't feel as comforting.

"Joscelyn, I'm worried about you."

"I know and I'm sorry, but I'm safe and I'll call you soon." Joscelyn disconnected the call. She was happy and relieved that Bonnie and Teresa were making it. So far, anyway. But she didn't like having to evade Amy's questions. Her friend deserved answers, just not yet.

The front bell jingled and Cade limped through the door. "Hey."

"Hi. I didn't expect to see you today." A bubble of excitement popped in Joscelyn's chest at the sound of his voice, chasing away her regret. She came out from behind the computer and stretched up to kiss him. "Aren't you supposed to be separating your cows and calves today?"

"Yeah, and Sadie was supposed to help, but she never came home from school. I thought maybe she stopped in here?"

Joscelyn frowned. "Nope. I haven't seen her for a couple days. Did you check Lisa's house?"

"Yeah. I called all the girls in the saddle club. None of them have seen her and she doesn't really hang out with anyone else." Cade picked up a book, pretended to look at it, and then tossed it back down. "I called my grandma and she hasn't seen her either." He shook his head.

"Did you call Trent?"

"Yep." He pulled his phone out of his back pocket, checking the screen. "He's working his cattle today, too, and she's not with him."

Cold concern washed her excitement away and Joscelyn picked up her keys. "Let's go ask around town and see if anyone has seen her." They stepped out onto the sidewalk. "Do any of the girls know how to reach that David guy?"

"I didn't think to ask."

"I'll send out a group text." She tapped the message on her phone.

Joscelyn and Cade walked up and down Main Street stopping in every open shop to ask if anyone had seen Sadie. No one had, so they went back to the library and called everyone they could think of. Cade ran his hand down over his face. "Why doesn't she answer her damn phone?"

Joscelyn brushed his cheek with her fingers. "I don't know. It's strange, I agree. Teenagers always have their phones with them. Maybe the battery died." She stood up and grabbed her purse. "Let's drive around town. We haven't checked the park yet."

They drove for an hour, through the park then on every street and cross street of the small town looking for Sadie. When Cade got to the far end of Flint River, he pulled over, reached for his cellphone, and dialed.

"Get me Sheriff Dietrich." He glanced at Joscelyn, then stared at the dashboard. "Tom, it's Cade Stone. Sadie's missing." He listened. "We've been looking for her all afternoon." He listened for another minute and then glanced at Joscelyn. "She might be with a boy who's new in town." Joscelyn could hear the sheriff's garbled response before Cade spoke again. "Yeah, Joscelyn saw it last week. It's some kind of compact like a Toyota or something." He turned to Joscelyn. "Color?"

Blood drained from Joscelyn's head and her stomach rebelled. Why didn't David want Sadie to talk about him? Who is David anyway? Dread overwhelmed her. Could David be Lenny? How could she be so blind, so stupid? "I didn't see the color clearly, but I think it was dark." She croaked out the words before she threw open the truck door and stumbled out to the dirt road. She bent over, her stomach screaming to purge. She thought she would retch.

Cade came around the truck. His hands clasped her shoulders.

"Josce, what is it?" He pulled her hair back as she dry-heaved. She wiped her mouth with the back of her sleeve and stared at the ground. "Joscelyn, I've asked you before and I'm asking you again. What are you not telling me?" His voice took on a steel edge.

Joscelyn raised wide, penetrating eyes to his face and tears choked her words. "Oh, Cade. I left Colorado because I was being stalked by a sociopathic former client who turned violent."

"What?" At first confusion clouded his eyes and Joscelyn watched as what she said began to register in Cade's mind. "The note... why didn't you say anything?"

"I didn't want to scare Sadie. In fact, I'd hoped I'd lost him. I wanted to believe the note was a prank." She stood, took two steps and said, "Maybe it isn't him. Maybe... " Joscelyn clutched at that hope. "We don't know it's the same guy. We shouldn't jump to conclusions."

"We need to talk to the sheriff. Come on." Cade rushed her to the truck and spun his tires in his haste.

~*~

Joscelyn told her whole story to the Flint River sheriff while his deputy took notes. Sheriff Dietrich called the sheriff back in Kiowa. "Tell me again, where were you when you last heard from this whacko?"

273

Joscelyn wiped her eyes. "He called my phone when I stopped for a break at a lake a couple of hours up the canyon from here. When he said he knew I was in Montana, I realized he was probably tracking my phone somehow, so crushed it and threw it into the lake. I never heard from him again. That was months ago."

"Except for the note in your glove box." Cade closed his eyes.

The sheriff looked grim. "If it's the same guy, he probably did track your phone. And it wouldn't take him long to search through the few small towns around here."

"But why would he be hanging around Sadie?" Joscelyn realized the answer as soon as the words left her mouth. "Oh, my God. Do you think he'd use her to get to me?"

CHAPTER 27

"We're searching for the car. I've called the Sheriff's Departments in the surrounding areas and all counties are on the lookout."

"I'm going back out. I can't just sit here." Cade stood so fast, his chair toppled over behind him.

Joscelyn grabbed his arm. "I'm coming with you." She almost didn't recognize the eyes that glared back at her. "Cade?"

He shook her loose and stormed out the door, but Joscelyn wasn't going to be left behind so easily. She ran after him and jumped in the truck before he opened the door on his side.

"Get out."

"No—I'm coming. I'm sorrier than you know, Cade, but we don't even know if Lenny found me." She hit the dashboard with both hands. "We don't even know for certain if it's the same guy."

"Suit yourself." Cade threw the truck into reverse, then jammed it into drive and flew out of the parking lot. He drove fast up Main Street and turned right past the Courthouse at the end of the road just as the sun sank behind the hills. Cade started at the north end of town and methodically drove up and down each street for a second time.

"Did any of Sadie's friends say they knew how to get ahold of David?" Cade's voice was low and menacing when he finally broke the silence.

"None of them do."

"Do *you* think that boy is your stalker?" His eyes flashed at her.

A heavy weight pressed in on Joscelyn's chest. "I don't know. I never got a good look at him. He was either too far away or in the shadows. But my client's name was Leonard – Lenny, not David." Joscelyn thought of the shed in her backyard. The cigarette butts and the blown circuit breaker. A sob caught in her throat.

The look Cade gave Joscelyn made her feel the full brunt of the stupidity of her comment and tears sprang to her eyes. "David is blond and Lenny has black hair," she added feebly. *How could I be so stupid? Have I come to love my life in Flint River so much that I stuck my head in the sand of denial?*

"If this guy was your client, then you know him best. If he has her, where would he take her?" Cade growled.

"I don't know. Let me think." Joscelyn's mind raced over her sessions with Lenny. She thought of his violent acts on her animals and how he threatened to run her down in her driveway. "He did his worst things in the night, so no one could see him, then he left the injured animals to be found." She drummed her fingers on her knee. "He never left any evidence at the scene... Think—is there anywhere in Flint River that he could take Sadie where he wouldn't be found? Any place out of the way? A place he could hide?"

Cade slammed on the brakes and jammed the gear shift into reverse. He spun around and stomped his boot on the gas. He turned left onto an old road that led up a hill into the pine trees. Before long, they were jolting along dirt roads that had no signs or buildings. Joscelyn gripped the armrest on the door and braced herself against the dash. Fear for Sadie tore at her between each lurch. There was no moon in the pitch-dark night. The only light bouncing along in front of them was cast from the dim headlights of the old truck.

They drove more than ten miles before Joscelyn asked, "Where are we going?"

Cade remained quiet for so long, she thought he wasn't going to answer. Finally, he said, "There's an old abandoned sapphire mine at the end of this road, about ten more miles."

"Oh, God."

"You said he was violent. Tell me what he did." He coughed away the emotion in his voice. "Did he hurt you?"

"No. No Cade, he never hurt me. As far as I know he hasn't hurt any people." She paused. "He hurts animals."

"This guy is a sociopath?"

She glanced at him out of the corner of her eye. "Yes, I think so. He was a client of mine, but I didn't have the skill to help him. I think he needed to be on medication and I can't prescribe. I'm not a medical doctor. So, I referred him to one. He thinks I quit on him. He felt betrayed."

"Christ!" Cade slammed on his brakes in front of a structure of old, rotting wood. He threw the truck into park and jumped out. A second later, Joscelyn realized he'd found Sadie. Tension eased out of her taught muscles only to be swept up and swirled together with the sharp chill of fresh terror when she saw the girl. Sadie huddled at the side of the road near the entrance to the old mine. Her arms were held tight around her legs and she flinched at the light, tucking her head away from Cade when he ran to her. Joscelyn shuddered.

An engine roared from behind the broken down mine structure. A car shot out and careened past Cade's truck, nearly swerving off the road to avoid hitting it. Joscelyn couldn't see the driver's face, but she knew who he was. She jumped out of the truck and ran to Sadie. The poor girl was crying, begging her Dad to leave her alone. Joscelyn approached and put a gentle hand on Cade's arm. Joscelyn appealed to him with her eyes and inclined her head, signaling him to step back. Breathing hard, he glared at her but moved away as she indicated.

"Sadie? Sadie, it's me Joscelyn. Your dad and I are here now. You're safe. We've come to take you home." The girl cried harder and rocked herself back and forth. "Sweetheart, you're safe now." Joscelyn touched her back and Sadie flinched. Not deterred, Joscelyn put her arm around her shoulders. All at once, Sadie lunged into Joscelyn's arms, sobbing. "Shh, shh, there now. We're here. You're safe. We've got you."

Joscelyn looked up and met Cade's eyes. He looked broken, a distant pain clouded his eyes. She knew she would need to take control. "Cade, help me get Sadie into the truck." He stared at her with distant eyes. "Now," she commanded.

Cade blinked and then moved to help. Joscelyn spoke to him over Sadie's head. "Cade, keep breathing. Tell me what things you see."

He gave her a confused look and then he remembered. He took a breath and said, "We have Sadie. She's safe. My truck, my phone, and you. I see you."

"Good, yes. Let's get Sadie in the cab." She held his stare. "I am here and I'm not going anywhere." He nodded and lifted his daughter into the truck. "I'll drive, give me your keys."

On the way back to town, Cade held Sadie in his arms and crooned comfort to her. Finally, Joscelyn asked, "Sadie, did he hurt you?" Sadie dissolved into tears again, trembling and though Joscelyn couldn't meet Cade's eyes, she simply said. "We're going straight to the hospital. You can call Sheriff Dietrich from there."

They drove to the emergency entrance and Cade carried Sadie inside where the nurses took over. Joscelyn leaned close to the intake nurse and whispered, "I think you might need a rape kit." The woman gave a solemn nod and left.

"Can I stay with her?" Cade asked.

"As soon as we check her over, we'll come and get you. She's in good hands." The ER doctor assured him.

Sadie cried out, frantic. "Joscelyn, please don't leave me. Please stay with me."

Joscelyn saw the stricken look on Cade's face. She apologized with her eyes and said, "It isn't you, it's a woman thing. I'll make sure she's okay and I'll send for you as soon as possible, all right?" He turned his back on her. Her heart ached for Cade and his daughter and the relationship she knew she was losing with Cade, but Joscelyn gritted her teeth and went to Sadie.

"I'm here, sweetheart." Joscelyn put her arm around Sadie and they listened to the doctor.

"Sadie, I'm Doctor Williams and I'm here to help you. Can you tell me where you are injured? There's blood on your shirt. May I look for any cuts or contusions?"

Sadie whimpered and nodded. She turned her face into Joscelyn's shoulder. Joscelyn stroked her hair. "Can you show us where you're bleeding?"

Sadie pulled up her shirt a few inches to reveal the bottom end of a long gash across her ribcage. Joscelyn's eyes flew to meet the doctor's gaze. Doctor Williams said, "Sadie, I know you're scared, but everyone here wants to help you. I need you to change into a gown so that I can give you a proper examination and treat your cut. Okay?"

Staring at her hands, Sadie nodded. The assisting nurse handed her a gown. "Please put all your clothing in this bag." She set an evidence bag on top of the gown. "We'll wait on the other side of the curtain until you're ready."

Joscelyn asked, "Do you need help or would you like me to wait with the doctor?"

"Stay."

When the doctor came back into the exam room she sat on a wheeled stool and looked up at Sadie. "I have to ask you some difficult questions."

Sadie's grip on Joscelyn's arm tightened but she nodded.

"Did your attacker harm you anywhere else?"

Fresh tears washed over Sadie's face but she shook her head. The doctor's eyes filled with compassion and she asked, "Sadie, did he rape you?"

Sadie whimpered, "No. He... he held a big knife to my throat." Overcome, she clung to Joscelyn who almost collapsed with relief. Sadie tried to continue. "He made me take off my shirt." Tears poured over her cheeks. "He... he cut my bra." She closed her eyes and the sound that came from her throat sent chills through Joscelyn. "He... he touched me, said horrible things to me... " She drew in a ragged breath. "I thought he was going to—you know... and maybe kill me, but he heard my dad's truck." She hiccupped with her next big breath. "He got angry and sliced my belly. Then he ran." Joscelyn held Sadie's head tight to her chest.

The doctor opened the gown only far enough to tend to the cut. "Luckily, this cut is mostly superficial. You will only need stitches in a few places. I'll take care of that and then after a complete exam, we'd like to keep you overnight for observation."

After the examination and confirming that there were no other injuries or tests that needed to be done, the doctor admitted Sadie for the night. Sheriff Dietrich came in and took Sadie's statement and then the doctor gave her a sedative. By the time Cade entered the room, Sadie was asleep.

Joscelyn went to him and put her arms around his waist. He stiffened and did not return the embrace. "Cade, Sadie is all right. You got there in time. The bastard ran away before he could do more. She has a cut across her ribs and belly, but it only needed a few stitches. She's going to be okay."

Cade pushed her aside and went to Sadie's bed. Joscelyn closed her eyes. "I'm sorry, Cade. I know you blame me."

"The sheriff is downstairs. He wants you to give him a full description and any other information you have." Cade's voice was so low Joscelyn hardly heard him. He didn't look at her, so she walked to the door.

She stopped and said, "Please let me know how she's feeling when she wakes up." He didn't respond, so she left to find Sheriff Dietrich.

After an hour and a half of painting a complete picture of Leonard Perkins and his antisocial condition for the sheriff, he drove her home. Sheriff Dietrich assured her he would put all the nearby counties on alert for Lenny's car. It was late when he dropped her off, but she doubted she would be able to sleep. Joscelyn understood why Cade blamed her. She blamed herself. How could she be so stupid? Poor Sadie.

Joscelyn let herself in the front door and turned the deadbolt. She flipped on the lights and let Teddy out back while she brewed herself a cup of herbal tea. Teddy came back in and Joscelyn latched the back door, set the chain and went upstairs to lay down. When she sat down on the edge of the bed, the tears came. They came hard and full. She cried with relief that Sadie wasn't raped, but also in anguish for the terror the girl faced. Tears came for the life she left in Colorado and her ruined relationship with Cade. He was special. He gave her a sense of belonging and she blew it. She agonized over being so dumb and unwittingly putting her new friends in such terrible danger.

Her tears stopped instantly when she heard the glass break downstairs.

CHAPTER 28

Teddy growled and barked. He ran down the stairs. His claws scraped and slid on the wood floor. More broken glass crashed against the floor below. Joscelyn's heart rammed against her ribs so loud she wasn't sure of what she'd heard. She tried to slow her breathing and her heart rate so she could listen. *Where is Teddy? Why isn't he barking anymore? Did he yelp? Were those footsteps crunching on the broken glass?*

Joscelyn ran to her nightstand drawer. She opened it and reached for her 9mm Ruger. Her hand clutched the cold metal and she willed her breath to slow. Something was wrong. The balance of her gun felt off. Her eyes darted to the bottom of the pistol grip. She flipped the catch to check the clip. It was empty! For one terrifying moment, frigid blood stilled in her veins. Then just as suddenly, her entire system screamed in red hot alert when she heard him.

"Josc-e-lyn," Leonard Perkin's voice oozed up through the stairwell, "where are you?" he sang. "Come out, come out, wherever you are." She heard his footsteps ascending the stairs. Resisting the urge to scream and drop to the floor in terrified tears, Joscelyn took a hard, mental grip on herself. She scanned the loft for options. The shower was a possibility but she figured that would be the first place he would look. The flimsy curtain would offer no defense. With no time left, she shimmied under the bed. Joscelyn knew he'd find her there, too, but the bed would at least keep him from her a little longer. *Teddy, where are you?*

She saw the steel toes of his black boots step onto the loft floor at the top of the stairs. "Josc-e-lyn, you're only wasting time. You can't escape me now."

It took all her strength not to cry. She concentrated on taking silent, shallow breaths through her mouth hoping he couldn't hear her pulse hammering like *The Tell-Tale Heart*. Joscelyn watched his boots thud across her floor and heard him tear the shower curtain off its rod. He uttered a frustrated grunt.

"Hiding like a little girl, under the bed, are you?" His sing-song voice crawled like cockroaches up her spine and over her scalp. "Don't you know there are monsters under the bed?" His laugh sent sharp jabs of terror through her nervous system. "Olly, olly, oxen free." He sang as though they were playing a child's game. He stalked toward the bed. Lenny tore the bed skirt away and dropped to his knees. His vacant, pale-blue eyes searched the dark corner for her. She curled herself into a tight ball, making herself as small as possible, still gripping the gun with white knuckles.

He reached her with little trouble. She kicked at his grasping hands. He clutched her ankle and yanked hard. She slid half way out from under the bed on the slick wooden floor.

Joscelyn screamed. "No!" She kicked harder and grabbed at the base of the box-springs. Trying to find anything to grasp to pull herself away from him. He tugged and again she screamed louder. Leonard pulled her all the way out and while she cowered on the floor he punched her, full force, in the face. Stunned by the blinding pain, her ears rang and she blinked her eyes several times before she screamed again.

"Shut up!" Leonard stood and kicked Joscelyn in the ribs with his steel-toe boot. Air from her lungs expelled in a groan. "No one can hear you. You are utterly alone. This boring little town is buttoned up tight." He wheezed a wicked laugh. "Rather convenient for me, by the way. Thank you."

Joscelyn curled protectively around her injured ribs. Moaning against the unbearable pain. She could hardly breathe. *Think!* Her eyes flashed wild, trying to find something she could use to defend herself.

"Finally, I have you to myself." Leonard sat down next to Joscelyn and tangled his hand in her long hair and yanked her closer to him with it. She whimpered, which brought a sneering smile to his lips.

With trembling hands, she aimed her impotent 9mm at Lenny. "Let go of me, Lenny, or I'll shoot."

His laugh came out in short barks. "Do you think I'm stupid enough to leave a loaded gun in your possession? You tried to shoot me once before, remember?"

Joscelyn pushed herself to her knees and with all her strength, swung the Ruger at Leonard's temple. He dodged her blow, but she caught him on his cheek and split the skin. Screaming in rage, he chopped down against her wrist causing her to drop the gun. He kicked it across the floor and tightened his grip in her hair, each root searing with pain.

Leonard touched his face and stared at the blood on his fingers. His dead eyes rose to meet hers. Without looking away, he felt for his carbon-bladed hunting knife. Joscelyn heard its whisper when he drew it from the scabbard tied to his thigh. Her stomach flew to her throat as he brought the blade to his lips and ran the flat side of it across them like a lover's caress. He gazed at the blade with lust in his eyes. He touched her cheek with the tip. Barely touching her skin, he drew the point down under her jaw. She shuddered as he stopped at the pulse throbbing in her throat.

Joscelyn closed her eyes. She lay deathly still. Her every nerve on high alert yet she was suddenly enveloped in an eerie sense of calm. Time seemed to slow. She became hyper aware of every sensation, every sound.

Leonard pressed the sharp knife into her throbbing artery just enough to prick the skin. Then he drew the tip down her neck, through the semi-circle space between her collar bones. He traced down her sternum to the top button of her blouse.

With a flick of his wrist the button popped and rolled across the floor. He smiled at that and continued the path with his blade to the next button.

"What do you want from me, Lenny?" Joscelyn surprised herself by the steadiness of her voice.

"I want you to make me feel better." His smile took on an evil cast.

Joscelyn swallowed, her heart pounded on her eardrums. "How can I do that?"

"I wanted your help, but you refused. You help *everyone* else." His voice grew louder with each sentence. "You spend time with people you don't even know. Let men kiss you. You go on trips with them. But you give me *nothing.*" He pushed his face into hers and shouted, "Now, the only answer is for you to die!" Joscelyn flinched as his spittle sprayed her cheek. He sprung another button.

Joscelyn wept in spite of her resolve. She trembled and thought she might vomit until she heard Teddy barking. At least she thought it was Teddy, but the sound seemed far away.

"Teddy?"

"Shut-Up!" Leonard screamed. "I am sick of how you care for everything, even animals, more than me. You make me feel worthless." Another button popped into the night stand. He slid the blade down the front of her jeans. Joscelyn sucked her belly away from the blade. With almost no effort, Leonard jerked his hand and the razor-sharp blade tore through the denim, splaying open the front of her pants.

Desperation shook her voice. "Lenny, you are not worthless," Joscelyn tried to talk him out of his insanity. "I know your parents left you and you were passed around in the system. I understand how that could make you feel unimportant, but you're not. You *matter*."

Leonard thrust his knife between Joscelyn's breastbone and her bra. He sliced and the lace fell away. He yanked her hair harder. "I don't matter to you. Don't lie to me. Do you think I'm stupid? You passed me off to another therapist. Then you tried to run away from me."

"You scared me, Lenny." Her voice was faint. "You're scaring me now."

A ghost of a smile settled on his mouth and his empty eyes watched his blade as he pushed the cup of her bra away from her breast. He pressed the knife into her skin and carved a shallow line tracing its curve. A thin line of blood chased the blade. Joscelyn cried out in pain and his smile broadened.

She attempted to pull away from him and kicked at his legs, but his grip in her hair tightened. Her scalp burned.

In a cold, unemotional voice, he said, "My knife is inches away from your heart. Do you think it wise to fight me?"

He edged his knife back up to her throat. "If you move, you will die. You'll bleed to death on this floor." He peered at her from under his lank, bleached-blond bangs. "Do you understand me?" Tears blurred her vision and she blinked them away. "Do you?" he screamed.

"Yes," she whispered.

"Good." He leaned over her and ran his tongue along the thin cut on her chest. He panted over her with hot breath. Joscelyn cried out in pain from her damaged ribs. "Like that, do you?"

"Lenny, please. Please, don't hurt me any more."

He stared at her in confusion. "I'm not hurting you, Joscelyn. I'm loving you." He let go of her hair and jammed his free hand down the front of her jeans. She cried out then felt the edge of the knife press harder against her throat. "Be still!" He shouted as he groped her.

"You didn't expect this from me, did you? You never expected much from me." His fingers tore at her, hurting her. "I've surprised you. My devotion has overwhelmed you. I loved you and I only wanted you to help me." His breath was hot and rancid on her skin. "I didn't expect you to love me back... how could you? No one does."

Lenny licked the blood dripping from her cut. "I even brought you gifts. You ignored the gentle ones—the flowers, the notes."

"I didn't ignore them, Lenny," she sobbed. "I told you it wasn't appropriate for me to accept them." Joscelyn tried to reason with his fevered mind.

"I wanted your attention." He chuckled. "The cat was the means. You remember the cat? I captured it for you. Now it will never leave your memory. You're thinking of it right now, aren't you?" His breathing grew heavy. "Hanging in your barn."

Lenny seemed to drift off into a trance state. Joscelyn buoyed her strength and twisted away from his pawing fingers. Catching him off guard, she elbowed him in the chest and bunched her knees. She kicked at his groin with both feet.

He reacted with a swift slice across her ribs, this cut deeper than the first and Joscelyn cried out. The blade returned to her neck and Leonard pressed the blade flat against her larynx. She couldn't breathe.

In a chilling, calm voice, he said, "Please do not move. I'm not ready to kill you yet." Leonard's gaze moved to the fresh cut and he smiled wistfully.

Lenny caught her wrists and pulled them up over her head. He straddled her hips. "Ever since I sliced your horse's neck, I wanted to do the same to you. His blood didn't show up on his black coat, not like yours—crimson on ivory." Lenny slid the point of his blade down her side pressing hard enough to draw another line of blood. Joscelyn whimpered in pain. "Beautiful," he whispered. His greedy eyes roamed her torso and slowly rose back to the pulse thumping in her neck. A slow smile spread across his face.

CHAPTER 29

Driven by his helpless fury, Cade wore a path on the tile of the waiting room. Mary and Trent arrived seconds later.

Mary stepped in front of Cade, halting his march. She gripped both of his arms. "How is she?"

Cade shook his head. "The doctor gave her something and she's sleeping right now. They say she's okay physically. She had a few stitches is all." His eyes closed and a wave of nausea rolled through him. "But I don't know if she'll ever be okay emotionally. She was so scared."

Mary took his hands in hers. "She's strong, Cade. Like you. In time and with all our love and support, she'll work through this."

Trent put an arm over Cade's shoulders. "Is there anything you need?" He glanced around the room. "Where's Joscelyn?"

"Who the hell cares. This is all her fault." Cade choked on his bitterness.

"What?" Mary and Trent said in unison.

"The psychopath who did this to Sadie has been stalking Joscelyn since she left Denver. She led him here!" Trent and Mary shared a strange look that Cade didn't want to analyze. He flung himself onto the narrow couch and held his head in his hands.

The doctor entered the room and seemed to sense the tension. "Mr. Stone, I want to assure you that Sadie is going to be fine. She will sleep for the next twelve hours or more. I urge you to go home and get some sleep of your own. Tomorrow, your daughter will need you to have all your energy."

Cade felt depleted. Weakness seeped through his bones. What would he have done if he lost Sadie? She was all he had.

The doctor continued, "The sheriff left Deputy Brown on guard outside Sadie's door, so she is perfectly safe and I promise to call you immediately if Sadie wakes in the night."

Cade finally agreed to go home. He needed to feed the horses and his dog anyway. He would get some rest and be back at the hospital before Sadie woke in the morning. Trent and Mary went with him to check on Sadie before they left.

When Cade climbed into his truck, he noticed Joscelyn's purse on his front seat. "Damn it." Cade didn't want to think about her right now. He'd been developing strong feelings for her, but that all was changed. It was Joscelyn's fault that Sadie was put in danger—that she was attacked. She could have been raped, maybe even killed. Would have been, if they didn't happen to drive up the right canyon at the right time. Cade wasn't sure he could ever forgive Joscelyn for that. He slammed his fist on the steering wheel and then rested his forehead against his hand. He couldn't think clearly and right now, he needed sleep.

It was two in the morning, Joscelyn wouldn't need her purse before tomorrow. He would drop it off then. *Or better yet, I'll give it to Trent to take to her. That way I won't have to see her at all. Trent can have her.* Cade started the engine and backed out of his parking space. *Good riddance.* He pulled out of the hospital lot and pointed his truck toward home. Driving south, he passed the courthouse and turned down Main Street. The buildings were dark and he drove past their buttoned-up storefronts. At this time of night, the town was quiet except for a dog barking.

Against his will, he glanced over at the library. It too was dark, but the loft apartment light was on. Cade shook his head and accelerated. It didn't matter to him if she was still up. A dark, furry figure ran in front of his headlights and he slammed on the brakes. "What the... Teddy?"

Cade put the truck in park and opened his door. "Teddy, what're you doing out here, boy?" Teddy rounded the truck and barked frantically at Cade. "Did you get locked out?" Cade squatted down and ignoring the sharp pain from his old injury, he reached for the upset dog. He ran his hand over Teddy's head and behind his ear. "It's okay, boy. Calm down." Teddy's bark was high pitched and he caught Cade's sleeve in his teeth and pulled. When Cade yanked his hand back it was covered in blood. "Teddy! What happened?" He moved so the dome light shined on the dog's head. Teddy had a cut over his left eye. "You're going to need stitches, fella." For a quick second, he thought about taking Teddy over to the vet's office himself and not telling Joscelyn. He *really* didn't want to see her. "What'd you cut yourself on, buddy?"

Cade looked across to the library door. He took in the broken glass and his heart stilled. "Oh, my God." A calm clarity came over Cade, one that he had been trained for and that had been seared into him during battle. He got back in his truck, turned off the engine and reached over to his glove box. He pulled out his Glock 23. Checking the clip, he slid the semi-automatic pistol into the back waist of his jeans.

Gently, he lifted Teddy into the truck and shut the door. The poor dog barked furiously, but Cade knew he was safer in the cab. Cade approached the front door and listened. He didn't hear anything, so he drew his gun and as quiet as he could, he opened the door. Stepping across the broken glass, Cade edged his way, silently down the hall.

"Please, Lenny. Let me help you now. It isn't too late." Joscelyn's plea sliced through the night. Her cry like shards of glass, pierced Cade's heart.

Leonard scoffed. "How does it feel to be the one begging?" Joscelyn screamed in pain which sent tremors through Cade, but he kept his focus, breathing deeply. He used the noise to disguise his movement and made it to the bottom of the stairs.

"I'm sorry. Did that hurt you?" Cade shuddered, the sickening sweetness in the psychopath's voice, cloying in his gut.

"Please, Lenny. Don't." Joscelyn cried. With that, Cade ran to the turn of the stairs on the landing. He could see one of Joscelyn's hands and a tangled mess of her hair. He took another step. The board creaked.

"Who's there?" Leonard shrieked.

"Help me!" Joscelyn screamed.

Leonard hit Joscelyn's jaw with the hilt of his hunting knife. "Shut. Up!" Blood flew from her mouth and sprayed across the floor.

Cade took another step and leveled his gun at Leonard's head. "Let her go." His voice steady and commanding.

Leonard howled a maniacal laugh. "Well, if it isn't the broken Prince Charming, come to save the fair maiden." He pulled Joscelyn into his lap by her hair and kept the blade of his knife at her throat. "You're too late to save her," Leonard spit, "but you're just in time to watch her die."

Cade kept his eyes on his target. "Drop the knife. There is no way out of this for you."

"I'm not going to let *you* have her."

"If you kill her, you won't have her either." Cade tried reason.

"I don't want her!" Leonard's eyes stretched wide. He took a breath and howled as he moved to slice Joscelyn's throat. Cade fired his pistol before Leonard had the chance. The bullet hit Leonard in the center of his forehead, mere inches from Joscelyn's face. His head snapped back and his body went rigid for a second before his arms went limp. The hunting knife clattered to the floor.

Joscelyn screamed and Cade ran to her. He knelt and scooped her into his lap. She sobbed, trembling violently. "Shh, shh. I'm here. You're safe. It's okay now." When Joscelyn's emotions settled to whimpering, Cade pulled a blanket off her bed and covered her before he pulled his phone from his back pocket and dialed 911. "Sheriff, this is Cade Stone. I've shot him. I'm in the loft above the library with Joscelyn. She needs to get to the emergency room. Now!"

"Stay where you are. I'll be there in two minutes." The sheriff yelled into the phone.

"Josce, did he...where are you hurt? There's blood." Cade's emotions began to flood over his situational resolve. He ground his teeth to fight through it. Now was not the time for him to lose it. Joscelyn needed him. He saw her blood, he saw J.T.'s blood. He squeezed his eyes shut, shook his head, and groaned. His grip on Joscelyn tightened and she gasped.

There were tears in her voice and it shook, but he heard her say, "Cade, what do you see? I'm here, what else?"

He opened his eyes and they darted around the room. Breathing hard against his intrusive flashback, he whispered, "You... your blood... my gun. Oh, God."

Boots pounded up the stairs. "What the hell is going on in here?" Trent flew into the room. He stopped and gaped at the bloody mess. After a stunned silence he whispered, "I was over at Tonya's and heard a gunshot."

CHAPTER 30

Hours later, after Joscelyn was checked out in the ER and refused to be admitted, both she and Cade gave their statements to Sheriff Dietrich, and Cade drove her to his ranch. Her physical injuries were minor and would heal with time, but her psychological trauma would take a lot longer. If only he could spare her from that. Cade lit a fire in the predawn chill and pulled a quilt over them both as they sat on the couch and stared into the flames. He was exhausted but knew he wouldn't sleep.

"You saved my life." Her eyes searched his face. "You had to overcome a lot of demons to do that." She smoothed her fingers over the scar on his cheek. "Your training and your bravery made you able to do that. You're so strong."

Cade gulped down the baseball-sized lump in his throat and pulled her gently into his arms. "You've saved my life too."

They held each other, staring into the flames until the sun came up and the fire died away.

Torn, Cade said, "I need to go the hospital to get Sadie. I asked my grandma to come over early to sit with you. Is that all right?"

"Do you want me to come?"

Cade touched the purple bruise on Joscelyn's jaw with the tip of his finger. His chest ached. "Yes, but I'm not going to let you. You need to rest."

His phone rang, he glanced at the screen. Kissing Joscelyn's temple, he stood and stepped out on the porch to talk. He came back inside and said, "Trent's on his way over with Teddy. He's been to the vet, had a couple of stitches over his eye, but he's fine. He has to wear one of those cones on his collar."

"Thank God, he's all right." Joscelyn's eyes glistened. She hugged a pillow to her chest and grimaced at the pain in her ribs.

Cade sat down next to her and took her hand. "He's okay, Josce. We're all going to be okay and we never have to worry about Leonard Perkins again."

She let a sob loose and nodded. "It's all my fault. How can any of you ever forgive me for leading him here?"

Cade held her close, careful of her tender ribs and cuts. Less than twelve hours ago, he had the same thoughts. He planned to never forgive her. Now, he was overwhelmed with gratitude that she was safe and in his arms.

"You didn't know," he murmured.

"I should have known." She leaned her head against his chest. "It's ironic, in my last session, I told one of my clients she couldn't always run away when things got hard. I should have listened to my own advice. I should have stayed and faced Leonard in Denver."

"But then we never would have met." Cade lifted her chin so she looked at him. "You wouldn't have helped me with my PTSD. I wouldn't have gone to see J.T.'s family. I would never have seen my need to get into therapy." He grinned and stroked her cheek with his fingers. "There'd be no library or saddle club, not to mention, Sadie and her friends would all be addicted to pot and on their way to heroin."

Joscelyn rolled her eyes and then she pulled his hand to her mouth and kissed it.

"I never would have fallen in love with you."

Joscelyn's eyes darted to meet his and a tear ran down her cheek. He brushed it with his thumb.

"The doctor said you and Sadie might have nightmares and trouble dealing with your memories from last night." His eyes stung as he studied her. "That sounds familiar. I'd take this struggle from you, if I could." His throat ached and he swallowed hard. "I'm sorry I wasn't there to protect you. I should have been there."

"No, Cade. You were with Sadie, which is where you needed to be—and you did save me." She gave him a wobbly smile. "We'll just have to help each other through the rough times ahead."

He nodded and softly drew her into his chest.

~*~

Trent opened the front door for Mary but Teddy bounded in first. He ran to Joscelyn and licked her from head to toe the best he could with the cone bouncing into the couch and table. She tried to throw her arms around him and caught her breath on the pain. "Oh, sweet boy. You're such a good dog. You helped save me, even though you were hurt." Teddy barked and wagged his tail.

Mary bustled in. "Trent, you get that dog some food and water. I'd like to look Joscelyn over and see that she is all right with my own eyes." Mary crossed the room. Cade stood and she took his place on the couch. "You boys go get Sadie. Joscelyn and I will be fine here on our own."

Cade gave Joscelyn a helpless look and she grinned. After they left, Mary took Joscelyn's hand. "Are you all right, honey? I mean, *really?*" She stared into Joscelyn's eyes and Joscelyn knew she wasn't' going to accept 'I'm fine' for an answer.

"Mary, I've never been so terrified in all my life. My heart is sick that Sadie had to go through anything even slightly resembling what I went through last night. I feel so guilty." She covered her face with her hands. "I don't know how any of you can even look at me."

"Darling girl, none of this is your fault. None of it. Do you hear me?" Mary put her arms around Joscelyn. She smelled like fresh cotton and sunflowers. Joscelyn began to cry into the comforting arms that held her. "That's right. You let it all out. You're safe and loved and right where you belong."

~*~

Cade let Trent drive. "This is like riding in a Cadillac, not a ranch truck." Cade narrowed his eyes at the computer console. "Or maybe a space ship." He pushed the navigation button and a map appeared on the screen.

Trent patted his dash. "Yep, she's awful purty, don't you think? Much better than that old, beat up hunk of junk you drive around in."

"Not true. I'll give you that these seats are soft and your engine's quiet, but my seat is perfectly formed to my ass and I can pull out my tool kit and work on my engine anytime. You'd need a computer engineering degree to work on yours."

Trent laughed, "That's the damn truth."

They road in silence for a while, simply being in each other's company.

Cade cleared his throat. "I want to thank you for seeing to my cattle while I... while I wasn't up to it."

Trent kept his eyes on the road and nodded. He lifted an empty energy drink can to his lips and spit tobacco juice into it.

"And for taking care of Sadie after Louanne took up and left."

"That's what family's for."

Cade shoved his brother in the shoulder. "Yeah, but you went above and beyond. I got the check in the mail from the Montfort Feed Lot for my steers you sent there. You got a great price, I know you kept them well fed over the winter, or they wouldn't have done so well." Cade knew that Trent drove to Wolf Run every day since Sadie's mom left to keep an eye on his ranch. He continued the practice even after Cade came home from the war. Which was a huge thing because Cade wasn't able to take up the job until now. He could have lost everything.

Trent's cheeks darkened and his voice turned gruff. "I just had your herd trucked in with mine. No big deal. You'd do the same for me." He coughed and said, "I never told you how proud I am of you, Cade. For what you went through for our country. Dad would have bust his buttons. That's for damn sure."

Cade had to close his eyes against the flood of emotion that washed over him. He and Trent hadn't said as many words to each other since before he joined the Marine Corps. They both kept their eyes forward, not daring to look at each other. Trent pushed a button on his steering wheel and the stereo filled the cab with Chris Young's *Who I Am with You.*

When the song ended, Trent spoke, his voice low and soft. "Did that son of a bitch... " he glanced at Cade. "Did he rape her?"

Cade closed his eyes and swallowed several times. Finally, he said, "No. He was headed that way, but I got there before... "

The brothers sat quiet, their thoughts hanging heavy in the cab of the truck. Cade finally broached the subject pressing on his heart. "You don't have real feelings for Joscelyn, do you?" he asked.

Trent hesitated. "She's a mighty fine woman. A man could do worse." He glanced at Cade from the corner of his eye.

Cade's stomach rolled and tightened. He clenched his jaw and cleared his throat. "You gonna do something about it?"

"Well, here's the thing." Trent slowed down and signaled to turn left into Flint River. "Gran has been harping at me to keep my nose in my own back yard." He turned onto Main Street. They drove past the library which was roped off with yellow crime-scene tape. Turning right past the courthouse, Trent resumed. "She thinks I'm always looking for something better when I've had what I need all along."

"Tonya?"

Trent let out a short laugh. "Yeah. She's put up with a lot from me over the years and she's been there through thick and thin."

"Do you love her?"

Trent tilted up one side of his mouth. "I suppose I do. I just haven't wanted to stop playing around." He let out a burst of air. "Maybe it's time."

"Maybe." Cade couldn't keep the relieved smile from spreading across his face. For the first time in years he looked forward to his future. Maybe he could have love and a family after all.

They pulled into the hospital parking lot and went inside. Tonya was in the waiting room when they got there.

"Hey," she said and stood when the brothers approached. "I figured you'd be out at Wolf Run and I didn't want Sadie to wake up and have nobody here. I hope that's all right?"

Trent pulled her into his arms. "Darlin', you are just what I need this mornin'."

"Is she awake yet?" Cade asked.

"Not yet. Whatever they gave her last night really knocked her out." Tonya answered.

"Good, she needs the rest."

They waited together for another hour before the nurse came to tell them that Sadie was awake and asking for them.

CHAPTER 31

That evening, everyone sat around the dining table at Wolf Run. Mary and Tonya served up a filling ranch-style supper of tri-tip steak, au-gratin potatoes, fresh green beans, and apple pie. The mood was quiet but comfortable and the adults sipped their coffee between bites of dessert. Sadie went to her room so she could FaceTime with her friends and fill them in on the horrible events of the previous night.

Tonya cleared her throat. "I have something I need to tell you all." Everyone turned to listen. "Joscelyn, I know you think what happened was your fault. It wasn't, but it might have been mine."

Joscelyn sat forward and cocked her head. "How could any of this have anything to do with you?" Her brows scrunched together.

Tonya took a breath and her eyes dropped to the table. "I saw David," she picked at her napkin. "I mean the man who attacked you. I saw him sneak into the library a couple of times when I knew you were out." She covered her face with her hands.

"What?" Joscelyn's mind swam, she felt like she was in another dimension. "You saw him? He was in the library?"

Trent's stood. "What the hell, Tonya?"

"I'm sorry. I didn't know he was a psychopath." Her eyes seemed to plead with Joscelyn and she spoke directly to her. "You were out with Trent and I was... well, I was jealous. I didn't know who the strange man was, but I figured if I gave you enough rope, you'd... well, you'd get caught with another guy and Trent would... " She couldn't finish.

Joscelyn's mind raced through the past few months. She remembered then, the mouse and the bird and, "Teddy. My sweet Teddy. I bet it was Leonard who hurt Teddy." She searched Cade's face. "That was the same night I saw Sadie talking to David on the street. David who was really Lenny." Her eyes bore into Tonya's. "I wish you had said something. Oh, Tonya, you couldn't have known, but I wish you had said something."

"Can you forgive me?" Tonya's voice trembled and sounded small.

Joscelyn stared at the woman across the table from her. Her mind racing through the summer months. "You didn't know." She swallowed hard. "Everything is clear now though. I can't believe I missed it all. I'm the one who needs to ask for forgiveness."

Cade took her hand and gave it a gentle squeeze.

Mary stood and began to collect the dishes. "It's all over now and everyone will be all right in the end. We're all here having dinner together and I believe that this is the way it's meant to be."

Trent glared at Tonya and shook his head. "I can't believe you, Tonya. Your manipulative games almost got Sadie and Joscelyn killed." He ran a hand down over his face. "You went too far this time. Why couldn't you just tell me how you felt? I thought maybe we could try again—but not now. We're through, Tonya. Finally through for good."

With tears spilling down her face, Tonya whispered, "I'm so sorry." She walked out the door to her car. After three tries, it started and she drove away. Trent refused to talk about it and he left to take Mary home.

Cade and Joscelyn sat together on a glider on the front porch of the cabin. They sipped their coffee and watched the sun go down. Birds sang their final nighttime serenades.

Joscelyn leaned into Cade. "Believe it or not, I feel bad for Tonya."

"I wouldn't feel too bad. She did make a mess of things."

"But she didn't mean to. I think she really loves Trent."

Cade scoffed. "Those two won't be apart for long. They never are." He reached up and twisted a strand of Joscelyn's hair around his fingers. "So, what are you going to do now that Perkins is no longer a problem?" His voice floated soft on the breeze. Joscelyn stared into her cup but didn't answer, she had given it a lot of thought but wasn't sure how Cade would respond. He stopped the rocking of the glider. "Will you go back home?"

Sadie burst through the screen door. "You *can't* go back to Colorado. We need you." She threw her arms around Joscelyn spilling coffee all over them and causing Joscelyn to cry out from her cracked ribs. "Oh, Josce! I'm so sorry." The horrified look on Sadie's face made Joscelyn laugh, which also hurt.

She pushed herself up off the glider and plucked her wet shirt away from her skin. "It's okay, it's only coffee."

"I'm sorry, I forgot about your ribs." Sadie ran to the door. "I'll be right back with a towel."

Joscelyn turned to Cade and he took her hand. "Well?" he pressed.

She searched his face, realizing it was better to love at the risk of losing someone than to not have love at all. "I'm done running. I love you and I don't want to be alone anymore."

Cade pulled her down into his lap. He cupped her face in his hands and his eyes dove into the depth of hers. He brought her face to his and kissed her. At first, his lips were soft and reverent but soon the kiss pulsed with urgency. Joscelyn melted into him, wanting him, feeling like she finally belonged.

When they heard Sadie pause on the other side of the door, Cade drew back. His breath came fast and his eyes pleaded with her. "Stay."

She nodded and answered him with a kiss. She smiled against Cade's lips when she heard Sadie whisper, "Yes!" right before she closed the front door and left them alone on the porch, wet shirt and all.

ABOUT THE AUTHOR

Jodi and her husband live on a small ranch southeast of Denver where she enjoys her horses, complains about her cows, and writes to create a home for her imaginings. In addition to life in the country, Jodi fosters her creative side by writing, painting in watercolor, quilting, and crafting stained-glass.

Other Books by Jodi Burnett

Letting Go

Jodi-Burnett.com

Made in the USA
San Bernardino, CA
25 May 2020